CREATURE FEATURE

A MONSTER ANTHOLOGY

EDITED BY
ANTHONY GIANGREGORIO

CREATURE FEATURE
Copyright © 2011 Open Casket Press
ISBN Softcover ISBN 13: 978-1-61199-028-7
ISBN 10: 1-611990-28-9

Table of Contents

FOREWORD

Instead of droning on with a boring foreword, I thought I'd get you folks warmed up with a short story before you get into the really scary stuff.

Enjoy!

MONSTER ARE REAL

ANTHONY GIANGREGORIO

John and Wayne—both eight-years-old—sat on John's bed, talking about school and friends. Finally, the conversation got around to other things, some real and imaginary.

"And I say monsters are real," John said as he crossed his arms over his chest to make his point.

"No, they're not," Wayne snapped back. "If they were, then we'd see them all the time and we don't. It's just something people made up to scare other people. Just stories."

"No, it's not," John rebutted. "Monsters are real. They're all around us; you just have to know where to look."

"Are not real," Wayne said.

"Are too."

"Are not."

"Are too."

"Are not, and unless you can prove it, you need to shut up!" Wayne yelled, angrily.

"Fine, I'll show you," John hissed, angry now too. "Mom! Dad! Wayne says monsters aren't real!"

Wayne frowned, upset that John would stoop to getting his parents involved. Footsteps sounded from down the hall, and a second later, John's parents were at the bedroom doorway.

"Wayne thinks monsters aren't real; he says I'm a liar," John said to his parents.

"Well, he is," Wayne rebutted, swallowing the knot in his throat.

"Go 'head, Mom, Dad, show him the truth."

Mom and Dad looked at one another, then nodded in agreement. Together, they reached up, grabbed the top of their hair, and pulled.

Their faces slid off like rubber masks, exposing large heads that reminded Wayne of a fly and an ant if they'd mated.

He had time for one quick scream before John's parents attacked him, knocking him to the floor and tearing him apart to feed on his flesh.

John sat on the bed as he watched Wayne being devoured.

"I told you monsters are real," John grinned and wiped away a gobbet of bloody flesh from his leg.

Only the sound of his parents' feeding answered him.

TREELINE

MATT KURTZ

Dan Simmons was pulled from a deep sleep by a tiny hand shaking him. He flinched awake with a start, lurching against his wife and scaring her half to death. They were both about to scold their son Robbie, who was standing beside the bed, until they saw the terrified look on his face.

"What's the matter, baby?" Christy asked, rubbing the sleep from her eyes.

"I heard scary noises in the woods."

Dan pulled his son onto the bed with them. "You were just having a bad dream, bud. That's all."

Robbie shook his head. "No, I was awake. And when I got up to look outside, I heard it again."

"Heard what?" Christy asked, yawning.

"Pops and cracks. Like bones breaking or something."

Dan and Christy stared at one another over the rather peculiar—not to mention grim—description coming from their seven-year-old.

"Come on," Dan said. "Let's get you warm and secure, and back in your own bed."

While tucking him in, Dan told Robbie that the noises were probably just some of the local teenagers playing in the woods with firecrackers. Or the wind blowing the old branches around, causing them to creak, pop, and groan under their own weight. "Kind of like the funny noises Grandpa makes when he stands up after sitting for too long."

Robbie was content with the explanation because in no time, his tiny lids were drooping. Dan kissed him goodnight and double-checked to make sure his closet door was closed and the nightlight on. Upon returning to his room, Dan paused at the hallway window that faced the backyard.

The large, well-kept lot was lost in darkness, devoured by the acres of woods beyond. It was a calm night. There was no breeze. The black trees silhouetted against the gray sky were dead still.

Well, so much for the theory of wind blowing around the branches, he thought

The following nights were just as calm, but that didn't prevent Robbie from waking them again and again because of the strange cracking sounds he heard echoing from the woods.

Dan crossed into the treeline that separated his rural two-story house from the surrounding woodlands to search for evidence as to what was spooking his son. After fifteen minutes of wandering aimlessly, he tossed his cigarette butt on the leafy ground and snuffed it out under his boot.

He glanced around the woods. A gust of the chilly late November air snaked down his collar, eliciting a hearty shiver.

Ah…screw it. There's nothing out here, he thought.

He checked his watch and figured there was still time to sneak in a late afternoon nap before dinner. Such was one of the many luxuries of owning his own business: extended vacations. Having recently returned home after winning an out-of-state bid on a three month job in Louisiana, Dan had racked up enough time to not feel guilty about practically taking off the entire holiday season. The construction business was slow during the winter months and the few gigs his company did get could easily be handled by his partner Jeff.

Dan's R&R after that job was well deserved, having dealt with all the resistance from conservationists who, understandably, protested the miles of forest required to be knocked down for the highway expansion project. It was Dan and his crew that was responsible for stripping the earth with their chainsaws and bulldozers so automobiles could eventually travel farther and unleash even more toxic emissions into the atmosphere. To help him sleep better at night, Dan often told himself that more highways meant more businesses springing up alongside it, which could only help out the piss-poor economy and high unemployment rate

At any rate, he was more than happy to finally be home. His plan was to relax, work on some minor projects around the house, and—of course—spend some quality time with his wife and son to make up for his absence during the summer months.

Stepping out of the woods, Dan trekked across the backyard, eventually making it to his house's wooden deck. He sat on the top step, lit a final smoke before his nap, and scanned the treeline that loomed over his yard like an army of wooden giants standing in formation. The line was cut straight as an arrow, running the perimeter of his property—only to return to acres of wooded area, separating him from the nearest neighbor a good mile away.

With the autumn leaves having already shed, his view into the woods went pretty deep.

Whatever's in there also has a better view of me, Dan thought.

He shivered again, questioning whether this time it was from the chill in the air. Smashing out his cigarette, he stood and headed for the sliding patio door.

He'd tell Robbie he had only found a bunch of rotting trees that had fallen, which were responsible for the strange noises the boy had heard.

A cracking in the distance sounded over his shoulder.

Dan whirled around. Because of the echo, it was impossible to determine which direction it came from. But one thing was for sure…it came from somewhere deep within the woods.

"I heard something this afternoon in the woods," Dan said.

Sitting behind the roll-top desk in the living room, Christy was paying the bills, scribbling away in the checkbook's ledger. "What, babe?"

"I heard something earlier coming from the woods."

She looked up to find him standing in front of the sliding patio door, staring into their dark backyard. "Oh, great," she sighed, raising an eyebrow. "Now you're starting?"

Dan checked the two entryways to the room to ensure they were alone. "I'm serious. I was gonna tell you about it before dinner, but I didn't want Robbie to hear."

"Well then? What was it?"

He shrugged. "Like Robbie said…bones breaking." She waited for him to elaborate but he only added, "I'm going back out there tomorrow to take another look."

Dan entered the treeline and continued into the woods, searching for anything out of the norm. About one hundred yards in, just beyond the edge of his property line, he found it.

He stared with mouth agape at the bare strip of earth. Someone had plowed away all the trees, clearing a fifty foot wide path through the land. The path stretched ahead at least half a mile, disappearing over a distant hill. He looked behind him to where the clearing abruptly ended.

If it continued on its present course, it would lead directly to his house.

"Oh, come on. What idiot would…?" He paused, looking down at the loose soil.

If this was a construction site, where was all the equipment? Where were the tracks from the vehicles and bulldozers? The deadfall of cut trees plowed to the side? And, more important, how come he hadn't heard any of this taking place when it was happening less than a football field's distance from his house?

Studying the ground again, he discovered an almost subliminal zigzag pattern throughout the soil, all originating from various positions along the bare earth.

Stepping back to take in the entire scope of the area, he saw where each tree had originally been standing and the paths they'd made to their new locations.

They hadn't been cut down. They appeared to have *moved*.

Slid.

His heart raced.

The newly arranged woods leaned at an outward angle on both sides of the parted path, forming a large V, as if making way for something.

Something very tall. Very large.

Dan stumbled over the uneven earth, walking across the clearing and looking up in awe at the towering trees around him. He felt like some dignitary visiting a foreign land that had their gargantuan wooden soldiers lining both sides of his walkway, saluting his arrival.

Kneeling at one of the trunks, he clawed the dirt around its roots. The wooden tendrils dug deep into the ground as if planted for decades…if not centuries.

His scalp prickled at the odd sensation of being watched. He sprung to his feet and whirled around. Although there was nothing there, his eyes shifted from tree to tree as a chill crept up his spine and exploded at the base of his neck. He shivered and gasped. And knew it was time to leave.

Sitting on the edge of the bed, Christy shrugged. "So…what's the big deal? Just make some phone calls tomorrow and find out what they're building back there." She continued lacing her running shoes.

Dan quietly closed the bedroom door to keep their conversation private. "I'm tellin' you, no one tore anything down. It's not a construction site. Don't you think I'd know if it were?"

"Then what happened?"

Dan shrugged. "The trees…just seemed to have… moved. *Shifted* by themselves. The soil was all ripped up from the roots pulling and breaking free. Which might explain all the cracking noises Robbie's been hearing."

Christy stared at him. "Moved?"

"I know. I know. But if you don't believe me, how 'bout we both go out there and you can tell me…"

"Sorry, babe, I want to enjoy this warm spell while it lasts. Get a good run in before the rain moves in. They're forecasting bad stuff, nonstop, for the next few days."

Dan sat on the bed beside her. He exhaled and rubbed his sweaty palms on his jeans. "I'm telling you, Christy, it was creepy out there. I felt like the trees were looking down on me. Watching me, you know?"

"They've probably been warned through the grapevine to keep an eye on you. Since your job *is* to tear down all their brothers and sisters."

Dan shot her a look. Was that supposed to make him feel better?

She winked. A grin stretched across her face. "Get it? See what I did there? Grape*vine*? Vine? Plant? Tree? Eh? Eh?"

"Yeah, yeah. I got it." He rolled his eyes and forced a smile.

"It's not even our property. As long as they don't cut down any of our trees or open up a nuclear waste dump, a dirty bookstore or some strip club, just leave well enough alone. It's far enough from us that we won't even notice it's there."

She leaned over and kissed him. "Remember, this is supposed to be your vacation. So enjoy it, damn it." She smacked his knee and walked out the door for her jog.

Dan flopped on the bed and stared up at the ceiling. Christy was right. The clearing was far enough away that it shouldn't be any of his business.

Still.

He remembered how the parted path was heading directly for their home. Yeah, far enough away…but for how long?

For the next couple of days, because of the unseasonably warm weather, the area was pummeled with heavy rain instead of snow or sleet. Dan stayed indoors, which wasn't all that bad because it kept Robbie inside with him. They made up for lost time by playing games, watching movies, and to avoid going stir crazy, playing catch with a football in the basement.

Robbie even slept better at night. Besides the occasional clap of thunder, there were no more 'bones breaking' in the woods to wake him. He actually seemed a lot more relaxed.

Unfortunately, the same couldn't be said for Dan. He tossed and turned at night with his mind wandering to the clearing beyond his property. When he couldn't sleep, he'd go outside for a smoke. He'd stare into the yard with his back pressed against the house so the overhang kept him dry from the heavy rain. Even with the flood lights on, his view barely made it halfway across the lawn. Everything beyond its immediate beam was swallowed by a wall of black. The visibility was just as bad in the daylight from the sheets of rain, mist, and the fogbank that rolled in.

Little did Dan know that all the bad weather was acting as a curtain onstage, hiding its performers as they took their places, waiting for their big reveal at the start of the show.

The elements eventually took mercy on the area, clearing out and allowing the morning sun to shine for the first time in three days. But it wouldn't last. Another front was approaching fast.

Garbed in his pee wee hockey gear, Robbie was on the back porch, waiting for Dan to take him to his seven a.m. practice. He was going to be late. Christy had already left for the office earlier than usual while it was still dark and had forgotten to wake Dan. Both of them raced to get ready with Robbie being the victor by a few minutes.

Dan rushed outside, sliding the glass door closed behind him. "Come on, champ. Let's get a move…" He froze in his tracks, his jaw unhinging.

Robbie stood on the edge of the porch, staring into the back-yard.

In the distance, the trees that bordered their yard had moved. Parted.

The clearing had made its way to their home.

Dan shook his head in utter disbelief. What he was looking at was impossible. But apparently it had indeed happened under the cover of the bad weather and claps of thunder. Because there it was, his grassy yard funneling into some muddy, wide-open trail through the woods. Just as before, the oaks lining both sides leaned outwards, away from the bare strip of earth.

But this time Dan got his answer as to why the trees were tilting.

In the far off distance, a single tree stood dead center at the end of the wooden corridor. It was enormous, almost twice the size of the oaks. While the trees around it were bare, their foliage shed since late autumn, the solitary tree was as green as the summertime grass.

"Dad? What's going on?" Robbie whispered with fear rattling his words.

Dan didn't have an answer. "Come on, son, let's…let's get you to your practice."

He put his arm around Robbie and guided him to the minivan. As they both walked to the vehicle, they glanced back, almost in unison, finding that the green behemoth seemed to have moved slightly closer.

With Christy at work and Robbie playing all day at a friend's house after practice, Dan had the entire day to himself. His original plan was to get as much yard work done before the new batch of storms rolled in.

Instead, he found himself cautiously approaching the leafy monstrosity in awe. At its crown, two enormous branches reached up toward the sky, giving the tree its Y-shape and in turn, a human form. A titan stretching to the heavens. Green ivy draped from its limbs and coiled around its trunk, completely concealing its bark.

It wasn't until Dan was closer that he realized what he thought were vines hanging from its limbs was actually Spanish moss.

Walking around its trunk for a look at the backside, he discovered tracks in the mud. Much like the marks left by a sidewinder in the desert sand, squiggly indentions in the wet earth trailed behind the tree the entire length of the clearing. The thing must have slid there from God knows where.

Actually, Dan had a damn good clue as to its possible origin.

His head spun just thinking about it. It was too much to take in. Too crazy. He stumbled away from the tree and across the muddy clearing to the safety of his yard.

Heading back to the house, he knew that after taking a few shots of whiskey, he was going to make a phone call to bounce his insane theory off someone.

Dan was waiting in the driveway when the Jeep Cherokee pulled in.

His partner Jeff, a portly man in his early forties, stepped out of the vehicle. "What's so important you couldn't tell me over the phone?" Jeff asked.

"If I told you what it was, you wouldn't have come. So follow me, I need you to take a look at something."

"Bastard kinda looks like its wearing one of those Ghillie suits that snipers wear," Jeff said. "Only one tailored for King Kong."

"You don't find any of this odd?"

Jeff stared at the parted trees and the green giant. "I think it's odd that someone plowed a path through your property without you knowing it. Even under the cover of all that thunder and rain."

"I told you, nobody did anything. This just happened. By it-self."

"Okay, so you got yourself a sink hole that already filled itself back in?"

"It isn't some sink hole. Those oaks lining the side just…*scooted* there… during the storms. And then that big green thing appeared."

Jeff chuckled. "Yeah, right. I think you got yourself cabin fever from being cooped in the house for too long."

"Just tell me something."

"What?"

Dan nodded at the green monstrosity. "Does that look familiar?"

"Ahh…sure."

"How? From where?"

"I don't know…" Jeff said, shrugging. "With all that Spanish moss it looks a lot like those trees in Baton Rouge."

"Kinda like the ones we cleared for the highway project, right?"

Jeff took a few steps closer and squinted. "Yeah. Sure. I guess."

"Okay then, for simplicity's sake, let's forget all this talk of trees moving on their own, out of the way. Let's just focus on what the hell a Louisiana swamp tree is doing right hear in my backyard!"

A phonebook sat on top of the kitchen table, opened to the local university's directory. Jeff stood at the kitchen counter and poured himself a steaming cup of coffee while Dan paced with his cell phone.

"That's the earliest you can get here?" Dan paused and glanced into the backyard through the kitchen window. "No. Yeah, yeah, I understand. I just appreciate that you haven't hung up on me already. I promise you'll see what I'm talking about when you get here. Hopefully you'll be able to make some sense of it." He nodded. "Okay. Thank you, Andy. Okay, goodbye." He snapped his cell shut and then the phone book. "Monday is the soonest he can make it out. The head of the department is gone for the winter break, but this Andy kid works at the campus arboretum and he can come out and take a look at it then."

Jeff shrugged. "So? That's it?"

"Who else can I call? 9-1-1? The tabloids? An exorcist?" Dan threw up his hands. "It's a tree for God's sake. I don't need anyone else calling me crazy."

"Hey," Jeff pointed at him. "If it gets any closer, you can always take a company chainsaw and cut the sucker down. Or better yet, use one of our bulldozers. Problem solved."

Dan forced a chuckle. Actually, it wasn't such a bad idea.

Later that afternoon, the gray clouds returned and the sky went dark. And once again, the rain fell in thick sheets, making it impossible to see anything beyond a few feet.

Right after nightfall, Christy arrived home with Robbie, picking him up from his friend's on her way home from work. They entered the dark living room and found the blinds closed on all the windows except the sliding patio door. Those were pulled open, providing a view into the rain-drenched, inky abyss that was now their backyard. A recliner sat in front of the door, facing outside as the windswept rain splattered the glass.

Dan sat in the chair, only the back of his head visible over the top of its cushion.

Robbie rushed over to him. "Daddy! Daddy!" The boy paused and looked down at his father's lap, where an axe lay. "What's that for?"

"Oh-ah…Daddy's just playing fireman, that's all," Dan said with a smile.

Christy giggled as she hung their wet jackets on the rack in the hall. "I thought fireman was *our* game." She approached her boys.

"Careful, Robbie," Dan said. "It's sharp."

Christy stepped in front of the chair, her back against the window. Looking down at Dan, her eyes widened when she saw the axe on his lap. Robbie was running his tiny finger along its metal head, approaching its sharpened edge. Dan took a hold of Robbie's hand. "I said be careful. That's the bad end."

Both turned and glanced out the window into the rainy void. A flash of lightning and crash of thunder made Christy jump.

"Is it for *that*?" Robbie asked, staring outside.

Dan nodded.

Christy's cheeks grew flushed. "Robbie! Go upstairs and play. Mommy and Daddy need to talk."

"But…"

"Go, Robbie!" she said.

"But, I wanna play fireman with Da…"

"You heard your mother. Now go. I'll be up later. After I'm done with Mommy."

Thunder rumbled and a shiver shot up Christy's spine, apparently from her husband's poor choice of words while holding a very large axe.

Dan kissed Robbie on the forehead. "Go on, bud," he told his son gently.

Robbie huffed but left the room. His footsteps were heard ascending the stairs.

Christy studied Dan, who silently stared out the window, ignoring her. She spoke very calmly and equally soft. "Dan? What's going on?"

"I want you and Robbie to stay at your mother's. At least for tonight."

She looked at the axe. "Okay. Fine. But why do you have that?"

"To protect us."

"From what?"

"From that," he said, nodding at the window.

Christy turned. A flash of lightning lit up the backyard, allowing her to see deep into their lot of land. Her mouth fell open.

"I can't believe you didn't see it on your way in," he said.

The yard went black again. She waited for more lightning to confirm what she'd just seen. When it finally lit the sky again, she stared in awe at the moss-covered leviathan. It was now out of the woods and standing in the *middle* of the backyard.

With his parents behind him and just over his shoulder, Robbie sat on his bedroom floor playing a video game. Christy went through her son's closet and dresser, packing a bag for him while Dan stared out the window, the axe at his side.

"Dan, I wish you'd come with us," she whispered.

"I can't. It's here for me. Not you guys."

"What?"

"It's like you said. I've killed enough of its brothers and sisters in my line of work. Maybe I've reached my limit. Maybe something had to be sent to stop me."

She shook her head in disbelief. Her eyes dropped to the axe in Dan's hand. "Okay, I'm not leaving you alone. If you want us to go, you have to come with us. *Please.*"

"If I run, it'll only follow me. I have to see what it wants. To put an end to all this."

"It's a tree, Dan! I don't know how the hell it's moving, but for Christ's sake…"

Dan guffawed. "It just slides. Inch by inch. I mean, think about it? Who stops to notice if a tree is out of place? Who really notices trees at all anymore?" Staring back out the window, he whispered,

"But I'd sure like to know how it crossed all those roads without anyone noticing."

"Dan, please…"

"You guys need to go now." He raised the axe, holding it with both hands. It wasn't a threat, but the action still made Christy shiver.

She snatched the bag off the bed. "Come on, Robbie. Let's go see Grandma."

"Hold on. I'm almost at level three," Robbie said, frantically pounding on the controller.

"Robert," Dan said forcefully. "Listen to your mother."

Hearing his father address him by his formal name, Robbie quickly powered off the game console and television. "Aren't you coming with us?" he asked, climbing to his feet.

Dan smiled and knelt before him. He placed the axe on the carpet and hugged his son. "I will when I'm done here." He kissed Robbie on top of his head and squeezed him tight. "I love you, bud."

"I love you too, Daddy."

Christy extended her hand to Robbie. "Let's go." She looked at Dan and nodded. "I love you."

"Love you, too," he said and picked up the axe. "I'll walk you guys to the car."

Dan watched the minivan roll down the driveway. Even through the torrential downpour, he could still make out Robbie's little face pressed against the rear window, waving goodbye.

When the minivan disappeared around the corner, he turned back to the house and looked up. A strobe-like flash of lightning illuminated the towering tree, now next to the house. His eyes shifted to the open garage; at what sat on the top shelf near his workbench. He nodded, knowing he had to work fast. He knew Christy would return after dropping Robbie off at her mother's. Her immediate concern, God bless her, was that of the safety of their son. To get Robbie away from the house, the colossal tree, and his crazy Daddy with the big axe. But she'd return to try to talk some sense into him. Get him to leave.

But he couldn't. Not yet. He had one last job to do.

Dan placed the axe on the workbench and grabbed the chainsaw off the top shelf.

Marching through the blinding rain, he rounded the corner of the house and stopped at the base of the massive juggernaut. Lightning flashed overhead and backlit the tree against the storm clouds. Rain fell in his eyes as he yanked on the chainsaw's pull cord. Again and again, he ripped the cord until the motor roared to life. He squeezed the trigger on it and the teeth on the metal chain spun at such velocity that they became invisible. He held up the smoking and screaming chainsaw. "I'm gonna cut you in…"

One of the top branches swung down and slammed into him, knocking the saw from his grasp. The power tool flew, end over end, into the air and disappeared into the void.

Dan landed on his back with a wet thud. He frantically wiped at the muddy water blinding his eyes. There was a loud rumble from above—not thunder in the sky, but something *within* the tree.

He scrambled to take flight. As he rose, the muddy soil around him moved from the tree's roots, squirming and slithering below the surface. He turned to flee, his heart ready to explode in his chest. Forget this! Forget even trying to make it to the house or the garage. His plan was to just run—run as fast as he could all the way to the safety of his neighbor's house miles down the road.

A few steps into his flight, something sprung from the mud and coiled around his legs, cementing him in place. Dan screamed and clawed at the thick tree roots wrapping around his limbs. With each struggle to break free, the roots only tightened their grasp.

The sound of splintering wood came from over his shoulder. Dan turned toward the noise and saw a long slit running down the length of the ivy covered trunk. The green gash pulsated and puckered like a hungry mouth. An enormous black tentacle shot out of the opening and flailed wildly in the night sky. He stared up at the appendage in equal parts awe and terror. More rumbling, then another tentacle snaked out. Then a third, a fourth, a whole series of them emerged until at least a dozen thrashed around the tree and into the murky sky.

The roots holding him in place suddenly let go, sucking back into the muddy earth like a fat man slurping a strand of spaghetti. He was free!

As he turned to run, one of the tentacles from within the tree trunk lashed out and wrapped around his leg. Dan wailed in agony at what felt like a million needles tearing through his flesh. It coiled around his leg, encasing it from ankle to thigh. He clawed at the tentacle, digging his fingernails into it. He ripped his hands back in pain, and saw they were swarming with insects. While trying to shake the bugs free, he screamed in horror as a series of lightning bursts finally illuminated what the tentacle consisted of…

It was a teeming mass of tiny insects and critters, all clinging to one another. Leeches, snakes, ants, locusts, spiders…every imaginable insect, arachnid, and small reptile that stung, pinched, spat acid, all biting into his leg. They slithered and scuttled over one another, their segmented and scaly bodies forming an interlocking appendage that stretched back into the quivering tree trunk.

The writhing limb threw Dan up into the air, and then slammed him back into the mud. He tried to move but the numbness was spreading in a wave from his leg to his upper body. Was he going into shock?

Paralyzed from the crushing blows? Or was the venom that was being injected by the insects taking hold?

Lying on his back, he could only watch as the other tentacles rose into the air, hovering directly above him.

A long overdue debt was about to be paid in full for all the trees that he'd destroyed—as well as interest earned for all the living things that once dwelled in those trees and could no longer call them home.

A web of lightning streaked across the sky behind the flailing mass. It was the last thing that Dan saw before the remaining tentacles came crashing down upon him.

And with that crushing blow, the first of *many* debts was finally collected.

Christy's minivan skidded to a stop in the driveway. Running through the pouring rain, she leapt onto the front porch and entered the house.

"Dan?"

Her call went unanswered. She yelled again and again for him, each time more desperate for her husband's response. She searched every room on both floors, including the attic and basement, her frantic calls echoing throughout the house.

Rushing into the backyard, she screamed for him. A series of lightning flashes lit up the property.

The yard was empty. The tree was gone. The only evidence of its existence was a rain-filled trench—left from its enormous weight—which led back to the edge of the treeline.

The other trees were all back in place, having returned to the exact positions they'd stood in for decades.

Christy fell to her knees and wailed for Dan, knowing that wherever the monstrosity had returned, it had taken her husband with it.

A month later, Jeff lay in bed with his mind racing. The stress of running the construction business without Dan kept him up most nights.

Eyes closed, he exhaled and flipped over on his stomach, hoping the change in position would help him sleep.

Then he heard the crack outside, somewhere in the distance. Jeff rose and ripped back the curtains. He peered into the dark woods outside his bedroom window. Another loud crack caused him to lurch away. It sounded like some local punks were lighting firecrackers out there.

He tilted his head and listened closer. Another crack! Then another!

No, the noise was more like…that unforgettable sound he'd heard when he fell off the Jungle Jim as a kid and landed on his arm.

The crack echoed again throughout the murky woods.

He shivered.

Yeah, he thought, *it does kinda sound like bones breaking.*

THE FLOODLINGS

KEVIN LEWIS

Last Monday, Jake Smith sat at his desk in his computer software company, COMPUTECH, showing all his coworkers more pictures of his baby daughter, Sarah. Last week was a good week. A dry week.

This week he sat in his basement, pumping water from the downstairs living room, back out to his front lawn. His wife, Beth, was on the couch, cradling Sarah in her arms. In one hour the two would switch places. This had been their routine for the past two days. There were moments when Jake thought that maybe he and his family should have done what the majority of his neighbors had done: evacuate!

"You were the one who wanted to move to New England in the first place," Beth said to him after Jake swore at the never-ending rainfall.

"Yeah, yeah," he retorted. "It'll all be over soon."

It wasn't over.

The rainstorm blew all of the meteorologists' forecasts away. The storm worsened and turned into a hurricane. By then the sewers had overflowed and flooded roads and backyards. Basements flooded and people escaped to their upper levels for refuge.

For Jake Smith and his family, their entire basement was flooded with over a foot of water.

Sarah slept with Jake and Beth, in their bedroom, while her frightened parents watched their daughter sleep. Watched and drank. Each held a bottle of beer in their hand and each had a horrified look on their face. Silently they crept over to the window, opened it, and glanced down at the street below. They both shook their heads in irritation and shuddered from the cool air. The street was an ocean of rainwater mixed with water from the lake down the street. That was the awful part of living next to a lake. If it flooded, everyone got the excess water. Not a pretty picture.

"When is it going to stop?" Beth asked Jake. She was practically on the verge of tears.

Jake stared at his beautiful wife of five years. Beth's hand rested against her forehead in agitation. Her black hair was all ruffled for she hadn't done it up in days.

He was concerned for her because she was an emotional wreck through tough situations. Jake had to be as calm as he could manage. "Soon, sweetheart. These storms happen. We live in New England, remember?"

They had moved from Florida to Barrington, Massachusetts three years ago to escape the hurricanes and flooding that seemed to plague the state every year.

Now they were right smack in the middle of a hurricane that seemed to have no end in sight.

"I know, but we haven't heard anything new from the local cable access station. They're never off the air during storms."

"When there are new updates, they'll inform us." However, Jake knew Beth was right. The cable access station never went off the air, even when they were repeating the same old information.

"HELLO OVER THERE!" a familiar voice shouted out.

Jake and Beth looked across from them. Sam Billings, their neighbor from across the street, leaned out his bedroom window.

"Hey, there, Sam!" Jake shouted back. "Want a drink?"

"Sure, why the hell not?"

Sam vanished from the window and emerged outside a minute later, where he hopped in his canoe that was tied to the front stairs, and rowed across the street.

"This is one hell of a storm, huh?" Sam said as he uncapped his beer bottle and took a swig.

"You got that right," Jake said, sitting down next to Beth.

Sam was getting on in years. He was in his mid-sixties but still kept active. Every summer he and his friends would stay at a cabin in Maine and go canoeing.

"I wish the TV station would return with more information," Beth said. She was really getting nervous.

"Honey, they will." Jake tried to sound reassuring to his wife, but figured he had failed in the attempt.

"You didn't hear?" Sam asked.

Jake and Beth looked at their neighbor.

"Hear what?" Jake asked.

"I heard from a friend of mine earlier that witnesses heard screaming from inside the station."

"Oh, my God!" Beth said. "What happened?"

"That's the strangest thing. The police aren't sure. All they said was the station was deserted. But that's not all the witnesses said."

Sam paused. He sounded as if he didn't want to continue the story.

"Go on, Sam," Jake urged. "What else did your friend say?"

"The witnesses thought they saw grotesque-looking heads surface out of the water outside the station, swimming away not long after the screams ended."

"That's crazy," Jake said. "What are you saying? That monsters slaughtered an entire local cable access station."

"Maybe. Christ, I thought it was a crazy story at first, but now I'm not so sure."

Sam Billings told Jake and Beth the tale:

"It happened when I was a boy. Right here in Barrington. My father was the police chief during the hurricane of '45. The entire town flooded. During the hurricane, my father was hot on the trail of a murderer. Freddy Barnes was his name. He was accused of killing his wife. Heat of passion or some crap, I don't really remember. Well, my father and a couple of his officers chased him down into the sewers. Why the hell Barnes ventured down there, I'll never know. Probably figured the cops wouldn't dare go after him. He was wrong.

"At some point, they lost sight of Barnes so my father suggested they split up, which was why his story was never corroborated. My father journeyed down a long tunnel that eventually led to an underground cavern. What my father told me he witnessed always gave me the shivers. According to him, he saw what he described as *fish* people eating the flesh of Freddy Barnes. My father figured that the creatures bashed Barnes' head in, killing him instantly; because he swore he never heard a scream. The fish monsters stood like humans but clearly had fish features: scales all along their bodies and dorsal fins on their backs. Their pectoral fins served as their arms and razor-sharp claws protruded from the pectoral fins. They weren't ordinary fish, though. My old man said they stood on their caudal fins, like a man standing on one foot.

"The creatures stared my daddy straight in the face. My father didn't know what to do. He wanted to run. He wanted to shoot the monsters. Hell, he still held the gun in his hand. But he couldn't muster up the courage. Instead, the creatures took what was left of Freddy Barnes and dove down into the water.

"No one believed my father, and any evidence washed away after the sewers flooded the streets. There was, of course, an investigation into what the hell happened. My father was found negligent. He simply lost Barnes in the chase. But my father still stuck to his story: that fish monsters devoured Freddy Barnes. The town laughed him right into a mental institution. I myself didn't believe him. Until now."

Jake, Beth, and Sam sat silently in the bedroom, Sarah still sleeping quietly in her crib. Rain continued to pour outside.

"That's unbelievable," Beth said, breaking the silence.

Sam shook his head. "That one incident tore my family apart. When my father told his side of the story, everyone looked at us differently. It was as if my family had become the black sheep of Barrington. We were outcasts. I remembered when my father was the respected chief and he and my mother would dress up and socialize with the town's elite. They would attend all of the popular functions. The mayor's fall and winter ball. I had so many friends, and people would whisper to each other when I'd walk down the street.

" 'That's the police chief's son,' they'd say. But when he told his crazy story, that all went away. No one wanted anything to do with us. My parents stopped receiving their annual invitations to the mayor's functions. I lost my friends because their parents were afraid I'd turn out just like my father. Hell, my mother refused to visit my father, her own husband, in the mental asylum out of embarrassment. And all because of a monster story. But now I'm not so sure. There's definitely something out there."

"But what could it be?" Jake asked.

"My father called them Floodlings, fish monsters that surface during floods. After the incident with the prisoner, he researched about fish monster lore. You wouldn't believe the folklore about this stuff. It became his obsession when he was finally released from the mental asylum. Nothing else mattered. I remember entering his study one night. I can still remember it vividly. It was during a horrible rainstorm, if you could believe it. My father was listening to the weather report on the radio in his bedroom, so I figured he'd never catch me. The walls of the room were cluttered with fish monster drawings, drawings he drew of the Floodlings appearance. Grotesque monstrosities, if you ask me. A pile of books lay on his desk with titles ranging from *Fish Monsters of the Deep: The Real Truth!* to *Earth's Monstrosities*. I thought my father had truly lost his mind. I was afraid he was becoming deranged. He needed to be sent back to the asylum.

"I heard footsteps in back of me. I turned around. My father stood in the doorway of his study. His face was filled with shock because I believe he didn't want me to witness his findings. He asked me what I was doing in his study. I wanted to run the hell out of there but I just stood where I was. I couldn't outrun my father. He was the ex-police chief after all. I simply told him that I wanted to find out what he was doing. He said, 'I'm trying to protect us. You, your mother, myself. Everyone.' He truly sounded like a lunatic at that moment," Sam said.

" 'From what?' I asked.

" 'From the Floodlings,' was his response.

"I told him he wasn't making any sense. My father said they were real. He had seen them in the sewer tunnels and that ever since then he'd been researching them. The Floodlings have always co-existed with us and we just never knew it. They're fish creatures that hide from the rest of civilization in the deeper depths of the ocean. My father said that this breed of Floodling came from hatchet fish. They can enter dry land for a little while, but like all fish, they thrive in the water. In fact, my father said these fish creatures have evolved so much that they can survive in oceans, rivers and lakes. He said this species of hatchet fish was called Gasteropelecus sternicla. They mostly swim with their own kind and thrive in South America in the Amazon River but he figured many of them migrated to Massachusetts years ago. He told me they were also known for gliding along the surface of the water, which makes them appear as if they're flying. I just couldn't believe what I was hearing. *Fish creatures?*

"I told my father that his theory was ludicrous. I was about to leave to get my mother when he said, 'You're just like the doctors. I'm not crazy.'

"That's when he left me alone in his study. I became nervous when I heard the front door open. My father had no reason to go out at night, especially on his own.

"I rushed outside and saw my father enter his car and turn on the ignition. He had a worried and frightened expression on his face.

" 'Dad, come back,' " I called to him. He ignored my yell and backed out of the driveway. He drove away into the night. I called for my mother who was asleep upstairs. She slept a great deal after my father returned from the asylum. My mother just couldn't cope with the fact that her husband had mental issues. She was so used to being the police chief's wife, Mrs. Socialite, that anything less was unbearable. It took a moment, but I finally woke my mother. She wearily looked up at me, her face tired and sad.

"She asked me what was wrong and I told her that Dad had taken off in a frightened state. She just stared at me without a care in the world.

"'He'll be home soon,' was her only response. She was in such a depressive state that my father's bizarre action didn't bother her one bit. An hour later there was a knock at the door. I answered it. It was Detective Joseph Crowley. He was my father's right hand man when he was chief and the only one who still treated my family with respect. In fact, it was Detective Crowley who brought my father home from the asylum.

"'Sammy,' he said. 'I need to talk to you and your mother.' I nodded my head and Detective Crowley entered my house. When my mother finally crept downstairs, Detective Crowley delivered the horrible news. My father had driven his car off a bridge and into the ocean. He'd drowned and all because he feared the Floodlings' return. And it looks like they have."

Jake felt sorry for Sam. Jake had always had a great relationship with his father and it saddened him to hear Sam, who was such a kind and thoughtful neighbor, talk about the disintegration of his father's state of mind as well as the destruction of his family. He still was undecided about whether he believed Sam and his fish creature story, but he still felt sorry for the old timer anyway.

"Oh, well," Sam said after a brief silence. "I'd best be going. Thanks for the beer."

Sam stood up and so did Jake and Beth.

"Anytime, Sam," Jake said. "You're sure you don't want to wait out the rest of the storm with us? We have plenty of room."

"That's very kind of you, but I'll be fine. I stocked up before the storm hit."

Jake and Beth walked with their friendly neighbor to the front door to see him off. When Sam hopped into his canoe, he turned to the young couple and said, "You need anything, you give me a holler, you hear?"

"Will do, Sam," Beth answered.

Sam picked up his oar, turned around, and began rowing back to his house. Jake was about to close the front door when he heard a squealing noise emanating from the street. "Did you hear that?" he asked Beth.

"Hear what?"

Jake shook his head, confused. "I'm not sure." He continued glancing around the street. Suddenly he eyed bubbling water in the middle of the street, next to the McClusky's house.

"You see that?" Jake pointed in the direction of the bubbling water.

"What is that?" a worried Beth asked.

He was about to respond when he noticed another bubbling eruption in the opposite direction. Sam was rowing in between them.

"Sam!" he shouted out to his neighbor.

Sam stopped and turned around. "What's up?"

"Turn around and come back toward us. There's something out in the street."

"Oh, hell, Jake, did my story scare you that much?"

"Sam, just do it!" He wasn't joking.

"Look!" Beth said; she sounded mortified.

Jake turned to where she was pointing.

Two heads bobbed up from the flooded street. They weren't human heads. They were fish heads and their glassy eyes were fixated on Sam. The old man finally came to his senses and started rowing back to Jake's house.

"That's it!" Jake shouted. "This way!"

Faster and faster Sam rowed, but the Floodlings swam with faster speed. It wasn't until Jake was staring intently at the monsters that he discovered why. The Floodlings weren't swimming. They were gliding along the surface, which gave them a quicker pace.

One Floodling that was in back of Sam eventually swam underneath the canoe, and moments later surfaced about five feet in front of the old man. Sam screamed as he jabbed his oar at the monster, but the Floodling grabbed it with its fin and bit it in half.

Beth screamed and the only thing Jake could do was to cup his hand over her mouth to cease the screams. He knew he was being selfish but he didn't want the creatures to come after them, too.

More Floodlings surfaced around Sam and they grabbed him, tearing apart his raincoat. Sam struggled with the creatures but he wasn't strong enough. Pretty soon the Floodlings' sharp teeth made contact with Sam's flesh and they feasted on the old man, whose father had warned everyone about the potential invasion of the underwater creatures.

Once there was nothing left of their dinner, the Floodlings dove back into the water, leaving the neighborhood quiet once more.

After witnessing the slaughter of Sam Billings, Jake and Beth returned to their bedroom. Both were silent and frightened; Beth wrapped her arms around her waist and shook uncontrollably. Jake covered his face with his hands. They sat at the foot of their bed and stared at the barricaded bedroom door. He didn't know if it would stop the creatures if they tried to get in, but it was all he could do.

"What are we going to do?" Beth cried. "Why isn't anyone coming for us?"

Most likely not everyone knows about the Floodlings, or the Flood-lings ate them, Jake thought but didn't bother telling Beth. In her state of mind, she didn't need to hear his inappropriate joke.

He comforted Beth, wrapping his arm around her shoulder. "It'll be all right, honey. We just have to wait it out."

In his mind, though, Jake wasn't so sure. *Those creatures out there tore Sam apart. If they had free reign of the flooded streets, what's to say they won't enter the house?*

"Let's feed Sarah. I bet she's hungry," he suggested.

Beth only nodded her head. They stood up and walked over to Jake's side of the bed, where they had placed Sarah's crib.

It was empty.

"Where is she?" Beth asked, horrified.

"I don't know. We put her right here, didn't we?" Jake's mind was wandering a mile a minute as to where she could be. Sarah couldn't have just vanished.

"Sarah!" Beth frantically screamed. "Where are you, sweetheart?"

No answer, not that they were ever expecting one because Sarah couldn't talk.

Jake removed the furniture from the door and they rushed out of the bedroom and searched the upper level. The bathroom was empty. That left the computer room, and the only other possibility would have been that Sarah had crawled down stairs into the living room or flooded basement. They prayed that wasn't the case.

As they exited the bathroom, they heard Sarah crying in the computer room. Relieved, they quickly entered the room only to stop dead in their tracks. Five feet in front of them stood a Floodling, standing on its caudal fin, its back facing them. It took a moment but it finally turned around, revealing a small object wrapped in a blanket that it held in its pectoral fins.

Sarah. The Floodling was everything Sam Billings' described. A total monstrosity. Its head was that of a hatchet fish, its sharp teeth grinning at the horrified parents. Green scales covered its body.

Jake was too slow to stop Beth from screaming. She flailed her arms in the air in horror as she advanced toward the Floodling and her child. "Give me back my baby!"

"Beth, no…"

Another Floodling lunged at Beth from one of the closets. Beth screamed as its teeth tore into her. Jake rushed over to attack the

Floodling but the creature swiped its pectoral fin sideways and smacked him across the room. He wearily stood up, dazed from his injury. Blood poured down his forehead. As he regained his senses, he saw that he was the only one in the room. Jake walked out of the room and back into the hallway, and heard squealing noises coming from the living room.

He slowly descended the staircase and saw two Floodlings' standing in front of the open front door. One held his baby girl and the other held his dead wife.

"Please, give me back my wife and child?" he pleaded.

The Floodlings stared at him for a long moment, as if truly contemplating whether to return them to him, but in the end, they turned around and dove into the water, leaving Jake alone.

He sank to the floor, tears streaming down his face.

Jake didn't know how long he lay crying on the floor, but finally he stood up and went to the open front door, the carpet soaked as the rain seeped in. As he stared at the empty, flooded street, thoughts filled his head. Where had they taken his wife and daughter? Although the idea sickened him, he concluded that the creatures would probably eat them. He was unable to suppress his tears. He'd just lost everything he ever loved, that made life worth living. No one was coming for him. For all he knew, everyone in the city had been slaughtered by the Floodlings.

Although Jake knew what lurked in the depths of the flooded street and beyond, the water looked soothing to him. Stepping out into the rain, he dove into the cold water. Moments later he surfaced, and when he did, he realized he wasn't alone. Near him, several Floodlings floated in the flooded street.

They stared at him.

They'd been waiting.

THEY CAME FROM THE CAVE

ADAM P. LEWIS

"Fire her up, man!" Ken finished tightening the last spark-plug and stepped back.

Bobby turned the key in the ignition. The engine rumbled to life as it thundered and shook the T-Bucket frame. Rick gave Bobby the thumbs up in admiration of a job well done.

"She's purring like a kitten," Bobby said, giving Ken the *okay* gesture with his hands.

"Like crazy, man," Ken smiled.

"You've outdone yourself this time."

"There isn't a T-Bucket in the area that'll take you down, Bobby. This baby is lethal," Ken bragged. He stood on top of the driver's side front tire and gestured at the engine with both his hands open. "She's a storming machine, man. Her Chevy small-block bent eight 265 engine is tuned up for maximum perform-ance. All four radials are pressurized. The fronts are ribbed and the backs are grooved. She'll hug the corners like a dame hugging your waist at a sock hop while bobbing up and down to Eddie Cochran."

"I dig, man, I dig!" Bobby clapped his hands together and smiled at the thought of a buxom blonde fitted in tight clothes that allowed her bullet brassier to almost poke his eyes out if he got too close to her breasts.

To his dismay, Bobby's imagination was interrupted. His drag opponent, Steve, pulled his T-Bucket alongside Bobby's. "You're eating my dust tonight, Bobby-boy!"

"Cool it, Steve. Your machine drives like a tank." Bobby waved off Steve's comment and lit up a cigarette. He took a long drag and blew the smoke towards Steve as if to say *go fuck yourself*.

Steve revved his engine out of spite. It burbled and nearly stalled before backfiring twice and settling into a soft rumble. His face became warm and reddened with embarrassment. The engine didn't sound intimidating, especially since it wasn't hopped-up like Bobby's T-Bucket with a small-block engine. Steve's engine was stock and the only modification was replacing the hot-air intake pipe with a cold-air intake pipe to increase horsepower.

Bobby rested his forehead on the steering wheel and laughed while smacking his knees with his hands. Amused, Ken lost his balance and fell off the tire and onto the ground. He wrapped his arms around his stomach and laughed.

"Keep laughing and I'll serve up a knuckle sandwich!" Steve threatened with fists curled and shaking toward Bobby and Ken.

"No need to flip out, Steve. You're a gas, man!" Ken laughed from his knees. He pushed up with his hands on the tire and calmed his laughter by faking a coughing fit.

"We'll see who has the last laugh when I win! I'll be waiting for you at the finish line!" Steve said, leaning his torso over the T-Bucket door.

"This baby will be burning rubber and lying patches up and back before you even start," Bobby said, patting the steering wheel and running his palms along the dash. "I'll have it made in the shade!"

"Can it, fellas," Jenny interrupted in a boisterous tone. "Before you two boys go ape, I've got to lay down the laws, ya dig." She strolled sensually between the two T-Buckets, pushing her hips side to side.

Bobby reverted back to his imagination when he caught sight of Jenny's body. Her large breasts were cocooned inside a tight bullet brassier under a sleeveless blouse with only the bottom three buttons snapped, which allowed her ample cleavage to be exposed. After getting an eyeful, Bobby's gaze shifted down her curvy waist to her wide hips. The way her fitted blue jeans swayed toward his T-Bucket, as if in time to an up-beat Chuck Berry record, was mesmerizing. Her swift walk teased him into thinking she was a fast girl who liked fast cars, fast music and fast times.

Bobby's gaze then followed back up Jenny's curvy body to her beautiful face. It reminded him of Eva Marie Saint: a round chin ascending into high pronounced cheekbones with an innocent smile negated by seductive eyes that suggested she loved it hot in the backseat of a roadster.

Jenny's French Pleat hairdo gathered her hair together on one side. It then rolled her hair up and inwards vertically against the back of her head. The ends of her hair were tucked into the roll to create a perfectly clean look. Bobby drooled at this. He loved that look on woman and nearly busted his belt buckle and through his zipper.

"Ain't she the bitter end?" Steve asked, patting his hand over his heart and sighing.

"A second balcony date with a dame like that's worth losing a pink slip for!" Bobby said, dabbing his shirt collar across his sweaty forehead.

Ken shook Bobby's shoulders, jarring him awake from his day dreaming and back into reality. "You won't have a set of wheels to paint the town red with a dame like that if you don't focus on the race." Ken's speech slowed. "Man, stop thinking about those curvy hips, that tight blouse and those full red lips…oh man, she's the bitter end!"

Jenny walked past the car and stood twenty feet beyond them. She pushed her hips to the left and rested her hand high on her voluptuous waist. She raised her opposite hand over her head. A white scarf flapped in the cool summer breeze. Her upper lip curled to the left and she winked at Bobby and Steve.

"This drag is for pink slips, boys!" Jenny yelled over the rumble of the engines. "To keep the race fair, there are two simple rules to follow. No swerving at each other's machines and the first to the top of West Mountain and back down wins!"

Loud cheers and claps roared from the crowd gathered to watch the drag race. Wagers were made for money and packs of cigarettes. Some of the girls were bothered by the loud rumbling engines and plugged their ears up with their fingers. Those that didn't cuffed their hands over their ears or acted as though it didn't bother them. That was how the boys acted. They didn't want to come off as soft to their girlfriends or the girls they wanted to impress.

Two fisticuffs broke out over which car was the meanest machine. To the horror of the fighters' girlfriends, the boys didn't stop fighting until the word *uncle* was muttered. The boy who lost was sure to go home alone after the drag race crowned a winner. There wasn't a single female there that wanted a boyfriend with a glass-jaw.

The girls who argued let cooler heads prevail and didn't swing fists at each other. They decided to let the cars do the talking.

Jenny stood motionless for almost a minute. The tension started to build. The low murmur swept over the crowd as they became anxious for the drag race to begin. Bobby's foot began to ache with nerves and excitement. He gripped the steering wheel so tight that his knuckles cracked. The suspense also got to Steve while waiting for the scarf to drop. His legs shook from side to side and he ground his teeth.

Jenny dropped her arm and threw the scarf to the ground in one quick motion. The drag race began.

Bobby slammed his foot onto the gas pedal. The back tires of his car tore up the dirt and shrouded the back of the car in a cloak of dust. Rocks kicked back and pelted the front row of the crowd. Grooves were dug into the ground. When his tires caught traction, his T-Bucket exploded through a cloud of dust kicked up by Steve's ride.

"Damn!" Bobby yelled. He stared in anger at the backend of Steve's T-Bucket.

Bobby hadn't lost a drag race and didn't intend on losing this one. All styles of hopped-up cars from his hometown and the neighboring counties came to Lake George to challenge him. But he hadn't torn into the dirt before. He was usually two car lengths ahead at the drop of the scarf. Now he had to catch up. He was in unfamiliar territory.

Bobby's tight grip on the shift stick turned his knuckles white. He squinted and kept his eyes focused on the road. His concentration was as solid like his nerves. The tension of the pre-race overwhelmed him but now that his wheels were rolling, his nerves were soothed. He thought of nothing else but the road before him. Every turn, every bump and every tight turn was memorized. He knew how fast his T-Bucket could take every corner without compromising the turn and careening off the road and rolling into a ditch.

He'd seen other drivers do so in his rearview mirror. He also saw them die. T-Bucket's were faster with the canopies retracted, resulting in deadly rollovers with the drivers being strewn from their seats. But their accidents didn't keep Bobby from blazing down the streets. He was fearless and confident.

Steve glanced into his rearview mirror to see Bobby's T-Bucket was gaining ground and was now half a car length behind him. He kept the gas pedal floored. "Come on, dig in!" Steve pounded his fist on the steering wheel. His T-Bucket rounded the first turn up

West Mountain. His tires lost traction, causing the back end to fishtail and skip around the corner, black skid marks left in the T-Bucket's wake.

Bobby rounded the turn smoothly and accelerated out of the corner and swung his T-Bucket to the left. He knew after the first turn that there was a stretch of straight road for half a mile. This was his only opportunity to take the lead. If he didn't, he'd have to wait until he reached the summit and whip his T-Bucket around and floor it. If Steve did the same, he knew he'd have to take a wider turn and wait until he rolled up to the straight stretch again.

Bobby skipped gears from second to third. His T-Bucket lurched forward and paralleled Steve on the right.

"Not this time!" Steve yelled over the roar of the engines.

Steve jerked the steering wheel. His T-Bucket swerved. Bobby stomped on the brakes, down shifted, and found himself two car lengths behind.

"Cheat!" Bobby yelled. He watched Steve's T-Bucket disappear around a bend in the road. Bobby slammed his foot on the gas pedal and peeled out. His T-Bucket fishtailed before catching the blacktop and continued screeching up the mountain road.

Steve looked over his shoulder and laughed. When he looked back at the road, his cigarette fell from his mouth and he yelled. He jerked the steering wheel. His car careened off the side of the road, crashed through the guardrail, and down an embankment. The T-Bucket rolled three times and came to rest upside down, a cloud of dust consuming it. Steve had been thrown clear and was laying partly-conscious fifty feet away from his car near the top of the embankment.

Rocks and dirt began to roll past his body. He heard footfalls on the ground. When the person came into view, he looked up. His eyes were blurred with tears and his eyelids fluttered and broke up the image. He couldn't determine who the person was but he knew no one else was on the mountain but Bobby and himself.

"Bobby!" Steve whispered. "Help me, man. Don't let me die here."

Steve received no answer. He closed his eyes and reached up his hand. "Please, Bobby…help me."   He felt a hand wrap around his wrist, then felt the ground beneath his clothes moving. He was dragged up the embankment. When he reached the top, he could hear the thunderous rumble of a small-block engine racing up the hill. Bobby hadn't dragged him back to the road. He opened his eyes and squinted.

"Who the hell are you, mister?" he asked.

The man lifted his foot above Steve's head and stomped down onto his face, shattering his jaw. His eye sockets buckled in. His nose broke. A large piece of the nasal bone broke free and pushed into his frontal lobe, killing him.

On the road, Bobby slammed his foot on the brake pedal. His T-Bucket skidded a hundred feet and came to rest half that distance from Steve's body.

He grabbed the windshield and pulled himself up. He locked eyes with the man standing over Steve's body. The man grunted and ran off into the woods.

"What the hell are you kids drag racing up West Mountain for? Don't you know it's illegal?" Sheriff Murphy inhaled a lungful of cigarette smoke and exhaled out of his nostrils.

Upon observing the way Sheriff Murphy exhaled, Deputy Frank straightened his uniform. He knew the sheriff wasn't amused with the situation at hand. Exhaling through the nostrils was the sheriff's way of relieving stress and showing annoyance and tolerance.

"We know, Sheriff," Bobby said. His head hung low and he kicked at the dirt with his foot.

"Like hell you do, son!" Sheriff Murphy flicked his spent cigarette to the ground. "You were doing it and now I've got a dead body bleeding all over my road!"

"Sorry, Sheriff."

"What did this guy look like again?" Deputy Frank asked. He held a notepad, ready to jot down the murderer's description.

"He was short, muscular and hairy," Bobby said, raising his hand off the ground near his shoulders to compare the height of the murderer to his five foot, ten inch height.

"What was he wearing?"

"He was only wearing shorts. I couldn't tell too much because it was dark."

"Which way did he go?"

"Into the woods." Bobby pointed in the general direction.

"So let me get this straight. You came around the corner and saw this guy crush the kid's face with his foot? And when he saw you, he took off running into the woods?" Sheriff Murphy asked. He rolled his eyes in disbelief.

"Yeah, that's what happened." Bobby nodded.

"Deputy Frank." Sheriff Murphy pointed an unlit cigarette at Bobby. "Take our pal here into custody. I want his car towed and impounded."

"What about the killer? You can't arrest me, I'm innocent, I swear!" Bobby pleaded.

"I don't believe your story one bit, son." Sheriff Murphy struck a match, inhaled the flame into the end of a new cigarette, and flicked the lit match at Bobby's feet.

"You think I killed him?" Bobby ran his fingers through his greased, black hair in stress and started breathing heavy.

"You greasers, I know your type. You race for pink slips. I bet you were losing and caused an accident and tried to cover it up with some far fetch scheme about a husky-looking killer." Sheriff Murphy turned and got into his squad car.

"I swear that's what happened," Bobby insisted. His head was guided through the rear car door frame by Deputy Frank.

"If I were you, son, I'd come clean when you go before Judge Matthews in the morning," Deputy Frank insisted, then slammed the door closed on Bobby's protests.

Rick climbed between the driver and passenger seats of his hopped-up '56 Chevy Bel Air hardtop and stretched out onto the back seat. Jane smiled and joined him. She lowered her pelvis atop Rick's and pressed her lips against his. Their legs intertwined as did their tongues. Between kisses, Rick could feel Jane's hot breath on his face and began to guide his hand down her torso. He found the bottom of her shirt and inched his hand up and underneath to her soft breasts.

Jane jumped and sat up. She looked through the condensation fogging up the back window.

"Sorry," Rick said. He sat up and leaned against the inside of the passenger door.

"It's not you," she whispered and pointed out the window. "I heard something, like a grunt. I think someone's watching us from the bushes. Maybe it's that guy who killed that drag racer the other day."

Rick wiped his palm across the condensation on the window and looked outside. He saw nothing but the dark silhouette of the trees and bushes swaying in the summer breeze.

"I don't see anyone." He leaned into Jane and began kissing her neck. He paused and said, "Besides, no killer is dumb enough to return to the area where he committed the crime."

"Maybe you're right," she said and leaned into Rick's body again.

"I know I'm right!"

Jane's head tilted back. She wanted to enjoy the ticklish yet sensual feeling of Rick's moist lips seducing her, but she couldn't keep her focus off the bushes. Even though Rick made sense by saying no killer would return, she still felt tense a while longer.

The spot on the window where he'd smeared the condensation had fogged over. The bushes behind the car were out of sight and now out of her mind. She closed her eyes and began to enjoy the kisses upon her neck. Rick placed his hands on both sides of her torso and pulled her down on top of him.

He grabbed the bottom of her shirt and lifted it up to her shoulders. Suddenly, Jane shot up again and wiped both of her hands across the back window and looked through the streaked condensation. She pulled down her shirt.

"I heard another grunt. It sounded louder this time. Go out and check."

"It's probably a raccoon," Rick said, unbuttoning her pants.

She grabbed his wrists and pushed his arms away. "Knock it off."

"Why the hell did I drive you up here if you're gonna act like a frightened baby the whole time?"

"Would you rather sit at the car hop and drink extra-thick milkshakes with your greaser friends than be with me?"

"I'd rather just get into your pants."

"If you want to get into my pants, you'll go see who's making that noise. I don't want some creep watching us."

"I don't care who's eyeballing us as long as I'm on cloud nine."

Rick sat up and climbed back into the front seat. He grumbled to himself, "I've got the fastest doll in town and she can't put out while wild animals look on, just my luck."

"Call me fast again and you can go back to that paper shaker ex of yours and watch her cheer from the grandstand at homecoming."

Jane wouldn't leave Rick and she knew it. She was too attracted to him. He had a fast car, James Dean looks, attitude and style. His leather jacket wasn't cracked or faded like other boys' jackets she'd seen; Rick's jacket was smooth like the way he presented himself to authority figures. He could get out of any pickle he found himself in.

Rick was equally attracted to her. She helped him win the pink slip for his Bel Air. When the drag race started, she whipped her scarf to the ground, signaling Rick and his opponent to put the pedal to the metal. She also flung nails from her scarf in front of the opposing car, which resulted in a blowout a half mile into the race.

Rick pushed open the driver's door. He adjusted the crotch of his pants and loosened the tightness created by the make-out session. From his back pocket he removed a comb and ran it front to back through his oiled-up hair. He walked around to the back of his Bel Air and froze in fright at the sound of a guttural grunt coming from the bushes.

He turned his head to Jane while keeping an eye on the bushes. "Hey, I heard it that time."

She leaned over the backseat and cranked the window up. She then locked the door. Rick looked in at her. "Why'd you lock the doors? I said it's probably just a raccoon."

The grunt rumbled from the bushes again and Rick's head swished around. "That sounded too big to be a raccoon."

"I told you," she said, cowering behind the passenger seat. Her fingers curled over the top of the seat. Only her head from the eyes up could be seen peeking over the headrest.

"Cut the gas, baby, hush," Rick covered his lips with his index finger.

"Don't have a cow," she replied.

"I said play dead! I'm tryin' to listen, out here."

Jane shut up and stared out the window. Rick was showing the attitude that she was attracted to. He was the typical greaser, slicked back hair, jeans rolled up to his ankles, cigarettes rolled up onto his shoulder within his undershirt, switchblade hidden in his sock and a screw the world attitude.

Rick bent over and lifted up his jean leg. From between his sock and calve he removed the switch blade. He pressed the switch. The blade sprang out, making a loud metal *clink*.

"You've got me pretty salty, bud, come on out of those bushes or I'll slice you up!" Rick demanded.

A raccoon charged out from under the bushes and ran. Rick breathed a sigh of relief and closed the blade.

"See, told ya it was a raccoon." He turned and smiled.

Jane's body suddenly went rigid. She pointed over Rick's shoulder and screamed. Before Rick could turn, a heavy tree branch, carved into the shape of a crude club, swung down onto his head. His skull split open and blood splattered across the back windshield and across the hardtop. Rick's collapsed to the ground, his legs and arms twitching.

Jane started whimpering. She scooted over into the driver's seat and pulled down the visor. Car keys slid down the visor and fell onto her lap. Picking up the keys, she fumbled them between her fingers, trying to find the ignition key.

A shadow appeared on her left and the driver's side window shattered, showering Jane with pieces of glass. An oversized hand covered in course hair with calloused finger tips and scarred palms reached into the car and grabbed Jane by the blouse, pulling her out of the car.

Jane landed hard on her back. She looked up and saw her attacker standing over her with a club clutched in his left hand. His brow protruded over his eyes, making them look recessed and black. His head rested atop a short neck, giving the impression his head was drooped. His nose was wide and flat. Beneath was a bushy mustache that faded into a matching beard.

His scalp was hidden underneath short nappy hairs, his shoulders were broad and molded into thick, muscular biceps and hairy forearms. His chest was covered in dirt and hair that trailed down to his pubic area, which was concealed underneath a deer pelt. The pelt hung a few inches passed his thighs. His legs were built the same as his arms, thick and hairy.

He grunted and swung the club up and brought it down onto Jane's skull, knocking her unconscious. Then he reached down, grabbed a fistful of her blonde hair, and dragged her away.

Sheriff Murphy shined his flashlight on Rick's body as he tipped his police cap back with the flashlight handle. "Clean this shit up before it hits the papers," he said to Deputy Frank.

"Poor kid," Deputy Frank said. "Who do you suppose did this, Sheriff?"

"The same maniac that killed that drag racer." Sheriff Murphy scratched his temple and lit up a cigarette. "Some junkie looking for money to buy a fix, probably."

Deputy Frank bent down and lifted up Rick's legs, then dropped them and pointed at the ground. "Golly, take a look at that!"

Sheriff Murphy shined the flashlight beam on the ground. Implanted into the dirt an inch from the body was a wide footprint nearly fifteen inches long. He shined the light on the footprints. The light followed them across the dirt ridge and into the brush.

"Call for backup. I want a roadblock set up. No one gets in or out."

"What are we going to do?"

"Follow those footprints. I'm hedging my bets that when we find the guy who made those tracks we'll find our killer."

A car rolled up to the murder scene. The engine shut off and a lanky young man with pock marks, wearing a button blue down shirt and matching slacks stepped out.

"Damn," Sheriff Murphy said while lighting up a cigarette.

"What's the matter, Sheriff?" Deputy Frank asked.

"It's that snoop Reed Smith, son-of-a-bitch is going to have this all over the front page in the morning."

"That's just what we need. People will be gossiping and heading up here to take a look at where the kid was murdered. The crime scene'll be ruined."

Flashbulbs lit up the gruesome scene.

Reed let his camera fall from his hands to hang from the strap around his neck. He pulled out a notepad and pencil from his back pocket, and tried not to look at the dead body as he asked the sheriff, "What happened here?"

"No comment."

"Any clue to who or what did this?"

The sheriff began to walk away but paused when he heard the word *what*. "What do mean *what* did this?"

"Come on, Sheriff." Reed smiled. "Don't you pay attention to what the kids are talking about at the car hop?"

"I'm the sheriff. I'm too busy for shakes and burgers. I've got more important business to tend to than to sit around at the car hop."

"But you just left there. You even have the tray still hanging off your window." Reed pointed the eraser end of his pencil at the squad car.

Angered, the sheriff swatted the pencil out of Reed's hand and grabbed his shirt collar. "Either you tell me what the hell you mean by *what* or I'll arrest you for obstruction."

"Okay, okay, Sheriff, relax." Reed straightened out his shirt. "I'll tell you. Word is there's some sort of beast living in a cave up here on West Mountain."

"What cave? Why the hell should I believe that some sort of beast is living up there?" The sheriff pointed up the mountain side.

Reed nodded at Rick's lifeless body. "That's all the answer you need. First Steve Williams and now this kid. That makes two teenagers killed this week in the same area. And the killer isn't that kid you arrested a few days back. He's still in jail. A new murder means that kid is innocent and he should be released."

"Don't tell me how to do my job." Sheriff Murphy removed his gun from its holster and opened up the cylinder. He turned it and checked to see if each chamber was loaded with a bullet, then closed it and returned it to its holster. He took a drag off his cigarette and blew it at Reed. "If I read about all of this in the paper tomorrow, I'm gonna run your ass out of town. I've got a maniac on the loose and you're talkin' about monsters. All I know is some murdering, lowlife drifter is living in a cave somewhere and I have to find him."

"Then why check your gun for bullets if you don't think what I'm saying is true. It's because that's what did this, a monster. Not some drifter. This is the story of the century, Sheriff. I could win a Pulitzer."

"I said keep it out of the papers."

"Then I'm coming with you to the caves."

"The only place you're going is back to your office."

"Fine, then tomorrow's headline will read, 'Cave Beast Slays Second Teen.' "

The sheriff sighed. "Fine, get in the squad car. I swear, for your sake, there better be a beast up in that cave or I'll seal you up inside and leave you till Christmas."

Another car pulled up. Mitch and his girlfriend Claire got out and ran up to the sheriff. Claire saw Rick dead on the ground, turned and buried her hands over her face, then her head into her Mitch's chest.

"Damn, Frank, didn't I tell you to call for backup. I wanted access up here cut off!"

"I called. It's not my fault they're slow getting up here."

"What happened here, Sheriff?" Mitch asked.

"You know him?"

Mitch nodded. "Yes, sir, that's Rick Anderson. His father owns Anderson's Hardware on Route 9."

"That's Pete Anderson's kid? Damn it, that'll tear him up. Pete's a good guy. A good bowler too," Frank said.

"Regardless. Do you kids know anyone who would want to kill Rick?" Sheriff Murphy asked.

"It's not someone; it's *what* did this to him," Claire said, wiping tears off her cheek with her blouse.

"You two in on this cave monster talk, too?" The sheriff rolled his eyes.

"It's not talk, it's the truth," Claire snapped. "It almost got us a few nights back. After Steve was killed and all, we had to go see for ourselves. We swore we wouldn't come up here again but rumors are spreading around town tonight that the monster got another one."

"You can help out by getting back into your car, turning around, and going home before you get yourselves hurt or killed," Sheriff Murphy ordered.

"But we know where the cave is," Mitch said.

"How do you know that?" Sheriff Murphy asked, surprised.

"We followed him."

"Him?"

"It's…I can't believe I'm saying this but…it's a caveman,"

"Goddamn it, now I'm supposed to believe there's a Neanderthal running amuck millions of years after extinction and killing teenagers?"

"We saw him, Sheriff. We know it's hard to believe but it's true," Claire argued.

"I don't like this situation at all." Sheriff Murphy exhaled cigarette smoke through his nostrils. "Caveman or drifter, it doesn't matter, either way I've got a killer to apprehend." He pointed to the kids. "You two are gonna lead me to this cave. Once we get there, you both head back home. Understand?"

"Yes, Sheriff," Claire said and Mitch nodded.

Led by Mitch and Claire through the woods, Sheriff Murphy, Deputy Frank and Reed followed the recently cleared terrain. Freshly matted down leaves and broken twigs littered the path. No footprints could be seen but the outline of feet where the caveman had stepped on the brush creating the path was visible. Along the sides of the path, scattered remnants of dead squirrels and opossum were found. Their underbellies were gouged out. Bite marks could be seen pressed into their small bones.

Sheriff Murphy shined his flashlight on the ground and ordered the group to stop.

"What did you find, Sheriff?" Deputy Frank asked.

The sheriff bent over and picked up a red scarf. "Did you kids leave this behind when you followed that man up here?" He showed them the scarf.

Claire shook her head and burst into tears.

"You recognize it?" he asked.

"It belongs to Jane. It was a present I bought for her sweet sixteen," Claire said.

"We better hurry," the sheriff suggested. "If we're lucky, he may be keeping her alive."

The group continued on another half mile before reaching the cave. The entrance was hidden behind large, freshly broken-off tree branches propped up crudely in front of the opening, as if trying to conceal it. Footprints similar to those at the murder scenes were found.

"Step aside." The sheriff pushed through the group. He pulled down the branches and exposed the mouth of the cave. He drew his gun and shined his flashlight into it.

Nothing could be seen but pieces of dust floating within the flashlight beam. No noises came from within. It was quiet, as though the caveman inside was hiding and knew there was danger at the entrance.

Mitch curled up his nose. "It smells like a wet hog in there."

The stench was faint with an underlying scent of ammonia.

"Turn your flashlight on, Frank," the sheriff ordered.

Together, both flashlights created enough light to illuminate the cave. It was deep with an approximate ten foot distance between the floor and ceiling. The light only reached twenty to thirty feet short of its natural range due to the amount of floating dust. The walls looked unstable. Pieces of rock and slate crumbled off in tiny landslides when the walls were disturbed. Large and small piles of dirt collected at the foot of the walls. Rocks of various shapes and sizes loosened and dribbled across the cave floor and some dropped down from the ceiling.

Large footprints with a drag marks on either side carpeted the ground. Sheriff Murphy bent down and shined the flashlight on the tracks, studying them.

"I'm no scientist but I know for a fact that these aren't normal prints. Maybe we do have a caveman in here. And by the looks of this drag mark, he took Jane inside with him."

"Now do you believe us?" Claire asked, snidely.

The sheriff pointed the flashlight into her face and then at Mitch. "If this is a prank, you'll all be locked up and sent before Judge Hopkins in the morning. You two stay here. I'm not in any mood to track you down if this is a joke."

Sheriff Murphy bent down and studied the footprints again. They were clear and showed more detail than the others he'd seen. When compared side by side with his ten inch long flashlight, one of the footprints extended half the length of the flashlight, estimating the footprint to be fifteen inches long.

The sole rounded off in a flattened oval. The sides of the footprints bulged out like a football and then curved back into the toes. The toes themselves were round and about the size of half dollar coins. They were separated and bent, suggesting they were broken and were never set to heal properly.

Deputy Frank pointed his flashlight beam at the drag mark left by Jane's body and asked, "If that was made by Jane, then what's this drag mark on the opposite side?" He repositioned the light.

The drag mark was over ten inches wide. The sheriff stood up and drew his gun. "A club, a large club like the one used to bash in the Anderson kid's skull. Keep your eyes open and your gun drawn, Frank. We may have to shoot."

Scanning the cave floor for more clues pertaining to the caveman, they spotlighted piles of rotting mush, the original of what they smelled when first entering the cave. Only now the smell was clear as to what it was. It was feces, black and oily and similar in size and shape to hotdog buns. Next to the piles, they found large puddles of mud.

"Urine," Frank said. "I bet that's urine."

"That's so gross," Claire said, squeezing her nose closed with her fingers.

Pressed into the wall were handprints. The handprints were large in size, about an inch or two shorter in length and width of the footprints.

The dust started settling and the flashlight was able to illuminate further into the cave. They saw nothing but the same bodily droppings and footprints, the same that were scattered at the cave entrance.

Together the group ventured deeper into the cave in a slow defensive manner, leery of the caveman. They glanced behind themselves every ten feet checking for it, more so from nerves. There were large holes in the walls that it could hide in. They didn't want to be surprised by the caveman jumping out at them.

Sheriff Murphy put his hand up, halting their movement, then turned and pressed his index finger to his lips, hushing them. Pointing up the cave and to the left, he whispered, "I heard something."

A saber-toothed cat emerged from the darkness, growling low. Before anyone could move, it sprang into the air and pounced on top of Deputy Frank. Its jaw opened wide and clasped down on the back of Frank's shoulder. The sharp teeth penetrated through the muscles and tendons easily. The cat powered its head up and tore Frank's arm clean off.

Sheriff Murphy staggered backwards, firing his revolver until each bullet was spent. The saber-toothed cat sprinted back into the darkness of the cave, the severed arm still in its mouth. Frank was already dead from blood loss.

"Frank, Frank!" Sheriff Murphy shook his unharmed shoulder.

"It's no use Sheriff, he's dead. Pour guy bled out," Reed said, somberly, eying the large pool of blood near the body.

Sheriff Murphy bent down and closed Frank's eyelids, then pried Frank's service revolver loose from his hand and stood up. "Caves, Neanderthals and saber-toothed cats; what the hell is happening here?"

"Seems we've took a step back into the past, Sheriff," Reed said, snapping photos of Frank's body.

"Stop staking photos, show some respect!" Sheriff Murphy covered his hand over the lens.

Reed pulled back. "Suppose we all die here in this cave tonight. At least this film will document what happened to us. I know I don't want my family not knowing how I died. I doubt any of ours wants to go to their graves wondering either."

"Fine," the sheriff reluctantly agreed, "but just don't take photos of a body unless it's that caveman and he's dead!"

"What do we do about Deputy Frank, Sheriff?" Reed asked.

"Leave him for now."

"What? We can't just leave him here!" Claire said.

The sheriff handed Frank's service revolver to Mitch. "You know how to use one of these, son?"

"Yeah, I do."

"You and Claire, pull Frank's body out of the cave. Only shoot unless it's absolutely necessary. Understand? Don't be a hero and shoot at the first bush that wiggles. Know what you're aiming at. You might regret pulling that trigger."

"Yes, Sheriff."

"And one more thing."

"Yes?"

"Don't shoot me by accident."

Mitch nodded and with Claire's help, they took hold of Frank's ankles and dragged the body out of the cave. A trail of blood in the dirt was left behind. Once they exited the cave, they pulled Frank almost fifty feet from the opening and covered his body with the branches used to seal up the cave.

Claire collapsed into Mitch's chest and wept. Her tears were absorbed into his shirt. He held her tight in his arms and rubbed her back with his left hand. In his right, he gripped the service revolver. His palm began to sweat and the steel felt cold.

Sheriff Murphy and Reed continued walking two hundred feet deeper into the cave without incident. The saber-toothed tiger had disappeared and the stench of excrement diminished. Neither man spoke. They kept their ears focused on any noise, fearing it would be the caveman or the tiger. A grunt, moan, yell. Anything.

Then they heard the caveman's voice. But it wasn't one voice, it was many voices.

They appeared to be talking in an unknown language. Their speech between them was a series of grunts and clicks with meaning only known to them. Although the sheriff and Reed couldn't understand what the Neanderthals were saying, they knew by the intonation, high-pitched and shaken, that the Neanderthals were stressed and scared. But soon the tone changed and they started to sound angry. They began to argue with one another. Yelling echoed throughout the cave. Wood clapped together, suggesting clubs were banging against one another.

"What do you suppose they're saying to each other, Sheriff?" Reed whispered.

"No clue." The sheriff tipped his cap and scratched his head. "But whatever they're saying, it doesn't sound good for us. We need the upper hand."

Beneath the arguing and wood banging, the soft whimpering of a female could be heard. Her voice was different from the Neanderthals. It wasn't harsh. It was pleasant even in a crying state.

"It's Jane, has to be," Reed said.

Sheriff Murphy nodded. "We've got to get closer. We need to get her out of there."

"And how are we supposed to do that? Jesus, sounds like there's a dozen of them in there."

The sheriff raised his gun. "A few rounds exploding around them and they'll scatter. We'll have, I don't know, maybe seconds and if we're lucky, a minute to get her out of there."

"Seconds don't sound very appealing to me."

"I'll chase them. You get to Jane and guide her out of the cave."

"What about you?"

"Don't worry about me, I'll catch up."

Reed followed the sheriff as he neared the Neanderthals. Again, the two men started to smell the thick stench of body waste. On the dirt walls, flames lit up the section of cave in which the Neanderthals were gathered. Churning on the ceiling, black smoke drifted and lingered, unable to dissipate due to the lack of ventilation.

Sheriff Murphy stopped. He pressed his back against the wall and peered around the corner. There he saw them, the Neanderthals. Their faces and bodies were just as described to him. Even the females and their offspring looked primitive and simian with large brows, flattened noses, matted and short hairs, thick lips and dark eyes. Some were fully nude and some wore only an animal hide around their waists.

The chamber they were gathered in was no larger than a five hundred square foot basement complete with a damp smell. The ceiling was higher than the ceiling leading to the chamber by about five feet. Large stones protruded from the ground which they sat upon. Toward the back of the chamber was a large opening leading from the chamber to an unknown area. The sheriff figured this to be the Neanderthals' only option for escape. They would follow it to either a back entrance or it looped around to the front entrance.

The women were tending to their children by either breast feeding or picking bugs from their hair and eating them. The men were banging clubs together and pushing each other around as if vying for dominance.

A fire was burning in the middle of the room. Lying on her back next to the fire was Jane. She was shaking in terror as one of the women picked at her hair.

Reed peeked around the corner and asked, "Where do you suppose they came from?"

"Some hermit family maybe. I bet they've been up here for a while," the sheriff suggested. He ducked his head back around the corner, looked at Reed, and whispered, "This is it. Once I start shooting, there'll be confusion. That'll be your opportunity to grab Jane. She's in the middle of the chamber by the fire. Run to her, grab her, and lead her out of the cave."

Sheriff Murphy breathed in deep, psyching himself up, then bolted around the corner. He fired his revolver. Following the pop of the gun, the Neanderthals screamed. Reed could hear their feet shuffling, the men grunting in anger as their home was breeched, and the women screaming in fear for their children's lives.

Clubs whirled as gunshots popped. Bullets began dropping the cavemen. Their clubs never struck the sheriff. He stood out of reach of them and they bounced harmlessly at his feet most of the time. Sensing they were in danger, the cavemen turned and followed their women and children through the opening in the back of the chamber. Close behind, the sheriff pursued.

In the confusion, Jane stood up, turning around in circles, not knowing where to run. All she knew was a gun was being fired. The next thing she knew, her arm was grabbed and pulled in the opposite direction that the Neanderthals were fleeing. The hand on her arm felt different. It wasn't coarse, hairy and bulky. It was smooth, thin and weak. She didn't fight it. She followed, knowing that the hand was benign.

When Mitch and Claire heard the gunshots, Mitch pulled back the hammer on the revolver and started for the cave entrance.

"Where are you going?" Claire asked.

"They're in trouble. I've got to help."

"You're going to leave me? Here, alone with a dead man? What if those things are coming for us? What will I do?"

Mitch knew she was right. He had to stay and protect her. Standing at the cave entrance, he looked into the darkness. He squinted, hoping to see the faint illumination of a flashlight coming into view, then crept closer to the entrance when he heard feet quickly scuffling along the dirt floor of the cave. He backed up and raised the barrel of the gun, pointing it into the cave.

"Something's running this way," he said in trembling voice.

"Who is it?" Claire asked.

"I can't tell. I can hear grunting." He began backing away from the entrance. Turning to order Claire to run, when he looked back she was already gone.

He kept the gun pointed into the cave. His finger twitched and began to pull back on the trigger, but he didn't have the will to pull it. He was too frightened. Whatever was coming his way was going to kill him. He knew it; he saw it play out in his mind. He saw cavemen swinging their crude clubs, bashing down on his skull and their thick hands pulling his limbs from his body and feeding them to the saber-toothed tiger. Not even the premonition of his own death gave him the courage to pull the trigger.

In the darkness of the cave, Mitch began to see figures coming at him. When he finally had gathered the courage to pull the trigger, he found he couldn't. The gun had slipped from his grasp. He pulled a phantom trigger and only then did he realize he was no longer holding the gun.

Mitch closed his eyes and prepared for the worst, waiting for the Neanderthals to pummel him to death just as he figured they must have done to the sheriff, Reed and Jane. He heard the gunshots, the screaming and the crying.

"Mitch!" a female voice called out.

He opened his eyes and before him was Jane. He smiled as she fell into his arms. He hugged her tight and consoled her as she wept.

Mitch looked up to see Reed and asked, "Where's Sheriff Murphy?"

"He should be coming out anytime now." Reed turned and looked back into the darkness and listened. He heard and saw nothing.

He stepped into the mouth of the cave, formed a cone around his mouth, and called, "Sheriff! Are you all right?"

Sheriff Murphy's eyes fluttered open. He gazed up into the sky. Above, he saw a flock of large-bodied winged creatures. Their snouts were long, thin and opened up, releasing a piercing caw. Arched cones protruding out of the top of their skulls extended to the mid of their backs.

Oversized talons dragged behind their stubby tails as they flew over the tops of strange trees of which the sheriff never saw before in text books or in the Adirondacks.

The trees towered taller than any skyscraper he'd seen. The leaves were the size of bus tires and as black as the rubber which the tires were made of.

The bark of the trees were gray and appeared scaly and shiny when the sunlight gleamed off them. Jumping from leaf to leaf were tree frogs ten times their normal size.

In the distance, he heard a loud growl and it made him shiver. He'd heard that growl before in the cave. It had come from the throat of the saber-tooth tiger.

The echo of the growl told him the carnivorous feline was far away, but circling near enough to attack if it built up the nerve.

When he looked down, he found he was naked. A throb on the back of his head and a dampness in his hair made him recall what had happened to him.

He remembered chasing the cavemen through the opening in the back of the chamber, then running through a bright light. Then he was attacked and knocked unconscious.

The taste of blood still lingered in his mouth from where he'd bitten the tip of his tongue. He began to feel a strain on his ankles and wrists. He fixed his eyes on his wrists and whimpered. They were tied to a thick branch that could support his overweight body which hung from the branch.

He rubbed his wrists and ankles together, trying to break the fibers that bound them together and to the branch, but the fibers were too strong. He couldn't escape.

He looked behind him and over his shoulder at the ground below. There he saw a pile of brittle leaves and sticks. Then he looked around. To the right he saw an opening to a cave. To his left he saw the Neanderthals. They were gathered around him.

They were grunting at each other and pointing at him. From the group, he saw one of the cavemen approach him with a blazing torch.

The brute threw the torch on top of the sticks and leaves. The dry foliage burst into flames and a second later the skin on the sheriff's back began to bubble and melt under the heat of the flames.

The Neanderthals were pleased that the cooking of the man from another time had begun…they were hungry.

THE LAST WAR

ANTHONY GIANGREGORIO

M*ark's Journal: entry 503*

We never saw it coming.

One year ago, while the people of Earth slept in their beds, or on the opposite end of the planet where they were working and playing, the aliens came out of the sky.

There was no warning, nothing. Our radar defenses were useless, their technology far beyond anything we had at our disposal.

And so too were our weapons.

We threw everything we had at them. Rockets, missiles, jet planes with smart bombs, nothing so much as put a dent in any of the fifty mother ships that hovered above the major cities of the world. The U.S. military was about to try nuclear arms but were destroyed before any could be deployed.

The most terrifying thing was why they came to our world.

They came because they were hungry.

The term 'monster' had been used in science fiction for thousands of years, but the aliens that visited our world were the very essence of what a monster should be.

The smallest one was well over seven feet tall. They had three eyes, and four arms. Other than that they were frightening similar to humans. The third eye was directly in the center of their oversized foreheads and their arms were in the same place humans were. The one main difference was their skin tone. Where Caucasian human beings were flesh colored, say pink for an easier reference, the aliens were as white as clean sheets of the same hue.

Which was how the slang name for them was created.

We called them 'sheeters.'

To anyone reading this who never saw one in person, the name might sound odd, but trust me, when you have a sheeter standing over you, ready to rip your head off so it can suck you like a silly straw, the name is very apt.

When they first arrived, we had hopes they were friendly.

There was even a large assembly on the front lawn of the White House, where the President of the United States and the alien commander gathered to discuss why they came to our planet.

But no sooner did the alien commander and its delegation arrive and stand before the President, then the commander reached out, took the President's head in two of its large hands, while the other two hands held the man by the waist for leverage, and pulled upward, tearing the President's head off like his neck was made of paper mache.

As you can imagine, pandemonium ensued as Secret Service agents began shooting. No sooner did the chaos begin than the alien delegation pulled out some strange kind of guns. They were short, stubby even, no more than four inches long, and they didn't shoot conventional bullets. They shot out a beam of light. Not a laser, but an actual beam of pure energy.

Wherever the beam touched human flesh, said flesh began to sizzle and then melt. Within a minute of the initial killing of the President, the entire crowd surrounding the podium had been turned into a pink ooze that soaked into the grass.

A few escaped and spread the word as well as what the cameras got before the operators were killed, melted like ice cream in the hot sun.

It was chilling to say the least.

From that moment on we were at war, and from the looks of the planet, this may very well be the last war ever fought here.

I suppose it's a small consolation that we as a world, as in mankind, didn't end up destroying ourselves, that it was an outside enemy that was doing it.

Small consolation, I know.

"Hey, Mark, it's time to leave, get a move on," Peter snapped out to me from across the room.

I looked up and gave him a wave, letting him know I'd heard him. Closing my journal, I came back to reality and where I was. I was in the underground vault and basement of a bank on West 54th with twenty other survivors.

As far as we knew, we were the only ones left in the city. The sheeters had been hunting humans more than normal lately and were taking out our camps by the droves. Some of us had decided to leave the city, to head to the mountains where there was a better chance of surviving. But most of us—the ones who still wanted to fight—who hadn't given up entirely, we stayed; no one was gonna make us leave our city, our home. This was our planet, and by God we would take it back or die trying.

Unfortunately, the latter was what was probably going to happen as we were overmatched, outgunned and low on supplies.

As a rebel unit we were pathetic and where we once would venture out to attack guerilla warfare style, now all we did was search the remains of the destroyed city for food and other essential supplies.

As I put my journal away, I let my eyes scan over the people who had become more than just friends to me; they had become my family.

Peter was our leader. He was a little over six feet tall with long blonde hair and a pale complexion. Before the sheeters arrived, he would have been considered to be a surfer boy. He had that look.

Next was Mary. She was short and stubby, with black hair cropped tight to her head. She wasn't very pretty, I'm sorry to say, and she was covered from head to toe in tattoos. She looked like a midget biker chick. But they say it's inner beauty that matters, and Mary had it in droves. She could make you laugh in a second and always had a smile for you, no matter how hard things had become.

The next of our ragtag group was Marty. In his late fifties with gray hair and a beer belly, he would be the last guy you'd think would be a rebel. He'd been in the Iraq war and he knew how to survive. He'd been a handyman in his former life and he was the one in the group who would keep things running, such as the generator we had. Truthfully, I don't know what we would have done without him.

The next in the group was Rose. She was in her late twenties but had a soul much older. She was like our mother. She would always be there when we lost someone on a raid or out searching for food, or just needed a shoulder to cry on in general. She was beautiful, and even with her face and clothes covered in dirt from lack of water from washing, she always seemed to look better than the rest of us. It was just her way.

There were others, too, but they weren't in my immediate circle of friends so I won't go into details on who they were or what they looked like. The ones I described were the only ones that *really* mattered to me. They were my family now.

I looked up to find Peter was standing over me, talking.

"Huh, what?" I asked.

"I said, snap the hell out of it and get your gear, we're leaving in five," he said and walked away.

Mary came over to me and I looked down on her. She was a foot shorter than me easy, though she wore boots with heels that added a few inches to her height. She handed me a pistol.

"It's all cleaned, Mark," she said. "It has a new coat of oil, too."

"Thanks, Mary," I smiled. "All I know how to do is point and shoot it."

"And you can't even do that too well," Peter called from over his shoulder. A few other guys within earshot chuckled but I ignored them.

"Hey," I said casually. "We all can't be action heroes."

"That's for sure," Peter replied, getting more laughs from any-one close enough to hear.

"Peter, that's enough. Mark does what he can, we all do," Rose said like a stern mother. "Now say you're sorry."

Peter looked down, like he was a child caught with a cookie before dinner. "Sorry, Mark."

"No problem," I replied.

Peter cleared his throat and clapped his hands. "Okay, let's get moving. Bruno and Garibaldi, you're coming, too."

Two disheveled men in their thirties looked up from where they sat playing poker in the corner.

"Seriously?" Bruno asked, annoyed.

Peter nodded. "Yeah, we need two more sets of hands. The last search party thinks they found the rubble of what was a super-market. If it's true, we'll need more men to carry what we can find back here."

"But we just got back this morning from a run," Garibaldi said.

Peter walked over to the man and pulled the cards from his hand, dropping them on the table.

"Hey, what the hell?" Garibaldi yelled.

Peter leaned over and went nose to nose with the man. "Listen up and listen good; in case you hadn't noticed, we're in a fucking war and we're losing badly. I don't care that you were out this morning, we need the manpower and you and Bruno are who I want. Now stop complaining, grab your gear, and let's go."

Garibaldi looked like he was going to say more, but when he looked past Peter's face to see Bruno looking at him, Bruno shook his head slowly, the gesture clear: 'shut up and do what you're told.'

Garibaldi merely nodded his head and Peter's face calmed. "Good, I'm glad we're on the same page." He turned and walked back to Mary, who was chuckling, a big smile on her face.

"For a second, boss, I thought he was gonna give you shit," she said.

"Well, he didn't, so let's forget it and focus on the mission," Peter told her. Mary nodded and went back to packing her gear.

Rose came over to me and rubbed my shoulder. "You okay?" she asked, her white teeth peeking out of her mouth. I never understood how she was able to keep them so clean. We'd run out of toothpaste more than a month ago and most of us had given up on dental hygiene altogether. Hell, on any kind of hygiene.

"Yeah, I'm fine, just another day in fantasy land, right?"

She smiled, the gesture going right to her eyes, making me feel safe and secure, even when I wasn't. "That's the spirit, it's not over till it's over. We'll beat them, we just have to find out how."

I nodded slightly, not commenting on her morale speech. Sure, we were going to find a way to kick the aliens off our planet, because the entire might of the Army, Navy, Air Force, Marines and every other military machine across the planet just didn't have what it took to get the job done. But our little band of rebels did.

With everyone getting ready to leave, I did the same, as Rose walked away to spread her high spirits to the rest of the group.

Two hours later found us picking our way through the rubble of what was once a U.S. city. On both sides of us was nothing but steel and concrete wreckage, the buildings destroyed by flames and sometimes artillery fire.

Bruno was on point, then came Peter, myself, Mary, and Garibaldi brought up the rear. Garibaldi carried one of our most prized weapons, a grenade launcher which was connected to his rifle. If we were attacked, hopefully that would do the job of taking down our enemy.

The sun was high in the sky as we made our way to the location Peter had marked on a map. If the last search party was correct, there could be canned food that our group sorely needed.

My palms were sweaty and I had to keep switching hands with my gun to wipe them clean on my pants. I wasn't a warrior, and never claimed to be one, but through simple circumstance I now found myself playing soldier, only this game was far deadlier than anything I might have played as a boy with my friends.

The enemy I was up against was ruthless. The enemy didn't want to just kill me, but if possible, wanted to capture me so I could be made into a meal.

We had all heard the stories of humans becoming nothing more than cattle and there were rumors of breeding camps near Australia.

Stolen pictures by spies who somehow managed to escape, showed aliens sitting at tables while human torsos were served up, much like humans cooked pigs whole. From what I'd heard, it was our eyeballs that were the cherished prize, a delicacy to the aliens. But though the eyes were popular, believe it or not it was male testicles that were the caviar to the enemy. I tried not to think about some alien sheeter munching on my balls as if they were fine chocolate, but the images I'd seen back when the internet was still up would stay with me forever.

Like most of the old life, the internet was long gone thanks to the aliens blowing up all of our satellites.

"I got movement at three o' clock," Bruno said and held his hand up to stop us.

I snapped back to reality and felt my heart beat faster in my chest. Man, I swear I wanted to piss myself right then and there and only force of will stopped me. Next to me, Mary gripped her M-16 tighter and grinned slightly. She was fearless and I had to say I was envious. Being scared all the time wasn't a good thing, though some said it was why I'd stayed alive for so long.

"Firing line, now," Peter snapped, and we all lined up beside one another so there would be no chance we would shoot a friend instead of the enemy by accident. If there had been more time we would have spread out so not to be such a close target, but no sooner did Peter give the order to line up, then we heard the rubble shift some more as something approached from around a large pile fifty feet ahead of us.

The soft click-clack of safeties coming off and weapons being cocked filled the air around me as I waited for what would come next.

Bruno was the first to speak as the origin of the noise was discovered. A dog appeared and walked closer, its hackles raised upon seeing us, while growling softly. "Oh shit, it's just a dog."

We all let out the breath we were holding as the mangy, half-starved dog stopped walking and stared at us, as if it was trying to understand just what the hell we thought were doing in its territory.

Bruno was about to say something else when there was a beam of light and the dog exploded into a hundred bloody chunks, gore and viscera splashing all of us, despite being more than twenty feet away.

"Jesus Christ!" Peter yelled as he wiped blood from his face.

Before any of us could do anything, no matter how small, an alien patrol appeared around the same pile of rubble, their white complexions standing out like an ink spot on a clean piece of paper. We were caught out in the open, there was nowhere to run to, and though we were sorely outmatched, all we could do was fight and hope for the best.

With a warrior's yell, Peter leveled his AK-47 and began spraying the alien patrol with bullets—there were six in all. Beside me, Mary did the same. I saw her bullets crawl across the ground then jump up and begin peppering a sheeter. The alien took the barrage stoically, barely moving. Other than taking a step back from the force of the rounds, it remained unhurt.

See, sheeters have body armor that our weapons can't penetrate. Only head shots will do the job. For some reason, sheeters don't wear helmets. I've never seen one with head gear, which is odd. Someone once said it was some kind of weird honor thing with them, as if they weren't afraid of the humans enough to wear helmets. But if that was true, then why wear body armor?

As soon as the patrol saw us, they began firing at us, too. But instead of the sound of gunfire, there was only the hiss of their beam weapons.

Falling to the ground, I began to shoot, though I don't know if even one of my bullets hit anything. I heard a thumping sound and looked over my shoulder to see Garibaldi fire off a grenade. I saw his face light up as he fired and then I saw that same face vaporized as a beam weapon hit him above the neck.

Like hot wax sliding off a mold, his face melted, the skin sloughing off to puddle at his feet. He didn't even have time to yell, the air in his chest sucked out of him from the heat of the blast.

The beam weapon began to go down his body, cooking him from the inside out. His clothes blended with his flesh and his internal organs popped before the man became nothing but a pile of ooze. Even his bones were melted.

The grenade soared through the air, the man who fired it dead before the grenade landed amidst the alien patrol. When it went off, four of the sheeters were caught in the blast, and their exposed heads received shrapnel, which shredded eyes and sliced their pale flesh.

Peter whooped in victory, thinking we had the upper hand, but no sooner did the whoop leave his mouth, then one of the remaining two aliens shot him. The beam weapon was set to a finer scope, and before Peter knew what had happened, he glanced down to his abdomen to find there was nothing there but a gaping hole about six inches in circumference. He felt no pain yet and there was no blood, the beam cauterizing the wound as it happened.

Peter reached down and put his hand through the hole in his body, and as I was standing behind him and to the side, I saw the fingers of that hand wiggling back and forth, almost as if the man was waving to me.

He turned to look at me, his eyes wide with shock, then he spit blood and crumpled to the ground, very dead.

"Come on, Mark, shoot the bastards!" Mary yelled from my side. I had stopped shooting, stunned at seeing Peter disemboweled without the weapon leaving a trace behind other than a hole in his body.

Mary got in another good shot, hitting an alien in its third eye. Its head snapped back and it dropped to the ground. There was one left and I began to shoot it, squeezing the trigger again and again until the clip ran dry. I was yelling, too, or at least I think it was me yelling. Looking back, I don't even know if it was actually me or if it was Mary.

All I know was that when I opened my eyes, I saw there were no more sheeters to shoot.

"Nice shot, Mark, I guess you're gettin' better," Mary said and walked over to the aliens to make sure they were all dead. "Check on Peter," she told me sadly.

I watched her shoot a couple in the head for good measure. They may have been alive or were truly dead, but I know Mary felt good shooting them again anyway.

"Uh, thanks," was all I could think to say to her compliment. I must have gotten lucky and one of my bullets hit where it was supposed to. I went to Peter. The instant I saw his eyes I knew he was dead. I knelt down and closed them, it was all I could do for him. There was no time to bury him, as the sheeters would have called in that they'd found us. We had to move and fast or we would be in yet another firefight.

I glanced at Bruno and Garibaldi, or what was left of them. I felt my bladder want to let go again as I thought how that could have been me. I was lucky today, that's all.

"Peter's gone," I said and stood up. Mary came over to me carrying a small suitcase. "That sucks," was all she said about Peter. "We lost three good men today, Mark, but I think it might not have been in vain."

My eyebrows went up, as I asked her a silent question.

She held up the suitcase. "I'm not sure exactly what this is, but I think we just scored big-time."

"Where'd you get it?"

Mary pointed to the dead sheeters. "It was with them. One of them was carrying it." She began to walk back to the bank, casting a sideways glance at Peter as she passed him. "Get Peter's and Bruno's weapons, they're still good."

I did as instructed and asked, "Where are you going? Are we gonna check out the supermarket still?"

She stopped walking and looked back at me. "No, that's irrelevant now. We need to get this back to the bank, and pronto. What I found may give us an upper hand in this war. Or at least do some damage."

Before I could ask her anymore questions, she turned and began jogging away.

Not wanting to be left all alone, I took one last look at my dead teammates, and quickly walked, then ran, to catch up to Mary.

I had to admit my curiosity was piqued. What could be in an old suitcase that was so powerful it could do real damage to the sheeters?

We arrived back at the bank more than three hours later.

Mary made us take a roundabout route back; she was worried we might be followed. As we approached the entrance to our base, a voice called out, "Halt, state your name!"

"It's Mary and Mark," she called out. "Returning from the field."

I watched a man appear as if from nowhere. He was camouflaged with bits of debris to look exactly like the wall when he was standing still.

"You're overdue. Where's Peter, Bruno and Garibaldi?" the guard asked.

Mary shook her head. "Dead," she replied flatly.

The guard didn't ask anymore questions. We had all lost friends and loved ones and it had become par for the course. Sure, we mourned their loss, but when people died constantly, a long grief period wasn't a luxury. There wasn't time. Sometimes, all the consolation the death of a friend would elicit would be a quick nod, a handshake, or a pat on the back.

"Go 'head, we're good here," the guard said and Mary and I walked by him to the hidden opening to the bank vault.

The opening was a three foot hole that we had to slide down. The top five floors of the bank were gone, sheared off as if a giant sword had sliced it. The lower half was intact, but the windows were all blasted out and the frame of the building was severely compromised. Truth be told, we didn't know if one day the entire thing would come crashing down on us.

Mary went first, sliding into the darkness, and then it was my turn. Feet first, I went down it like I was a boy playing on a slide in the school yard. The only thing I had to remember was that I needed to keep my back pressed to the slide or I might end up without a head by the time I reached the bottom.

As I went downward, the wind whipping the sweat dry on my face, I felt the air grow cooler. Then white light blasted me and I closed my eyes, knowing I had reached the bottom. Mary wasn't there, she had already headed off to the command base, or what we called the command base, which was the vault, which I stated earlier. It was funny in a sad way each time I entered the vault. I had seen all the jewelry, money and bonds that filled the safety deposit boxes, and now, most of it littered the floors of the vault. They had been searched in hopes of finding guns or ammunition. But the contents of the boxes were pretty much worthless to us. If you couldn't shoot it, eat it, or drink it, it was all a waste of space.

I arrived in time to see Mary had placed the suitcase on a bench. With tools already in hand, Marty was looking at it, while Rose and Mary talked.

When I entered, Rose looked up at me and smiled, "Good to see you in one piece, Mark, we lost too many good people out there today."

"Yeah, I'll miss Peter, he was a good guy," was all I could think to say.

Rose nodded, turned to Marty, and asked, "Well, what is it?"

Marty was concentrating on the contents of the suitcase and he whispered to himself as he touched this and fiddled with that. I noticed a small red light start to flicker and off near the bottom, but it meant nothing to me. I watched Marty connecting a few wires and then more lights lit up. He had fixed something, I knew that. Man, he was some handyman.

Finally, Mark looked up and with a deep frown and said, "It's a backpack nuke. A dirty bomb."

"I fucking knew it," Mary said, proud of what she'd found.

"A bomb?" I said, amazed. " You're kidding. What would the sheeters be doing with that?"

Marty shrugged. "They probably raided another camp somewhere and found it. Before the communication lines went down, we were gonna use our nuclear arsenal, my guess is whoever made this was planning to do just that."

"Okay, so what can we do with it to help us fight them?" Rose asked.

Marty rubbed his chin as he considered it. "That's a tough one. See, when this thing goes off, nothing for miles in every direction, including straight up, is gonna be able to live for a long time. The radiation spreads fast. That's why it's called a dirty bomb. It's fucking nasty. Some have timers so the guy who sets it can get away but this one doesn't. It has a 'dead man's' switch." He pointed to a black button in the center of the dials and gears. "Press this button and 'boom,' no more whatever you want to kill."

"So, what? We have to kill ourselves if we want to use it? That's crazy," Mary said.

Marty nodded in agreement. "It might be to us, but to someone else, it was the only thing that made sense. The only way to make absolutely sure this baby will go off is to activate it manually. Timers and radio signals can fail. Someone went to a lot of trouble to make this. Hell, where ever they found the radioactive waste probably killed the people who got it. Probably at one of the destroyed reactors near the shore, I'd guess."

"So whatever we do with this bomb will be a suicide mission for the team that uses it," Rose said, frowning deeply.

I was about to raise a question when an alarm bell began to sound.

"They've found us!" someone yelled. "They're right above us!"

"Shit," Marty spat. The bastard's found us." He turned and his eyes shot daggers of accusation at Mary. "They followed you back here, you dumb bitch, it's the only explanation."

"I didn't do anything of the kind!" Mary yelled back as an explosion rocked the very foundation of the bank and the ceiling shuddered.

Rose spoke up. "It doesn't matter how they found us, they're here and we have to fight them off and escape. Pass the word, anyone who can get away, fall back to Base C on East 23rd Street." She waved her gun in the air and turned to me. "Mark, you're with me and Mary. Marty, get everyone you can and form a defensive line. They may be bigger than us, but down here that should be a disadvantage to them."

I knew what she meant. There was so much stuff stacked everywhere that the larger sheeters would have a hell of a time maneuvering around, while we could squeeze between piles of supplies.

"Now go!" she yelled and we headed out. Marty took the dirty bomb with him and disappeared down a corridor.

Rose led, Mary followed, and I had took up the rear. As we moved through the corridors, I could hear gunshots and people screaming, and even over their shrieks I could hear the hissing of beam weapons.

I didn't want to, but I felt my bladder let go and I peed my pants. Embarrassing I know, but everyone was a little busy to notice, and for all I knew, the rest of the camp was pissing themselves as well.

We came out in a small lobby that led to a set of stairs that would bring us to the first floor. We had blocked it off with rubble and debris but I could see there was a large section now missing, having been blown apart by the sheeters.

They were pouring in by the dozen. I counted over twenty before I think the onslaught slowed.

My God, we were so fucked.

More than a dozen of my people were firing at the sheeters, the sound of gunfire deafening. Rose and Mary each went to a marble pylon and I did the same, coming up on Rose's right side.

As Rose and Mary began to fire, I found I was frozen. All I could do was watch the battle, too scared to contribute.

I watched a man jump up from behind a stack of flour cans we'd liberated from a food warehouse and begin spraying the sheeters. The man held a riot shotgun, a Remington 870. The weapon had a short barrel and no butt stock so he could easily carry it around. It was coated black so it wouldn't catch the light and on human beings the #1 buckshot would have been deadly.

But against the sheeters it was as if the man was shooting ping pong balls.

As the man ran out of ammunition, a sheeter fired its beam weapon at him. The beam caught the man straight on, and with one yell of fear or pain, the man began to melt, becoming a puddle of goop in less than three seconds.

The shotgun dropped to the floor, the severed hands that hadn't been in the beam still attached to the weapon. The gun clattered on the floor once and remained still.

All around me was a nightmare, one I prayed I'd never be thrown into. People were screaming, some partially melted from being hit, and they dragged severed bodies across the floor. A woman I only knew as Tina had been sheared in half. She was crawling slowly away from the battle, her intestines dragging out behind her like tied cans on a wedding car. A sheeter walked up to her and stepped on her intestines, but instead of stopping her, her entrails began to spool out, reminding me of a garden hose being unwound. The sheeter raised and lowered its shoulders and I wondered if that was how they laughed. Then it grew bored and shot her in the back of the head, the face and skull disintegrating, leaving only a torso with arms.

"Come on, you fucking coward, fight!" Mary yelled when she saw I wasn't shooting. But still, I was frozen. Anger flared in her eyes because I wasn't helping, and I saw Mary swing around with her rifle to shoot me.

She would have killed me then, but a sheeter popped up behind her and grabbed her by the head. She was lifted up as if she was a doll in a child's arms, and as I stared in horror, the sheeter popped her head off her shoulders. As blood geysered out, the sheeter began lapping at it, an ambrosia of the most horrific kind.

I began to back way, too frightened to think straight, not realizing that I was walking out into the open. My eyes went to the pylon where Rose was supposed to be, but she wasn't there. I cast my eyes to the left and right and then I found her, or what was left of her.

"There's a fucking mother ship over us!" someone yelled, who had a two-way radio. "We are so screwed!"

Before I could do anything, I felt searing heat on my right side and I casually looked down, like when a fly is on your arm, and my mouth fell open in absolute horror.

Where my arm was supposed to be, right up to my shoulder, there was now nothing.

A beam weapon had caught me and my arm was gone, the wound cauterized at the shoulder. There was no pain as it had happened so fast, but as each second ticked by, my body came to the realization that there was definitely something wrong with it.

As the first bout of pain filled me, I screamed. Then, out of my mind in pain, I turned and ran. Disintegrating rays sizzled past me, the smell of the air being superheated coming to my nose. But I could smell something else, too. I could smell the odor of my own dissolved flesh.

I ran, the sheeters right behind me, their heavy boots clopping on the floor.

The entire bank rumbled as the mother ship settled into a holding pattern and I knew I was going to die. Off a side corridor, the ceiling collapsed, the foundation finally giving up, dust and grit filling the air, making me cough.

I rounded a bend in the corridor and tripped, falling face first to the floor. My nose was smashed and I began to taste blood. It dripped down my chin and I rolled over to see what had tripped me.

Marty was on the floor, his chest a raw mass of meat and bones. He'd been shot and the hole was similar to the one that killed Peter, only this one was more primitive, as if the beam had been set to a lower setting and the wound wasn't cauterized as well.

I reached out with my one hand to get up and my palm came down on something hard. Grabbing it, I pulled it close and saw it was the dirty bomb.

The sound of running boots came to me again and I knew I had seconds before I was caught. I was blinded by pain now, my body not happy about losing a limb. In front of me, where I had been running, the ceiling collapsed, blocking my escape route.

I did the only thing open to me, an option I would have never thought I could possibly do.

I opened the case and pressed the button to activate it.

The instant I did, it began to hum, as if something was cycling up or perhaps counting down. Then the sheeters appeared at the end of the corridor and I heard them saying something in their native language. They didn't shoot me, knowing I was helpless.

You know, I'd like to say I was being brave. That in the end I was the most heroic person in the base, but I'll be honest as I have seconds left to live and there's really no reason to lie now, not to me or anyone else.

It's easy to be brave when you're gonna die anyway. When there's nothing left to lose, thinking of the greater picture is simple.

As the humming grew louder and the sheeters walked closer, I glanced down at the bomb once more and realized that the small red flicking light must have been a tracking chip.

It had all been a setup so we would take the bomb back to the base. The only thing is, the sheeters didn't figure on Marty getting it to work. They didn't think a simple handyman might have the knowledge to fix the bomb, nor that a coward would have the fortitude to do what was right, despite the consequences.

That's the funny thing about wars. Many times, the side with the superior technology thinks that because they have cooler toys, they're stronger and smarter.

But sometimes, they're wrong.

The humming came to a stop and there was a blinding white light that seared my eyes from my skull.

What happened next?

Sorry, I can't tell you that.

SEND IN THE...

SCOTT T. GOUDSWARD

"You're sure of this?" Charles asked and paced around the small dressing room. The tent flaps and thick canvas did little to instill a feeling of privacy. He checked over his shoulder often while he paced.

The hay strewn, gray concrete floor crunched with each step. Frank's shoulders drooped a little as he applied another handful of white base makeup to his forehead and smeared it down over his cheeks.

"Very sure," Charles said, staring at Frank's reflection in the mirror. He noticed what might be a slight tinge of resignation in the older man's brown eyes.

"If you'll excuse me, Charles," Frank said, turning back to the mirror. "I need to finish getting ready for tonight's show." Turning to leave, Charles reached for the door flap, then stopped and spun on his heel.

"We'll need to practice, you know." Charles shot back over his shoulder.

Frank stretched the latex bald cap over his thick, graying hair and secured it with spirit glue. "Perhaps you should go prepare for your own act?"

"It's magic. It's the same gig every night: smoke bombs, card tricks, floating women..." Charles threw up his arms and eased past the flap.

Frank turned back to the mirror, filled in the white-face, and started drawing large, red diamonds around his eyes and a red circle around his mouth. Milo the Clown was almost ready for his act

* * *

"Are you kidding me?" Mary Alice yelled. She slammed a manila folder down on her cluttered desk. "A parade? You want me to cover a goddamn parade?" Alan tossed his hands up and gave her *the look*. "Oh no, that look may work on the junior reporters, but not me."

"Look, Mary," Alan said, sitting on the corner of her desk. "We need someone to cover this. I have a cameraman all set up and ready to go."

She flopped down in her chair, exhausted at the brief exchange. She reached through the piles of papers and grabbed the folder, then flipped it open and let the papers spill out over her desk.

"That's what I think of this story, Alan. You're wasting me, putting me on this."

"I need someone to cover this, Mary Alice," Alan said slowly, almost forcing out each word. "How many times have I gone to your side when you ducked under a police line? How many times did I pull your ass out of the fire when you were going balls to balls with the cops?" He loosened his tie and unbuttoned the collar of his shirt.

Mary Alice slid forward in the chair and dropped her face on her desk, her forehead resting on the keyboard of the PC. "Who's the camera guy?" she asked.

Some of the red eased out of Alan's face. He ran a hand through his thinning brown hair.

"How 'bout Patrick? He's good."

Mary Alice shook her head, threatening to unleash the sandy blonde curls from their scrunchy prison. "We went out; I kicked him in the nuts on our second date." She sat up and began gathering the spilled papers from the folder, cringing with each recovered sheet.

"What about Kevin?"

She shook her head some more.

"Is there anyone in the photo department you haven't dated?" he asked.

She looked around the bustling press room and pointed to an intern sitting in a chair behind the review desk. "Him," she said and glanced at the papers. "What's his name?"

"Jason or Justin or Jared, something like that," he guessed.

"You so owe me for this, Alan."

Frank grimaced as he steered the clown car back through the big top, towards the stage entrance. All the others who had piled in after him had safely disappeared down the access tunnel beneath the raised floor. The small, bright green and red car looked like a Christmas abortion as it disappeared from the area. The crowd erupted with applause. The car came to a stop off-stage, and Frank all but pried himself from the tiny vehicle. Each movement, every step, brought a fresh crack from his joints. He'd been Milo the Clown for too many years.

He pulled off his red foam nose and stood in the shadows of the doorway, and as he watched, mobile trampolines were rolled out and staging was set up. A pack of acrobats descended from the ceiling on coils of cloth as the lights dimmed. They stopped and floated, suspended from the ceiling inches from the ground, all dressed in colorful red and orange, which was supposed to represent human flames.

The lights went out, a spotlight lit the center ring to the "ooh's and aah's" of the audience. A plume of gray smoke erupted within the circle of light, and when it cleared, Charles was standing there in a dramatic pose. The acrobats bounced on the trampolines, preparing for their part of the act. Charles twirled and his sequined cape floated to the ground almost in defiance of gravity. He shot a quick wink to Frank and turned back to the crowd.

Frank turned on the lights surrounding his mirror, oblivious to the ones that were burnt out. Outside the confines of his cloth room, the animals were led to pens and soon the cleaning crews would flow into motion, sweeping, shoveling and hosing down the performance floor and disposing of the soiled hay.

He took a damp cloth and wiped it across his forehead, exposing a swatch of skin beneath. Looking at his reflection, he jumped a little. The makeup he was used to, but the green wig and the purple fedora always got to him. He dropped the foam nose into his bag and started to 'de-clown.'

"What do you think?" Charles asked, slinking in through the flap in the tent.

"You were made for that gig."

"I was made for headlining in Vegas, not a traveling circus." Charles took a deck of cards from his pocket and shuffled them with one hand.

"You controlled the audience. Kept their attention and probably helped sell a couple dozen DVD's tonight."

"You know what I mean, Frank."

Frank sighed and dropped his white cloth, now stained with makeup, onto the table. He spun to look at Charles, his face looking like a mish-mash of half-peeled flesh. "Can't this wait?"

"Nope." Charles flipped the cards into his pocket and walked closer to Frank. "Think about it. No one will know but us and Billy." He looked over his shoulder, expecting the ringmaster to walk in. "Billy has to know about it. You know his motto."

"No surprises," they both said in unison.

Frank buried his face in a hot, damp towel and rubbed at his skin until it was the same color all around.

"And if I say yes?" Frank started and pulled the latex from his head and dropped it in his pack.

"then we get news coverage; maybe sell some more DVD's and more publicity for the circus. Go out with a bang instead of dissolving into obscurity."

"Charles, I'm close to fifty-five. I don't know how many more clown cars I have left in me. Pretty soon, I'll be one of those guys with the barrels on wheels with a broom and a shovel, cleaning up elephant shit."

"I can guarantee that once this goes off, we'll get so much press that we can both go to Vegas. You can be my emcee and I'll get my stage show." Charles smiled as he thought of the future.

Frank kicked off his oversized shoes and slid the suspenders off his shoulders. Beneath the clown get-up, he wore a Metallica concert shirt and nylon pants. He sat down after hanging his costume on a rolling metal rack. "You really think this will land us a spot in Vegas?"

"Absolutely. But I need us both and I need us to rehearse, at least once."

Frank sighed and wiped makeup from his neck. "Okay, I'm in."

Mary Alice stalked across the press room floor, a folder tucked under her left arm, a purse clenched in her right hand. She stopped halfway to the intern and fixed her hair in the reflection of a laptop screen. The intern sat on a bench and fiddled with his camera settings, snapping some random shots across the room.

"Look, Jason..." Mary Alice began but was cut off.

"You've been teamed up with me because they don't know what else to do with me." He finished her sentence.

"In a nutshell, yes," Mary Alice said, eying him up and down.

He stood up for a second and looked her over as well. "And it's Jared, not Jason. He extended his hand. "And you're Mary Alice." She cocked her head at him. "I heard you talking over there."

"You know the gig?" she asked.

He nodded and put the camera into a padded bag hanging from his shoulder.

"Anything you don't know?" She eyed the young man carefully, from his worn sneakers, socks that needed new elastics, jeans with holes and the paint-stained t-shirt. *What might lie beneath it?* she contemplated. Buzz cut hair, not blond but so short it was hard to tell the color of and eyes like stormy skies. A little sigh escaped her red-painted lips.

"Okay, here's the deal. I'll be speaking into a digital recorder through all of this and you'll snap pictures of what I tell you to. With any luck, we can both be done and back before anyone notices that I'm...I mean 'we're' there."

"It's a parade. I don't get it. Marching bands, guys in kilts, people on stilts in lame costumes, some un-original floats..." He shrugged.

"It's a circus parade, Jared not Jason. Animals, acrobats..." She shivered a bit "...And clowns."

"First off, Mary Alice, you got me wrong. I don't do stills, this is a hobby," Jared said, patting the camera bag. "I do live video feeds. Get me a good shoulder-mounted camera and I'll follow you into a riot or a volcano."

"Didn't I mention that?" Alan said, jogging over. He slapped Jared on the shoulder and took a moment to catch his breath. The room droned on, too many people talking on phones, too many other people yelling over cubicle walls. "You'll be in news chopper 8."

Frank sat in the belly of the float as it trundled down the street. Charles walked beside it doing street magic. It was a three-tiered structure that looked vaguely like a Mayan temple, if you crossed it with banana custard. On the bottom two tiers, acrobats were doing tricks on trampolines built into the superstructure.

Frank took a long drag from his flask and let the empty container slide from his red and white gloved hands. His reflection in the container was of a concave abomination. The side of the flask was smeared with white makeup and the mouth of the bottle had a generous coating of red lipstick. He belched, scratched his clown crotch, and started the long climb up the ladder to the top of the float and the trap door waiting for him.

Mary Alice screamed as the helicopter dipped towards the street. Jared was next to her in the open doorway of the aircraft, both strapped in with safety harnesses. Jared had started filming long before they reached the parade route.

"This is Mary Alice Sullivan reporting from Beacon Road and Broadway. We're all geared up and waiting anxiously for this special parade. This day marks the fortieth anniversary of the Collins' Family Circus and tonight, the very last showing of the circus will be totally free to the public." Jared panned back to behind Mary Alice, where preparations for the parade were in progress. "In just a few short hours, this grand spectacle will be underway and all the tickets to tonight's final show will be passed out as the parade progresses through the city's streets."

Mary Alice let out a final scream as the helicopter banked to the right and began to hover. Jared zoomed in on the parade, which looked like a giant misshapen snake waiting to devour the city's residents. She straightened her headphones and tried to fix her hair.

"When are we live?" she yelled.

"Five minutes!" Jared yelled back. "I'm just getting some stock footage."

"Did I mention I'm afraid of heights?"

"Only about thirty times."

"What about the noise on the tape?" she asked.

"There is no tape, it'll be live." Jared paused. "Okay, there's a tape but only for the records or if we lose the feed. The news van should be able to kill any background noises and swears; there's a five second delay."

"I guess Alan forgot to mention that, too." She sat back in one of the small seats and let Jared do his thing. "A live broadcast," she muttered. "In a helicopter, covering a circus parade." She watched Jared grasping the door handle with one hand for stability, and holding onto the camera with the other. "I'm going to castrate him when I get back."

Frank reached the top rung of the ladder and held on for dear life. Sweat rolled down his scalp and got trapped under the latex flap on his head. His heart pounded in his chest; it wasn't the fall he was afraid of, it was the landing.

He grabbed the handle of the trap door and waited for the signal. Through the plaster/chicken-wire frame, he could hear muted voices and muffled canned music. The float rumbled to a stop, and from the control booth, the driver signaled Frank by flipping him off and smiling.

Frank turned the handle, then eased open the door just a little to peek out as the smoke bomb went off. He clambered out of the float and closed the door just as the green smoke blew off, thanks to a light breeze.

He waved to the crowd and bowed to their applause as Charles climbed the stairs on the far side of the float. As he ascended, the acrobats started their routine.

Small hidden nooks in the float slid open and colored smoke and sparks shot out, all swirling into a vortex powered by hidden fans mounted on the top of the float.

Frank took a deep breath and coughed. He saw the wires and headset on Charles, realizing he was rigged for sound.

Frank stood up, let the smoke surround him, pointed to the news helicopter, and waved.

"In 3, 2, 1." Mary Alice nodded at Jared, and he started filming. "Good afternoon, this is Mary Alice Sullivan reporting to you from high above the parade route. We're here today to celebrate and bid a fond farewell to the Collins' Family Circus. If you look down towards the street, you can see what looks like a show about to begin. Standing high atop that sacred temple are two of the circus' performers; The Amazing Charles and the always lovable Milo the Clown. Let's watch for a moment."

"Welcome to the show!" Charles said into his microphone.

Nearby, Frank danced around the top of the pyramid, hamming it up for the people on the street.

Each footfall that danced him through the swirling smoke made him cough and gag, but he hid it from the viewers almost thirty feet below.

He stopped to point and clap with his gloved hands at the acrobats, and honk his red foam nose.

"We have something very special for you tonight folks." At his words, air cannons slid out from the undercarriage of the float and shot bundles of paper tickets into the air at the gathering crowd.

The crowd scrambled for the tickets as they fell like confetti to the pavement. Frank stepped back into a cloud of orange/green smoke and doubled over coughing.

Charles amplified voice laughed and said, "Right now, in the middle of this street, I'm going to make Milo the Clown disappear! Then I will bring him back tonight during the live show!"

"Is that guy okay?" Jared asked as he watched Frank stumbling about. "Every time he goes through the smoke he doubles over like he's sick."

"Guess they weren't expecting quite the bird's-eye view." Mary Alice said and pointed at the float. "Look, I can see the door on the top of the float."

"He looks drunk; staggering all around like that. There's no harness, that clown's gonna fall off that float and break his neck."

"Well, if he does, it'll make a great story," Mary Alice whispered then realized she was being recorded. "Hey, can you guys in the van delete that last comment?"

* * *

Frank staggered back from the side of the float and got hit face first by a cloud of red-blue smoke; he began coughing, gagging on the foul cloud.

Charles dramatically whipped out a long piece of cloth from his inside pocket. He held it out to the crowd and shook it on each side of the float. Frank took the cloth and played it up, trying to blow his big foam nose on it, only to have Charles pluck it from his grasp. Charles then pulled several vials of colored liquid from his coat and gestured over them, and one by one, smashed them on the float. Each one created another ball of colored smoke. Each one caused Frank to grab his guts and try not to fall over. It wasn't one of Milo the Clown's finest moments

"What are you doing, Frank?" Charles said, covering the microphone. He took off the headset and let it drop. "Have you been drinking?"

"The smoke is killing me. It's like my gut is full of razors." To keep the show going, Charles smashed the last jar of fluid and a small purple mushroom cloud of smoke appeared, and Milo the lovable clown, fell over dead.

"Something's wrong down there!" Mary Alice said, excited. She yanked on the safety harness to make sure it was secure and leaned out of the helicopter, her fear of heights forgotten. "On me, quick!"

Jared swung the camera in place and focused on her. "Go!"

"We're still high above the streets of the parade, where a magic trick meant to enthrall and entertain has gone horribly wrong." She leaned out of the door a little further. "From what we've seen, the trick that was centered around colored smoke and some props, meant to make Milo the Clown disappear, has failed and the poor clown has fallen ill, or worse." She motioned for Jared to zoom in on the float.

Below, Charles was bent over Frank, trying to administer CPR.

"As you can see, it's a true tragedy. More details as they arrive." She slid the headset off and waited after about a minute of watching through the side view pane of the camera, then called 9-1-1 on her cell phone.

Charles pounded on Frank's chest, trying to get anything from the man. Colored smoke swirled around them as he tried to work CPR. But the only training he'd received was from watching ER. "Don't die on me, Frank." He stood and went to the side of the float, and signaled to the acrobats to stop and get help. One of the pair jumped down to the next level, while the other started her way up to the top. Charles spun as Frank groaned and sat up coughing.

"Oh, thank God," Charles gasped and rushed over to Frank to help him stand. Frank looked around confused at his surroundings. Something was wrong with his eyes.

"You okay, buddy? The show must go on and all that," Charles said.

The trap door opened and Billy the circus manager popped his head out. "What the hell is going on up here?" he barked.

"Slight situation, boss," Charles said while holding up Frank. "Frank had a moment and fainted but it's all under control."

Frank broke away from Charles and staggered over to Billy.

"The bastard's drunk," Billy said, disgusted. "If we weren't shutting down I'd fire your ass, Frank." Billy went to close the trapdoor, when Frank leaned over and bit a chunk of meat out of his throat. Billy screamed and tried to cover the hole in his neck and fell off the ladder and down thirty feet into the understructure of the float.

Frank turned to Charles, scraps of Billy's bloody skin still in his teeth; blood ran down his painted white face and stained his costume with gore.

"Jesus, Frank, you should have just punched him," Charles said in shock.

The female acrobat in her body stocking and colored spandex suit screamed as Frank lunged at her. She slipped free from his clumsy grasp and hopped over the side of the float to the trampolines below. Frank turned slowly, looking at the stairs to the street or at the morsel of meat in front of him. He growled and hissed, then charged Charles.

A scream from the crowd erupted from the street as Billy ran from the float, blood pouring from the hole in his neck through his fingers. But also because Billy had the severed hand of the float driver clamped in his mouth as he gnawed on it like a dog with a bone.

"From up here it looks like Milo the Clown has gone crazy. He's attacked one man who was inside the float and now he's attacking The Amazing Charles," Mary Alice said, trying to take in the situation without smiling, thinking about this on her resume. "The pilot is going to try and drop us down for a better look at what's happening."

Jared changed camera angle and focused on Billy as he bolted into the crowd of people.

He zoomed in to capture the look of crazed hunger on Billy's face. Then the first scream came, followed by the beginning of mass panic.

"Back off, Frank. Sure this is all my fault, but somehow it's more your fault." Charles jumped as a gunshot rang out. When he turned his gaze just for a second, Frank was on him, shredding and ripping at his outfit, digging for the soft flesh beneath. Not knowing what else to do, while trying to scramble away from the incensed ravenous clown, he smashed handfuls of the small glass vials against Frank's head, creating whirling storms of chemicals and color. Frank buried his face into Charles' abdomen and started to chew.

Charles screamed and screamed as Frank ripped into him, tearing apart the soft tissue, going for the real meat within. Frank pulled out fistfuls of organs and flesh, chewing maniacally while Charles spasmed and died.

Frank was dead.

Long live Milo the Clown.

"I can't tell exactly what's going on now." The wind from the helicopter's rotor whipped at her hair. Mary Alice leaned out. "We have one man dead on the street, and we believe it's the same man that Milo the Clown attacked, and has been shot to death by the police. And Milo has attacked The Amazing Charles on the top of the Mayan temple float and we believe him also to be dead."

Jared again zoomed in on Milo feasting on the pile of meat that was Charles. Milo was in a puddle of Charles' blood; both hands prying his ribs open so he could jam his head deeper into Charles' abdominal cavity. As if sensing the helicopter, Milo looked up, his gore-encrusted hands grabbing at the sky.

"He's moving, I think he's looking at us," Jared said.

"The only thing you have to worry about is keeping that in frame."

Jared reached out with his free hand and grabbed Mary Alice's shoulder and shook her. "Look, something's happening." Milo fell backwards and convulsed while blood bubbled from his mouth. "Is he growing?" Jared asked, and let the camera slide from his shoulder, until Mary Alice noticed he wasn't filming and slapped him.

"Are you fucking stupid? You keep rolling and don't stop."

"You can explain that swear to Alan, this is still a live feed. I'm sure he'll enjoy paying that fine," Jared said. He rested the camera back on his shoulder, then focused on the scene below.

Milo the Clown's body was growing fast. The clown costume ripped as his limbs stretched and grew. Milo screamed and gurgled. The top of the pyramid was now totally covered by the expanding undead clown. Milo rolled down the side, leaving a trail of gore behind him. The stragglers on the street below shrieked and ran from the horrible sight.

"From our vantage point above the street, Milo is dead!" Mary Alice yelled into the microphone. "And unbelievable as it sounds, his body has grown to the size of six or seven car lengths. He seems to have stopped moving. His body is currently on the street. We still don't know what caused him to attack and kill the others and also what made him grow." Mary Alice swung to the side in her harness as the chopper dipped low.

"What are you doing, Randy?" she screamed at the pilot.

"Taking you in for a closer look. Everyone ready?" Randy dipped the helicopter low towards the street, hovering barely ten feet from the pavement. Patches of bone and skin were visible through Milo's flaking white makeup. The green wig matted with blood sprouted at odd angles from his head. Mary Alice took out her cell phone and snapped off several stills of the gigantic undead clown.

"Can I get to the street?" she yelled.

"I wouldn't recommend it," Jared said. People were still running in panic, some of them oblivious to the helicopter hovering in the middle of the road.

"Get your shots fast!" Randy yelled. "I don't know how long I can hold her here."

"We're here at street level and you can see from the frightening images on your TV what's happened. Milo the Clown still isn't moving, and the streets are awash with panicking people, all trying to escape the carnage." Jared zoomed in past Milo's giant colorful boots, where his toes jutted out like jagged rocks. Two policemen were trying to control the masses. "And far off down the road, the police are failing to control the situation." Mary Alice stopped for a moment and pressed her ear piece in tight, trying to make out the news van trying to communicate with her.

Jared grabbed her arm, squeezed hard and said, "Look!" He pointed out the helicopter's door.

Milo's fingers were twitching and she cocked her head to get a better view. Slowly, the massive digits moved on one hand, then the other. The massive head turned, rubbing skin and white face makeup on the pavement. Clouded eyes opened under rotted veined lids and with enormous effort, Milo the Clown stood up.

"I am so getting out of Dodge," Randy said, pulling the helicopter up.

"Swing around, we need a shot of the whole body of that thing," Mary Alice said.

Randy banked the helicopter around so Jared could get the shots of the giant clown. Two lone policemen were firing wildly at the giant clown, and when their clips were empty, they took off on foot, yelling into their radios for backup.

Mary Alice was too afraid to speak, in her mind only one thought echoed: *Pulitzer*. She looked at Jared busy filming the giant undead clown. Milo took a first thunderous step and his giant foot flattened the cooling body of Billy. Randy banked again, as Milo swung an arm at them.

"Thank God it's Romero and not Boyle," Jared muttered, though no one understood what he was talking about.

As Randy lifted the helicopter higher, they passed by Milo's face. His mouth was oozing dark blood, and his tongue flopped from side to side in his mouth, the cold wind of death flooding into the helicopter. They watched Milo taking futile steps, trying to follow them, but the aircraft was too fast.

"Wait? You're saying we should kill it?" Randy asked, replying to Mary Alice's suggestion. The helicopter was sitting on a rooftop five blocks away from the parade.

Far off between the buildings, they saw the giant clown's peeling, rotted head bobbing between structures. The green hair swayed in the breeze like demented weeds.

"Exactly. We kill it, and get the footage. Just think of it. Do you know how much the networks would pay for that kind of footage?" Mary Alice said.

"I'm thinking of it now and I'd rather not," Jared added.

"How are we supposed to do this?" Randy asked, dollar signs in his eyes.

"No idea. How do you kill a giant undead clown?" she asked.

Each footstep of the clown was a massive drumbeat, getting closer and louder every second.

"Is he...it, coming for us?" Jared squeaked.

The massive head turned in their direction. The ash-gray eyes highlighted with yellow veins seemed to focus on the helicopter.

"Oh God...it is coming for us," Jared said.

"How do you kill a forty foot zombie?" Mary Alice wondered. For the first time, real hysteria was creeping into her voice. The confidence of hanging out of the helicopter for the story and getting the break on it was now waning. Jared shrugged and got the camera into place on his shoulder, just in case the clown did something newsworthy.

"Artillery? Grenades?" Randy suggested.

"No, stupid, it has to be something we have. You could crash the news chopper into it. Kill the brain and it dies, right?"

"Sure, in zombie movies that's the way to kill a zombie. Destroy the brain the zombie dies. *If* it's a real zombie." Mary Alice looked puzzled at Jared so he explained, "Zombies pass one what they are by biting, in theory. But that clown just went crazy, then shot up three stories. Right before it started, that magician guy was covering him with chemicals. It's induced."

"How do you know all this shit, kid?" Randy asked.

"I got no life, no girlfriend; I watch a lot of movies...a lot of 'em, okay?"

"Suggestions people. It's getting closer."

"We wait for the police, Army, National Guard, whoever shows up first?" Jared said.

"We get a cannon," Mary Alice said. They both turned to look at her, as she took out her compact to check her makeup. She tried to fix her hair with her fingers. "It's a circus parade, they were going to shoot a man out of a cannon, from one float to another float, then catch him in a net."

Jared put the camera down and stumbled to the side, imagining the clown stepping into the building's parking lot. "You want us to lure the clown to the human cannonball and do what exactly?" Jared asked.

"Well, we can fill it full of anything we can find and shoot it," Mary Alice said, tucking her compact back into her purse. "Don't give me that look. It could work."

Jared grabbed her sleeve and pointed through the buildings where the clown could be seen. "We're running out of time."

"Well, then, what do you suggest?" she asked Jared, who shrugged. He looked along the rooftop, spotting the parking lot to the building below the helicopter. The yellow and white paint for each space reflected the sun's light.

"Behead it, fill the mouth with salt and sew it shut."

"Not gonna happen, kid," Randy said.

"Then I got nothing," Jared answered and then jumped as the rooftop shook a little bit. "I can feel the vibrations through my feet!" They all ran to the edge of the roof. Milo was getting agonizingly close. A foul wind blew over them as the undead clown turned towards them.

"Three more blocks and we're dead," Jared said, his voice shaking from fear.

"Get in the chopper," Randy said. "At the very least I can put some ground between us and him. Maybe even lead him out of the city." Randy ran to helicopter, jumped into the cockpit, and started the engine; the rotors slowly began spinning.

Mary Alice stood cemented to the roof in fear as she watched the clown head bob up and down, as it made its way through the city. The sounds of crashing, screaming and rending metal filled the air as the clown destroyed everything its path.

Deciding she just might die in the next few minutes, Mary Alice decided to throw caution to the wind and live a little. She grabbed Jared's arm and looked deep into his eyes, then pulled his head in and kissed him hard. Jared put the camera down and moved in close to return the kiss when she broke contact. He stood there, his lips pursed, too surprised to move.

Milo spotted the helicopter on the roof and moved in closer. He reached down to the street and picked up a handful of screaming people trying to escape; there were three of them, scrambling and fighting to escape, two women and a man. They punched at the giant dead fingers, their blows doing nothing to affect the over-padded gloves.

"Thank God most of the costume grew with him," Mary Alice said, the wind from the rotor whipping at her hair. "A giant rotting wang is not what I wanted to see today."

Milo moved his fist close to his mouth. The people screamed in fear and pain as the fingers tightened. The clown opened his massive mouth, the bloated black tongue flapping against his red-painted lips, and he shoved the people into his mouth as if they were jelly beans. Gore and blood rained downed to the street below as the clown chewed messily, organs and viscera sliding between his cracked lips.

Jared grabbed the camera and dashed for the helicopter. Mary Alice stood in stunned silence, then vomited all over her shoes, and finally turned and ran to the waiting helicopter and hopefully, safety.

Milo followed the helicopter out of town, his massive steps crushing people and cars the entire time; he was indiscriminate in the violence. The few who didn't get crushed beneath the enormous red boots fell victim to his appetite.

Randy set the helicopter down in a school football field.

"You two, get out!" Randy barked.

"No way, dude," Jared yelled. "I'm stayin'!"

"Look, kid, I'm gonna finish this. I can't believe how long the damn police are taking to get here. My house is…my wife and daughter…they live no more than a mile from here. If that thing isn't destroyed, that monster could go there next. It would kill them. I won't let that happen."

Jared took out his cell phone and dialed 9-1-1 but all he got for his trouble was a busy signal. He tightened his harness and clipped it onto the metal bar over his head.

"Look, I think I know what you're gonna do and I get it, but I'm coming so I can get the footage. I'll be rich; I can sell it to any network I want, name my own price. I'll be set for life!"

"But you'll die."

"Not necessarily. When I get enough footage, I'll get on the winch and jump out. It doesn't have to stop me, just slow me down enough so I don't break every bone in my body when I hit the ground. Then I'll unlatch and you can finish."

"You're either brave or stupid, kid. I don't know which," Randy said.

"Nah, just greedy," Jared said with a smile.

"Don't I get a say in this?" Mary Alice asked.

"No!" they both yelled at her at the same time.

"Get yourself up that fire escape to the roof of that school," Jared said. "Then call the news station and tell them to broadcast."

Mary Alice watched the helicopter take off from the field. She stood on the two story rooftop and waved as Randy headed back towards Milo. She dialed the station on her cell phone and waited.

She swallowed hard, feeling the building vibrate as the giant clown made his way through the city.

"Yes, it's Mary Alice," she said when the news station answered. "I'm on top of a school, waiting for the news chopper to explode when it hits a giant zombie clown. Now for Christ's sake, put me on the air!"

Jared attached the winch clip to his harness and leaned out to get the footage. "I feel like Fay Wray back here." He switched on the camera and got ready for Randy to take them both in dangerously close. Randy went in low, circling around the clown's red feet.

The giant shoes were getting more ragged with each step. The knees and thighs of the once bright, plaid, baggy pants were tight against the cold dead flesh beneath. The suspenders had broken and now swung like rubber snakes from Milo's waist.

Through the ripped fabric of the shirt, Milo's gray skin and rib cage were visible. Jared was tossed to the side like a child's yoyo as Randy dodged a mistimed grab from Milo. And then that face, the horrible face. The green wig had merged with the pale skin. White pasty makeup fell off in giant flakes. The bloated tongue wiggled back and forth like a giant slug, the lips enormous and vile, and the constant ooze of brackish fluid from the mouth rained down to the ground as if it was a waterfall. The teeth were jagged and broken. There was no more recognition of what was red paint and what was rotting flesh. And the eyes, clouded over, almost solid, yellow veins cross-crossed across the surface.

"That's your cue, kid!" Randy yelled.

"You sure about this, Randy?"

Randy nodded and tossed Jared his wallet. "Give that to my wife."

Jared got the last bit of footage and jammed the tape and memory card into his pocket. He punched the control on the winch and watched the cable unwind into the cabin. Without a second thought, he jumped out of the helicopter. The cable fed out until the winch jammed.

Jared was jerked back suddenly, and he felt something break inside. He groaned and started to tug against the cable, hoping to get some slack. He could feel the helicopter gaining speed and altitude as he hung from the cable. He was supposed to unhook himself and fall the remaining distance to the ground but the latch was jammed, he was stuck, he couldn't break free!

Randy pulled up, seeing Jared below was still attached to the cable. But Milo also saw Jared and reached out for him. Jared managed one loud scream before the winch was ripped out of the wall mounting of the ceiling of the helicopter as Milo pulled on the snack and stuffed Jared into his mouth

He spit out the harness and cable as if they were watermelon seeds.

"This is Mary Alice Sullivan, broadcasting live from the top of the William Wallace Junior High School. I have no video and Jared, my cameraman, who has been with me through this entire ordeal, is dead. He's been eaten by the giant zombie clown, the once beloved Milo, maybe a city block from where I stand on this roof." She took a deep breath and checked her phone battery. There was no point in faking tears; no one was going to see them. There was still some shock, and terrible rolling waves of fear and nausea as the tremors from the giant clown's steps shook her deep into her soul.

"News Now helicopter, being piloted by Randy…uh…" *Oh God, I don't know his last name!* tore through her mind. "Is as I watch even now, circling the clown, and gaining speed. None of us here know how to kill this abomination, but brave Randy is taking a chance while we wait for some kind of help to arrive."

She let her free hand slip down to her waist; the cell phone was clutched greedily in her other hand while she thought of the next words to say.

The helicopter climbed and she could just make out the dark shape in the cockpit that was Randy. The side window opened and he stuck his arm out and gave a thumbs up.

He pointed the nose down and gathered as much speed as he could. Mary Alice sat on the roof, unable to stand anymore.

Milo the Clown took a slow swing at the helicopter before it crashed into his face. There was a loud, almost-scream that escaped Milo's lips, as the rotors dug into his skull and tore off the top of his head.

Great flaps of painted skin flew everywhere. Then the fuel tanks ignited, liquid flame covering the towering forty foot clown. In seconds, Milo became a giant torch.

The massive body faltered and teetered, then crashed to the street below. The flames shot outward, catching nearby buildings and cars on fire.

Mary Alice looked at her cell phone and pressed the disconnect button as the wail of sirens echoed in the distance. She checked her face in the compact and again thought: *Pulitzer*.

ATTACK OF THE BED BUGS

P. A. DOUGLAS

Carl Pritchard and the boys loved to hunt. They did so every weekend and even on the occasional weekday. With the Pritchard family farm and home seated on the small town's prime estate for hunting of almost any kind, it was no surprise that Carl and the boys always got first pick when setting up camp each morning to go hunting, whatever the season.

Although the Pritchard's farmland was vast, covered in various forms of vegetation and livestock, a bustling twenty acres was devoted to the sport. Carl didn't care much for the local competition of hunters, but let it slide seeing as to how they paid him to hunt on his land.

"Would you two quiet down already?" Carl hissed, lifting the barrel of his Remington pump action. From behind him, his two sons, Tim and Chad, nearly grown men themselves, pushed and shoved one another in the bushes.

The two boys, already in their mid-twenties, suddenly came to a halt. Not having paid any attention to their father's words, the rustle of foliage several meters ahead had halted their playful banter.

"Shhhh…" Carl whispered as the brush shifted, and he raised his focused aim.

Before the unsuspecting creature had a chance to pounce or flee, Carl fired. The shot rang out, echoing through the silence. In a simultaneous procession, the high trees jerked and jittered as countless birds erupted from their hiding places.

"Hit," Carl said, lowering his shotgun with a grin.

"What yah hit, Daddy?" both of the boys said in a harmonious call.

As the three men, decked out in camouflaged attire, stood up, the dying creature spilled out into view from behind the foliage.

"Brewster!" Tim leaped forward, passing his father. "You hit Brewster!"

Brewster was the family hound who had been on countless hunting trips on and off the Pritchard property. He came hobbling out of the brush. The fatal wound slowly claimed his life, as Brewster slumped forward into the arms of Tim Pritchard.

"Dammit," Carl hissed. "What the hell was that damn dog doing out there like that?"

"Looks like we'll be cuttin' the trip short today, huh Daddy?" Chad sighed.

Already darting toward the truck with the hound in hand, Tim began to panic. That dog had been alive for almost as long as he had and it was easily considered a younger brother to the boys.

Carl jumped in the truck with his two sons and they headed off to the vet to see if there was anything he could do for old Brewster.

At the small town's local vet, Carl and the boys impatiently waited in the lobby for inevitable bad news. The shot was fatal and Carl was surprised to find that Brewster had enough fight left in him to make it to the vet still breathing.

Behind closed doors, the two men, a veterinarian practitioner and an assistant stood over the bloodied remains of the deceased pet.

"Are you seriously considering this right now, Doctor?" the assistant asked, questioning the vet's moral judgment.

"Of course I am. We talked about this time and time again. Who knows when we'll get this type of opportunity again? We need to act if we expect to see results." The doctor quickly injected the dead animal with a mixture of pesticides. Pyrethroids along with a fusion of dichlovors and malathion thickly slid into the slowly decaying hound dog. "Resistance to pesticides has increased significantly over time as you know and there are concerns of negative health effects from their use. So why not try them out now on something we can no longer harm?" he insisted. "This animal was infested with Cimicidae bugs. Just look!"

"I'm aware, Doctor, but that doesn't give us the right to toy with someone else's…"

Before she could spit it out, the doctor removed the syringe, interrupting her.

"What's done is done, Carol. And besides…if we manage to pull this off, you know how much money we'd make? We'll just hold the dog overnight and review the results in the morning. No harm done."

"And if the bed bugs do die off that easily, do you really think your FDA connections will come through for you?" Carol asked.

"We'll cross that bridge when we get there! Can you imagine… being the ones to solve the world's worst parasitic infestation?"

Later in the lobby, the doctor's assistant relentlessly attempted to reason with the bereaved pet owners on the need to keep the dog overnight.

"Not going to happen, lady," Carl said angrily from his side of the lobby's front desk.

The persistent back and forth of this topic left the assistant with no other choice but to fetch the doctor to help explain the situation. Not having gotten through to these camo-covered men in what seemed like a ten minute debate left the assistant flustered with irritation as she stepped away from the desk.

Walking around the desk and through a set of double doors, Carl and his boys stomped in rhythmic stride with the white coated woman, refusing to release their dead family member.

"Hey, they can't come in here!" The doctor jumped up from behind a small gurney with a cat strapped down on top.

The assistant looked back startled, not realizing that the men had followed her into the back of the building.

"No way in hell are you about to keep Brewster. He's comin' home with us, now," one of the boys said as Carl lifted the dead dog into his arms, already headed back the way he'd come.

In seconds the three men were gone, leaving the doctor and assistant standing together, looking at one another.

"Well, that's great. What now, Doctor?" Carol asked.

"Looks like we'll be busy tonight digging up a dead dog!" the doctor said, already making his way to the computer to pull up the pet owner's records.

"What do you mean 'we'?" she said angrily.

With Brewster long buried, Carl and the boys cleaned up and went to bed, resting up for another day filled with farm work.

Outside, doctor and assistant crept through the night, each holding a shovel. With flashlights scanning the ground around them, they slipped unnoticed through the Pritchard property, looking for signs of what might be a freshly laid burial plot.

How in the hell did I get talked into this, the vet's assistant thought as she quietly stepped through the back yard of the Pritchard's home. "Doctor, we could get shot if they find us back here, you do reali…"

"Shhh… I think I found it," the doctor whispered. "Here, help me with this."

The plot was an unexpected easy find behind the house. With several other plots and little head stones already placed together in a designated location, there was really only one place to look. They dropped to their knees next to the fresh soil, small garden shovels grasped in gloved hands. As the doctor took a closer look at the new plot, something seemed off, out of place. The dirt had been tampered with, the dog already missing, a hole where the grave should be.

"A raccoon or something, you think?" Carol suggested.

Still on bent knees, they waved their lights around them in search of the perpetrator who might have disturbed the hound's final resting spot.

Nothing.

Without warning, the ground at their knees began to rumble and shake. With flashlights focused, they leaned in to get a better look. Reaching her hand deep into the already soft soil, Carol shuffled through the empty grave.

A single bug crawled up her hand—a bed bug.

"It's a Cimicidae," she said, recognizing the species of creature. *Strange,* she thought. *Adult bed bugs are reddish-brown and flattened, oval and wingless. Bed bugs have microscopic hairs that give them a banded appearance. Adults generally grow to four to five mm in length and one and a half to three mm wide. This is way too big to be what I think it…* Before the thought had time to register in her mind, the almost three inch bug bit down on her hand, instantly burrowing deep into the flesh. It wiggled and squirmed with furious rage. Before the young woman had time to let out a single sound of terrified agony, over two dozen more, over-developed bed bugs rushed out of the open grave and swarmed over her. They covered her body like a rushing wave. Crunching and biting, the creatures dove down her mouth, burrowed into her eyes and dug deep beneath her skin, burrowing deeply.

The doctor opened his mouth and screamed at the sight of his assistant being attacked, but before he could get out another, the bed bugs were inside his mouth, clogging his throat and making him gag. They burrowed down deep into his esophagus and lungs, feeding on the man's insides. The doctor coughed softly and gagged, looking down at his shirt, he tore it open to see the bugs crawling beneath his skin, little waves of undulating flesh as they fed on him. Though most had gone down his throat, a few had burrowed upward, to begin tunneling into his brain.

As the doctor gasped and choked in death, his vision went out and a second later a pair of bed bugs popped out of each eye, their small mouths devouring each juicy orb. They fell out of the gaping sockets to run across the ground, then turned and dove back onto the fallen doctor to continue feeding.

By now the man was dead, more than half his body gone, bone glistening in the pale moonlight.

The mutated bed bugs devoured the one hundred and seventy-five pounds of meat and bone in a matter of minutes, pulling what remains were left underground through the small hole of Brewster's grave.

The distant scream of the doctor woke Carl from his deep sleep. He quickly dressed and woke the boys, all three soon making their way downstairs with guns drawn.

The rear door to the house opened and all three men stepped outside, weapons scanning the land around them.

After a solid half hour of searching their land, both front and back, they found nothing.

Little did they know, as they made their way back into the house to call the fruitless hunt done for the night, over a dozen oversized and mutated bed bugs had burrowed beneath the house and into the foundation. Crawling through the walls and under the floorboards, the blood sucking parasitic creatures crept into every nook and cranny, hunting to feed, hunting for sustenance.

As the two boys lay down in bed once more, Carl was already passed out in his bedroom, snoring softly.

Chad leaned over in his bed to look across the room the boys shared. "You think Brewster was a happy dog, Tim?"

There was no reply. Only the light sounds of Tim chewing away at his Doritos's, the nibbling crunch steady.

He must still be taking it really hard, Chad thought.

"You know, Daddy's gonna have your hide if he finds crumbs all over the bed again," Chad said before rolling over in his bed to face the wall. "Well anyhow…good night, sleep tight, don't let the bed bugs bite." Chad said and dozed off.

THE GREAT KAIJU

BRENNON THOMPSON

The water bubbled and the strange beast burst through the surface. Almost in slow motion, the giant monster rose from the bay, towering over the docks and buildings of the city.

From a window on the top floor of a high rise building further inland, a group of people watched, as the enormous creature lumbered and sloshed its way into the harbor. A tall, handsome man in his mid-twenties shook his head. With a sigh, he turned to face those assembled in the room.

"That's the third time this month!"

A ripping sound, followed by a loud crunch caught his attention. He looked out the window just in time to see a warehouse get flattened like a child's model by a giant clawed foot. The electrical wires wrapped up and hanging in its enormous fist shot out fountains of sparks in every direction and cast the monster in a blue glow. Across the harbor, the electricity to the high rise building ceased. Lights went out, fans stopped, and phones went dead.

The good looks of the man contorted into frustration as he slammed his fist on the desk, causing everyone in the room to jump. "This has got to stop!"

An older man, seated at the desk, looked up and nodded his head vigorously, causing his round spectacles to slide down his nose. "Yes. Yes. I agree. But what can we do against that horrible beast?"

"For starters, you can do something besides sit behind that desk!" the younger man snapped back.

The older man's mouth opened and closed like a fish, but remained silent. His only response was the pushing of his glasses back on his face.

The small group of people stepped forward in the old man's defense, each voicing their dislike of the younger man's accusing tone:

"Look here, you can't talk to him like that!"

"Inspector Daisuke is a great man."

"You have no right to treat him that way."

"You should be ashamed of yourself, young man."

"I think we all should just... calm down."

"The inspector has been a big help to this city. He's done many great things."

"It is not the inspector's fault."

"Enough!" the young man barked. Turning, he stormed from the room, slamming the door behind him. In the quiet of the darkened hallway, he lit a cigarette and tried to calm down. "Why does this keep happening?"

"I think I might know."

The young man instantly recognized the voice behind him and turned to see the inspector's secretary, Suki, staring back at him, almost on the verge of tears. He liked Suki, she was cute, had a great smile, and smelled nice. The inspector on the other hand, seemed to only like her because she was reliable and loyal to a fault.

He had never cared for the way the inspector took advantage of Suki. He always felt sorry for her. And looking through the gloom at the tears in her eyes now, it made him feel for her even more. "What is it?"

"Who." She corrected. She dropped her head, refusing to make eye contact. She shifted her weight nervously from one foot to the other, her low voice stammering and stuttering to continue, but no more real words came out.

The young man grabbed her by the shoulders and asked, "*Who* is it? Suki, *who* is responsible for that monster?"

She stepped back hugging her arms around herself and sobbing quietly. He instantly regretted the forceful tone in his voice. He put his finger under her chin, gently guiding her eyes to meet his. "I'm sorry, Suki."

She looked up, tears flowing down her cheeks. "It's Inspector Daisuke."

The young man gasped. "What?" He didn't believe his ears.

Suki dropped her head again, her voice barely above a whisper. "Inspector Daisuke is feeding the monster. He's been doing it for months now. He doesn't think anyone knows, but I do."

The young man turned back around, and gazed silently over the guardrail into the dark abyss below. Knocking the long ash from his almost forgotten cigarette, he took one last drag, before stomping it under his foot.

A woman's scream from inside the room echoed down the hallway. Taking Suki by the hand, he led the way. "Come on!"

Opening the door, they were met by another scream. "What's going on?!" he demanded.

"It's Inspector Daisuke! He's climbed out on the ledge," a frantic man said, pointing at a fluttering curtain. A trembling woman stood by the open window, screaming and clutching at her face.

"What?" The young man looked out the window but was unable to see the inspector. What he could see, however, was the monster swatting a fighter jet out of the sky, like an annoying fly, sending it exploding to the ground.

The monster grabbed a second jet as it buzzed by, stuffing the aircraft into its giant mouth and biting down with a loud crunch. The Army tanks at the monster's feet were fairing no better, firing volley after volley of shells, with little effect. The shells exploded in what looked like puffs of smoke from tiny firecrackers on its scaly chest. The loud noise doing little more than anger the already enraged creature.

Roaring, the monster stomped on the tanks, crushing them like tin cans. The soldiers scurried away from the devastation like little bugs. Stepping over some and on others, the monster devastated the army, leaving the military forces in shambles. It continued with its rampage, flattening a brick building less than a block away.

"Quick, everyone get out of here, the monster's getting too close. It's not safe to be here, I'll take care of the inspector," the young man said.

With a swipe of its massive tail the monster laid waste to a large communications tower just across the street. Fortunately, for the people in the building, the tower fell to the left, sparing them from being crushed by the steel structure. Some on the ground were not so lucky.

The screams of the hysterical woman was now so loud that the young man had to strain his voice just to be heard. "Go!"

With little protest, the group of people filed out of the room, the screaming woman leading the charge.

"I guess you plan on staying?" he asked Suki. Standing beside him, she nodded.

Leaning their heads out the window, they spotted the inspector on the ledge, clinging to the corner of the building.

"Hold on sir! We're going to help you!" Climbing up on the window, the young man attempted to reach the inspector, but the old man was too far away. "Suki hold on to me!" he called.

Her hands closed around his ankles, and he could feel her soft, dainty fingers against his skin. It felt nice. Despite the situation, he couldn't help but smile. Pushing the happy thought away, he refocused his mind and shimmied further out onto the ledge, his left arm outstretched. "Sir, take my hand!"

"Stay there! Don't risk your life for me. I'm not worth it, not after what I've done to the city." Daisuke gazed out at the destruction and shook his head. "This is all my fault." He sighed. "It seemed so harmless, I just wanted to make it my friend." He pulled a small bag from the inside pocket of his coat and stared at it. "I fed it these." He held up the bag and chuckled. "Rhinoceros beetles. These are its favorite." The inspector smiled weakly as tears filled his eyes. "It started out so small, so helpless, I had no idea." Taking a deep breath, he adjusted his glasses and looked back at the two by the window. "You're right, young man, this has to stop." Shifting his gaze to his assistant, he smiled. "And, Suki, thank you." Turning back, he held the bag up and called to the monster.

"Sir, no!" the young man screamed.

"Let me go, I know what I'm doing!" The old man took off his jacket and stood there with a strange looking belt around his waist.

The monster was now right below them. "But, sir, the monster!"

"Go! Take Suki and get out of here! Let me help this city for a change! After all, that is my job!"

With respect to his elder, the young man did as he was asked, and slid back into the room to be with Suki. They both stood still, together and helpless, unable to do anything else.

Inspector Daisuke called to the monster again, in soft cooing tones. The monster looked up at him. Clutching the bag of treats tightly in his left hand, he threw himself from the ledge right into the gaping maw of the colossal creature.

The two gasped, and Suki clung to the young man, her teary face buried in his manly chest.

As the cavernous mouth of teeth closed around him, the inspector pushed a small red button in his right hand.

The explosives strapped to the inspector's body detonated with an enormous, hollow thud inside the beast.

A great ball of fire erupted from the monster's mouth as it roared in pain, throwing its arms up.

The Great Kaiju rocked for a moment, stumbled, then slowly fell to the ground, dead.

TOXIC WASTE IS SO PASSÉ

SUZANNE ROBB

Jennifer walked along the pathway as she did every morning. With her headphones turned up, she rocked out to music, and held the leash for her dog, Loki, when she felt the animal start to pull hard. Lifting her head to look around, she barely missed falling into a giant crater, one she knew wasn't there yesterday.

What the hell? she thought.

She called out to her dog, but Loki was more interested in the crater than her. Jennifer walked as close to the side as she could get; it had to be a meteor crater of some kind, or perhaps an alien ship had crashed?

Looking around, she kept alert for alien invaders or spore creatures newly released from their meteorite homes. However, all she saw were hundreds of oak trees uprooted, and crammed into the giant hole.

"Loki, I bet it's those damn loggers! I'm calling Green War now."

Moving forward wasn't an option since the crater had to measure at least ninety feet wide by eighty feet deep. She had no intention of trying to go around it, only to find another ditch, or perhaps an angry logger. Walking at a brisk pace back to her house, she felt something watching her.

Slowing her pace ever so slightly, she bent over to tie her shoe and did a casual scan of the area. She'd seen enough spy shows so that she felt practically like one. Eyeing a rabbit from the corner of her eye, she disregarded it as a threat and stood back up.

If she'd looked up a little further, she would have seen the large human-like hand reaching down for her. Loki barked furiously, and then took off in the opposite direction, her leash no longer in Jennifer's hand. Turning to see what freaked out her dog, Jennifer saw one of the most ferocious and terrifying creatures ever created, a giant squirrel with glowing green eyes and thick black saliva dripping from its mouth.

She stared at it in a daze. It had large fangs, beady eyes, whiskers well over twenty feet in width, and thick black fur covered its body. The worst was the smell, it reminded her of rotten food, trash, and dead bodies all rolled up into one hellish type of potpourri.

"Oh my God!"

Taking a page out of Loki's survival skill set, Jennifer started to run. Unfortunately it was too late; the creature had her in its paws within seconds.

"Help! Something's trying to eat me!" Her screams were heard by a young couple hiking nearby, but they chalked it up to kids having fun and continued on, plus a huge crater prevented them from doing anything anyways.

Jennifer tried to pry the massive paws off her, but failed. Then she watched in horror as the squirrel brought her closer to its face. She decided then, it would be in her best interest to scream like crazy.

The giant squirrel, with a chunk of its right ear missing, stared at Jennifer with interest. She felt something familiar about the monster, but she couldn't put her finger on it.

She soon found herself being rolled around in the large spongy mouth, then stuffed among the oak trees in the crater. She'd seen squirrels do this often, not the stuffing people in giant craters thing, but the putting nuts in their mouth and rolling them around; the saliva scented the food so they could find it in the winter.

Rumor had it they could smell through twelve inches of snow, though why this squirrel concerned itself with the possibility of snow in Nevada confused her. Then the reality of her situation dawned on her—Jennifer now resided in a winter stockpile.

She felt the dark and sticky fluid covering her.

Damn, I hope the smell washes off, she thought.

She sat in the crater, grateful for the yoga classes her mother insisted she take. Waiting until the heavy footprints of the giant squirrel went away, she began the task of trying to climb out of the crater. Being covered in copious amounts of tar-like squirrel saliva made things significantly more difficult.

Man, I better not have rabies now.

An hour later, she reached the top of the crater. Loki stared down at her, waiting with a tennis ball in her mouth.

"Fetch? You left me to die so you could get your ball? I thought you were supposed to protect me?"

Loki stood looking at her with big brown eyes. Jennifer gave in, she never could say no to that face. She threw the ball, and walked as fast as her saliva-soaked clothes allowed her, the substance making her feel like she'd been covered in glue. She needed to make some calls, people needed to be warned. There was a giant squirrel creature on the loose. And it was preparing to store them all for the winter!

"Don't people realize how serious this is? They're acting like I'm the crazy one," she said to herself and slammed the phone down in annoyance.

Jennifer sat back in her chair and looked out over her backyard. Her birdfeeders were full, there were nuts out for the cardinals, and suet and corn for the squirrels. She loved her little corner of nature.

Every week she went down the street to the farmers' market, and bought all sorts of things for her animals. Well, it wasn't a real farmers' market, just a place where the locals sold goods for extra cash, so you never really knew what would be there, where it was from, or how exactly it was grown. These were minor issues to her; the organic signs all over-reminded her she was making the healthy choice.

Really, how dumb did you have to be not to recognize good fruits and vegetables?

She knew she spoiled the critters around her house, but for reasons unknown to her, no man would stick around longer than five minutes into a conversation with her. Aside from Loki, the forest inhabitants were all she had.

"Loki you believe me right? Then again you saw it, too." Loki simply looked up, a tennis ball in her mouth.

"It's not every day you see a giant squirrel. You'd think the police, Green War, even park services would want to be on the ball before someone gets hurt."

Jennifer stood up and paced back and forth. She kept smelling herself, wondering if at any moment the giant squirrel would rip the top of her house off because it smelled some of its food.

Going to the refrigerator, she grabbed one of the organic apples she'd bought from a man named Jed. At first hesitant, she had never seen one quite that color. Jed reassured her cross breeding apples was all the rage.

Always one to go along with new trends, she bought a basket full of the gray apples, along with the orange corn, and pink peppers. Chewing on the apple thoughtfully, she tried to devise a plan to warn people about the giant squirrel.

The police and other agencies were going to hold her last warning of alien groundhogs against her. She knew it would just be a matter of time before that story broke though. Jennifer had seen the crazy little critters last month. They were trying to carry away her bird bath.

She'd chased them off with a broom and alerted the authorities. A deputy had arrived moments too late, finding nothing out of the ordinary. He'd told her to call if she needed anything, she'd took him seriously, and called him saying that she needed a date.

Oddly, the deputy never returned, nor answered any of her calls. She figured he was busy and planned on trying again later tonight.

Loki sat in her dog bed watching her master. For the last few months her master had started acting strange. She ate funny smelling food, chased things that weren't there, and worst of all tried to get her, a dog, to eat organic food.

The only way to prevent it was to keep her ball lodged in her mouth at all times, lest a nasty smelling red carrot got jammed in there when she wasn't looking.

George and Margaret Harrison had been married for forty years. Every day they took a walk along the path behind their house. They brought bread for the birds, and on occasion would bring some peanuts to leave on the ground for squirrels and daring chipmunks.

George took a seat on one of the benches along the way, so Margaret could go and feed a few birds. He closed his eyes for a quick nap and enjoyed the fresh air. A breeze came out of nowhere, and it felt nice. But before he knew what was happening, a second later he found himself spinning through the air, then knocked unconscious by what appeared to be a large paw.

Margaret turned around to point out a bird to her husband, only to see a large bushy black tail heading towards the top of the path, her unconscious husband slung across the creature's shoulder.

Margaret squared her shoulders and started to head to the top of the path. She would find her husband and kick that monster's butt for taking him.

George woke up in an awkward position, his face far too close to his crotch, and his arm twisted in the wrong direction. He also noticed he seemed to be covered in some sort of sticky liquid. He tried to move his arm, which caused knife-like stabs of pain; it was broken, dislocated, sprained, maybe fractured, too.

He thought of his dear Margaret, and hoped whatever devil creature got him didn't get her as well. He didn't want her to meet a fate like this. In fact, he needed to get back to her to make sure she was okay. He tried to move and thought he might die from the pain. Margaret would just have to live without him.

Jennifer hung up the phone after leaving a message for the deputy…her deputy He never answered his phone, and the station said he was out on the streets to try and quell some of the rioting. She felt like the department really took advantage of him, and as soon as she got this squirrel-demon-creature business taken care of, her future deputy boyfriend would be her next cause.

The sun began to set, and she knew time was getting short. She had to go into action now. Grabbing a flashlight, a camera, and bear mace, she felt prepared to deal with whatever that creature threw at her. She also donned an entirely black outfit, and packed a bag of food in case she got hungry.

"All right, Loki, let's go."

The dog looked at her, its head cocked to the left.

"Come on, let's go play fetch."

The dog didn't move.

"Fine, then stay here and guard the house."

Loki raised the equivalent of a doggie eyebrow at Jennifer, watching her master head into certain death.

Minutes later, Jennifer crept through the woods, a nagging feeling at the back of her mind. There was something about the mega squirrel familiar to her, she just couldn't place it. *How does a squirrel get that big anyways?*

Carl Myers and Mike Rogers were out on their usual dumping route. They arrived at the turn-off for Gypsum Dypsum, the most out of the way place one could go in Nevada. They turned off the truck engine and went to unlatch the back of the pickup truck. Hopping inside the rear bed of the truck, they kicked, pushed, and shoved several barrels with stickers reading **Hazardous Materials, Caution—Radioactive Contents, Dispose of Properly**, onto the ground.

They ignored the warning stickers, and the large sign indicating long term exposure could result in mutations. They rolled the barrels into the gorge, and watched as they cracked open, leaking green ooze into the ground.

Mike's favorite part, he loved watching the glowing green stuff. He and Carl had been doing this route for almost five years. Of course they were supposed to take it to some proper processing place out in the middle of nowhere, but that was such a hassle, so they just dumped it here, then they had more time to go to the local bar and drink.

The warnings were all bogus; Mike looked at himself as proof. He loved the green stuff so much sometimes he would go and play with it. Poking it with sticks was fun, because the ends melted.

The sizzle and pop sounds were awesome. It was a lot like acid and he would throw his trash into it, watching it hiss and steam.

The fact he was bald, looked fifty, and had a toe growing out of his armpit didn't faze him at the age of twenty-seven, but if he knew he couldn't have kids due to unexplainable sterility and impotency, he might have changed his tune.

He blamed all the stuff liberal hippies complained about on pesticides, and the organic food craze. Nuclear waste dumping was passé, a very 80's thing to blame problems on.

As the glowing green ooze snaked its way through the cracks in the ground, it drained into the water table. The water table fed several of the nearby towns, including a couple of farming ones.

"Hey, Mike, I don't think that's normal."

"What?"

Roger pointed to a giant thing, its teeth were at last ten feet long, and as it neared the two men they noticed large, clawed hands. The face looked angry, and all of a sudden it started slapping its tail on the ground, making a weird clicking noise with its mouth. Both men started screaming, covering their ears with their hands as they fell to their knees.

The giant creature swatted the two men and they fell down the hill and into the pile of radioactive waste. The two men tumbled and turned in the ooze. When they tried to stand, they discovered they couldn't because their feet were melting.

Carl looked at the giant thing staring them down. He'd never seen anything like it in his life. He smelled something burning and realized it was himself, his body melting. Moments later, a pulpy red mess sat next to another red pulpy pile.

Margaret felt her blood racing, she needed something new in her life, something to liven things up. She would show that spineless excuse of a husband exactly what she was made of, tougher stuff than him to be sure.

I'm going to stop this thing; no one eats my husband and gets away with it, not on my watch!

Times like this she thought of her daughter. Disappointingly, she'd taken after her father. Such a shame; she'd had high hopes for her.

A noise in the bushes caught her attention. She immediately stopped and got into the defensive position for when facing an attacker; she'd learned the move in a self-defense class at the local high school.

Jennifer walked at a slow pace, marking her path with lip gloss. It was the best she could do on short notice. Since it had glitter in it, she assumed it would work rather well.

When she was standing about a hundred feet from the edge of the crater, she heard screaming coming from inside of it.

Throwing caution and her lip gloss to the wind, she broke into a sprint. When she reached the edge, she called out, "Is anyone down there?"

"Yes, please help me! I can barely move, and I think my arm is broken and dislocated."

"Give me a few minutes to find your exact location. I have a flashlight."

Jennifer started to scan the crater, but saw no movement, or a body. She needed to go in. "I can't see you, I'm coming in."

As she made her way down, she slipped a bit and fell a few feet. When she stopped and regained her bearings, her flashlight caught on something. She focused on it and screamed.

"What is it? Is the monster back?" The man sounded scared.

"No it's just a dead body, looks like a hiker."

She pulled herself together and pressed on through the crater. She balanced on branches and trunks to get to the other side. There were other things her flashlight caught glimpses of, but she decided it best to ignore them.

"Keep talking, I'm going to follow the sound of your voice." She waited a few seconds for the man to say something.

"Over here."

Over here, like that was helpful when you were in a giant crater made by a freakishly large squirrel, she thought.

Jennifer continued on in hopes that she would stumble over the man, or find him unintentionally.

"I'm near a tree trunk I think."

Does this guy have his head up his rear or something? she wondered.

"Okay, I think I'm getting closer."

"Hey, I saw your light, you're close."

"Okay, hold on a second, I think I know where you are."

Margaret was still in her defensive pose; she'd taken Pilates classes for the last six years, and could crack walnuts with her thighs.

It was a party trick of hers when she drank too much.

She hadn't even broken a sweat yet. Whatever waited for her, she could wait longer.

Then to her astonishment, she felt the ground start to shake.

An earthquake? she wondered.

Then it was over, just as quickly as it began. She eased her pose a bit as a shadow came over her.

She looked up until she saw some sort of black furry monster with huge fangs. It was huge!

She watched as the monster brought something up to its mouth that looked like a tree of some kind. The creature stuck the entire thing in its mouth, then began to roll it around.

When it finished, it spit out the trunk and shoved it where Margaret couldn't see.

With the monster distracted, she made her move. Nut cracking thighs or not, she wasn't stupid enough to take on this giant beast. She started running, away from the monster's direction.

Rounding a bend in the path, she glanced over her shoulder to see if the beast was following her, and when she turned her head to the front once more, she found herself falling down a hill she was pretty sure wasn't there the day before.

With a muffled curse, she began to fall end over end.

Jennifer reached the man just in time to hear cracking above her; the squirrel creature had returned, putting another tree in its stash.

"Don't move," she said.

"Not a problem."

Jennifer could hear the sarcasm in the man's voice, and once again something seemed familiar.

"Okay, I think it's leaving. We gotta hurry up and get you out of here." She turned her light on the man, still moving towards him.

As she got closer, she leaned down to get a closer look. Then something came rolling down from above and landed on top of her. She screamed.

Margaret got to her feet immediately, re-positioning herself defensively, knowing she was in for the fight of her life.

"Mom? What the hell are you doing here?"

"Jennifer, is that you?" Margaret raised her hands to protect her eyes against the beam of the flashlight.

"Yes it's me. Now tell me what you're doing here."

"Listen, young lady, it's way too dark out, just what do you think you're doing out here?"

"Uhm excuse me, don't mean to interrupt, but can one of you help me out," the man said.

"George? What are you doing down here?" Margaret asked.

"Dad, that's you?" Jennifer asked, surprised.

With a few quick moves, and several screams from George, mother and daughter had him free and in a standing position.

"I think your arm is broken, I'll wrap it for now," Margaret said.

"Margaret, I was hoping you wouldn't get trapped in here, too. I wanted you to be safe," he said.

Margaret didn't reply as she pulled a knife from her shoe and sliced part of her polyester track suit. She used it to make a temporary sling for her husband's arm. Jennifer stood next to her and pulled a matching knife out of her back pocket. Margaret felt a moment of pride.

"You just wanted the adventure for yourself, always so selfish," Margaret mumbled to George.

"What the hell are you talking about? That thing put me in its mouth, then stuffed me in this bottomless pit!" he replied.

"Oh, I thought…well never mind, glad to see you're well, honey."

"With parents like you it's a wonder I turned out normal," Jennifer said.

Both Margaret and George looked at their daughter with a sympathetic look, Margaret thinking the exact opposite.

"Honey, I know talking about feelings is important to you, but this isn't the time. There's a monster on the loose," Margaret said.

"I think it's a giant squirrel, Mom and it's storing things in here like oak trees and hikers!"

"Well, there's no reason to get all huffy." Margaret tied off the sling and George winced.

Margaret looked at her husband, he always stayed quiet when she and Jennifer talked. This fact annoyed her; why didn't he choose to participate in these family discussions, or at least take her side?

"And by the way, what feelings are you talking about? I don't like talking about feelings, although now that you mention it, I feel as if you look down on me, don't take me seriously, and view me as a disappointment."

"Dear, this isn't the time or the place, let's get out of this hole, shall we?" Margaret said.

"See, you never want to talk about feelings," Jennifer huffed.

How long is this going to take? I wonder if the monster will kill me if I ask it to, Margaret thought. She watched George, who walked towards the side of the hole they were in, apparently looking for a way out.

"Dad, what are you doing?" Jennifer asked.

"George, she's right, you're just going to break something else."

The ground started to shake, and all of a sudden something came raining down on them. They were hit with a hailstorm of acorns!

"Incoming, take cover!" Margaret yelled.

All three tried to cover themselves, but were pelted with several thousand acorns as the squirrel creature shook out an oak tree over the crater.

"We need to hurry. This thing is storing anything it can. I saw at least a dozen hikers shoved into nooks and crannies getting over here," Jennifer said. She needed to think, she wasn't planning on babysitting her parents while she hunted the giant squirrel.

Margaret mentally wrestled with herself. She didn't want to have to deal with her family while she rid the world of the squirrel.

George wondered which one of them was going to die first.

Jennifer used her flashlight and panned it around the area they were in.

"All right, let's go up this way, it looks the easiest."

The dysfunctional family of three made their way up the side of the crater. Every now and then, George used his other hand to help his daughter and sometimes Jennifer offered a hand to her father. Margaret tried to help, but had a hard time since it was a foreign concept to her.

Finally, they reached the summit, all three dirty and annoyed. Looking around, Jennifer felt they were safe, relatively speaking.

Then the ground began to shake again, and a rhythmic warbling like noise could be heard.

"Oh Christ, it's calling out to the others…the war is on!" Margaret yelled, then hit the ground.

As Jennifer joined her mother and father in hitting the deck and covering their ears, she thought that the noise sounded familiar. *I know I've heard something like that before…but where?*

The massive squirrel looked at the three things it had dealt with all day. Two of them had already been scented, the other one smelled like nuts.

Thumping its tail in warning, it hoped the other squirrels would be notified to the danger around them. It made the war cry, too, just in case some of them were out of its thumping range.

From the strong vibrations, the other squirrels in the area were holding onto their shaking trees for dear life, or had fallen out of their nest, cursing the giant one.

Ever since it had showed up there had been problems. First, they noticed their food trees were missing. Then they noticed there were fewer hikers than normal, which meant less feeding by the humans.

Now they had to deal with the tail thumping, and warbling whenever the giant got nervous, or wanted to warn them. Didn't it understand it was fifty feet tall?

Didn't it understand nothing was going to mess with it, and warnings were pointless?

The giant squirrel stopped its warbling and tail thumping; it was late and time for bed. It headed up the northern path to the quarry, the only place large enough for it to lie down and actually get some cover. The shelter also happened to be one of its favorite places. It had played there since being a baby.

Entering one of the old mining caves, the squirrel curled up and cleaned its tail of debris, pulling out a few arms and legs, chewing on them happily. Then it sighed sadly and closed its eyes.

The squirrel missed its mate, and its little friends. It had no idea what had happened, how it had become so large, but it knew it was different now, and that the others squirrels were scared of it. Its size made it scary, and a bit clumsy, but it also made it the guardian of the forest family. It took that role seriously, and anything which tried to hurt them would answer to it first. As the squirrel closed its eyes to sleep, a green glow was seen in the back of the cave. The drip was small and had been there for years.

Margaret maintained her defensive pose, George cradled his arm, and Jennifer scanned the forest with her flashlight.

"I think it's gone for now," Jennifer said with more confidence than she felt.

"What was all that ruckus about? Why didn't it kill us?" George asked.

"I think it was doing the standard squirrel warning; waving its tail and making that clicking noise." Jennifer said and noticed her mother ease out of her defensive pose and look at her. She wondered if her mother was proud of her for checking the hikers they'd passed on the way up. She hoped her mother thought she and her were more alike than Margaret realized, and started respecting her.

George looked at his wife and daughter, the two most important people in his life and also the two people in this world that couldn't stand him the most. He hoped the squirrel-thing, whatever the hell it was, came back and killed him.

After touching all those dead hikers, Jennifer sanitized her hands with some wipes she carried. She had a theory as to why she and George were chosen by the squirrel, and she had the proof. They both carried a bag of nuts, each a different kind. She always brought them when going on her walks.

Margaret's pockets were also full, but she hadn't been taken, which was strange, though Jennifer didn't think it was a stretch to think that even a giant squirrel wanted to avoid her mother.

Loki sat in her bed, a tennis ball at her side. Her master had gone crazy, and it was up to her to protect the house, unless the giant squirrel came back. The dog knew there was going to be some serious payback for all the times she'd chased it up a tree, or into the woods. She never would have tormented it that way if she'd known it was going to grow that big.

The three of them sitting around the edge of the crater, George watched his daughter pull an apple out of her survival kit and start to eat it.

"Hey, kiddo, you got another one of those for your old man? I'm starving."

"Sure, Dad." Jennifer tossed another apple to him and he caught it awkwardly with his good hand. He lifted the apple to his mouth to take a bite when he noticed the color; his eyes had to be wrong. The lighting was off; there was no way he held a gray apple.

"Honey, why is this apple gray?"

"Cross breeding apples is all the rage at the organic farms up in Gypsum Dypsum. They have all sorts of things; want a pink pepper or a red cucumber sandwich?"

"Uhm, no thanks."

George raised his arm to toss the apple away when Margaret walked up to him and asked. "Food? Where did you get food? Didn't even offer me any, of all the…"

"Here, I have some for you, enjoy, it's a special cross-breed of apple," he said with a smile.

"Ooh I've heard of these, been meaning to try some," she said.

"Well, go talk to Jennifer. She has all sorts of interesting organic foods to choose from."

George watched as his wife took a big bite of the apple, turned, and walked over to where Jennifer sat. George was a grocery store kind of man. He didn't care if it was free range or open range.

Jennifer was showing her mother some green almonds when she started to smell something.

"Do you guys smell that? It smells like smoke."

"It does, doesn't it? George, I thought you quit?"

"I'm not smoking, dear. Take a look over there, where the smoke is coming from," he said.

Both Margaret and Jennifer turned as one to look towards the smoke. There was a huge fire in the town center.

"And the fires of Hell came down!" Margaret said in a booming voice.

"Mom, we need to do something."

"We will, dear. I'm stopping that creature no matter what I have to do. Come on, follow me."

The two women started to sprint, Jennifer's flashlight beam bouncing from side to side wildly.

George watched them go, wished them luck, and decided to take a nap. If the Apocalypse was coming, he wanted to sleep through it.

The two women raced down the path, tripping and falling most of the way. As they neared the town, they could see several of the local stores on fire. People were running around crazily. A crowd had already gathered and stood watching as the fire department worked at putting out the blaze.

Jennifer saw her deputy and made a beeline for him. He didn't notice her until she was right on top of him, tapping his shoulder and yelling directly into his ear.

"Deputy, I'm not surprised to see you working. No wonder you never answer your phone. You need a vacation."

Deputy Frank Holmes looked at the crazy woman with a wary eye. He'd been debating a restraining order, but was told she was harmless. As he looked at her now, dressed in black, a knife sticking out of her boot, and cuts and scrapes all over her face and arms, he didn't agree with that assessment.

"Ma'am, can you please step back, please."

"Yes of course, you're working. We'll talk later," Jennifer said with a smile.

Jennifer walked back over to where her mother was talking with a group of women. It looked like her book club, but Jennifer wasn't sure.

"Find anything out?" she asked her mother.

"Jennifer, these are my Pilates buddies, and no, we don't know what's going on. Apparently, the grocery store burst into flames causing a chain reaction. Of course the rioters throwing Molotov cocktails didn't help. Now the locals are blaming the organic farmers, and the police are blaming the owners, saying they wanted insurance money."

Margaret's speech was short by the ground shaking. All of a sudden a dark shadow appeared, and as gust of wind blew the smoke away, a large, beady-eyed face was revealed. Long sharp teeth, whiskers, and human-like hands with five foot long claws were hovering over the screaming townspeople.

The creature looked angry.

The giant squirrel was about to fall asleep when it smelled smoke. It was the squirrel's duty to guard the forest now. Seeing the blaze, it went into action.

Turning its body, it started swatting the burning buildings with its tail. It was helping with the fire, but also sent multiple fireman and volunteers flying all over the place. It began thumping its tail to try and crush the buildings on fire, but unfortunately, it crushed several firemen inside.

Soon the fires were out, but the swatting had caused several other buildings to catch fire. The squirrel went into a stomping frenzy, only one thought on its mind: *fire bad*!

Jennifer and her mother watched in horror as most of the town burned, only to then be crushed by the giant mutant squirrel.

The local police showed up to try and help, but the moment they laid eyes on what they were up against, they got back in their cars and left. The National Guard could handle this, as far as they were concerned.

Jennifer watched the squirrel and realized why it seemed so familiar, it was her little buddy.

A couple of years ago, a squirrel would come and sit with her on the back deck in her yard every morning and eat the organic fruit she put out.

She knew it was that particular squirrel because of the nick in its ear.

A tear came to her eye as she realized what had become of her little buddy. She needed to do something to help it somehow. How could this have happened?

"Jennifer, snap out of it and pull yourself together. We need to get this situation under control," Margaret snapped.

"Mom, we need to help the squirrel," Jennifer said, looking at her mother with pleading eyes.

She's finally gone insane. I wonder if there could have been a mix up at the hospital when she was a baby, Margaret wondered. She looked at her daughter with a grave expression.

The town was on fire, people were being squashed into piles of red goo under the mad squirrel's stomping feet, and her daughter wanted to save it. *Why me?*

"Honey, we can't save the town, and the giant squirrel at the same time. You do understand it's killing people, right?" Margaret said.

"But, Mom, it's not the squirrel's fault, look at it. Nothing grows to that size without something human related being involved. It probably ate something radioactive, or was experimented on or was hit with gamma rays."

"Jennifer, you know very well animal experimentation only involves rats and mice, and do I need to point out that everyone in this town is excessively healthy, so I highly doubt there's any radioactive dump sites nearby. Really, dear, you watch too much television."

"Where's Dad, he'd believe me. I bet he would even help."

The two women looked around for a second, then back at one another.

"I don't see your father anywhere. Maybe he was crushed under that thing's foot, or ran away screaming like a little girl."

"Okay, we'll find him later. Let's work on a plan to save the giant squirrel."

"Jennifer, take a good look around you. See that red smudge over there? That was Cassidy Jenkins. And the divot over there? That was the bank."

"I know you think it's a monster, but I'm telling you that it's just an innocent squirrel, and I'm going to do something to save it! It didn't mean to crush all those people, and I know it didn't intend to destroy the town. It was just helping, don't you see?"

Margaret looked at her daughter and wondered once again where she went wrong. *I breast fed her, I coddled her, and when she was four, I told her she was responsible for herself. What better mother could I have been?*

Hell, Margaret practically deserved an award for mother of the year.

Jennifer turned away from her mother and began to walk towards the forest.

She had no idea how she was going to save her little buddy, but she had to come up with something fast. Perhaps she could build a giant cage and lure it in there.

Or maybe she could train it with giant peanuts.

As her daughter walked off, Margaret had a surge of motherly love. It was that or the gray apple wasn't sitting right with her. She decided to help Jennifer against her better judgment.

We're both going to die anyways, and I sure as hell don't want to die alone, she thought.

"Wait up, dear, I'll help you."

Jennifer turned around, all teary eyed.

"Uggh don't cry, don't make this about feelings."

"Okay. Thanks, Mom. It's just that you really do love me."

"Can I have another one of those apples?"

Jennifer nodded her head and reached into her bag.

The giant squirrel saw the two humans from earlier. One had gotten out of its storage place. Now that the fires were out, it needed to collect its renegade food. The squirrel started to follow them to see where they were going. When it realized they were heading for the forest, it knew they were a threat.

Thumping its tail and making the warbling noise again, it tried to warn the others that danger was coming.

Jennifer and her mother both fell to the ground, covering their ears as the warbling filled the air. Jennifer tried to motion to her mother that they needed to find cover, but was frozen in fear.

The monster squirrel stopped what it was doing, picked up a few of the bodies from around town, and put them in its mouth to scent them. These humans were so strange, they all smelled strange, but in a tasty way. It decided it would eat these ones as a midnight snack.

Margaret saw the giant creature put several bodies in its mouth and looked at her daughter. "Jennifer, the damn thing is eating people, there's no saving it. We need to stop it at all costs!"

Jennifer glanced over her shoulder and remembered her own turn in the spit wash.

She's right, we have to stop it.

"Okay, Mom, so what do we do?"

"I have no idea, maybe blow it up or use poison. Shouldn't the army or the police be dealing with this?"

Jennifer thought about these options, ruling them all out. Poison was an obvious no go, and blowing it up, well, there was a high chance they would blow themselves up in the process. And it's not like either of them were demolition experts. Hell, she wouldn't even know where to get the explosives. They would have to out think the squirrel creature somehow, lure it into a trap.

Then Jennifer had a stroke of genius. A few miles down the road, an old quarry stood empty, abandoned years ago. If they could get the squirrel to go there, they could trap it in one of the tunnels. That involved explosives again, but then she saw the deputy and had another idea.

"Deputy…Deputy, over here!" She called, trying to get his attention not realizing he was in shock and wasn't hearing a word she said.

Deputy Holmes had just missed being squashed by a huge furry foot and was busy wetting himself. Now the crazy woman was talking to him again.

He did everything right. He'd called in for back-up, but they left when they saw the monster. He'd notified the State Police, and the Army, but apparently they had bigger things to deal with. Giant monster sightings were being reported at an alarming rate all of a sudden.

He was exhausted, so when the crazy lady approached him, he just didn't have the energy to fight her off.

"Deputy, you poor thing, you're so tired you can barely stand. You really need to let me take care of you," Jennifer said.

"Look lady, I don't know what you think is going on with us, but…"

"Hey, buddy, don't you *hey lady* my daughter. She has her stuff together, unlike you. Now you're going to show some respect and help us kill that damn devil rodent before more of them come. You got me?" Margaret might think her daughter was an idiot, but that didn't mean other people could.

As the deputy nodded, at that precise moment a severed head rolled past them. The trio looked up at the squirrel, who reached for them with large, gore-infested paws, and even larger claws. They froze in terror. Margaret tried to get her feet to move, but they wouldn't and Jennifer had the same problem.

Then a loud gunshot rang out and a small chunk of the giant squirrel's claw was blown off, causing it to pull back. Looking around, Margaret saw George standing nearby with a shotgun.

"George?" Margaret was obviously shocked.

"Sorry I took so long. Why are you all standing there? We have a giant squirrel to kill."

"Dad?"

"Yeah, it's me. Don't act so surprised, I just saved you all, didn't I? Now stop gawking and let's get a move on, we need a plan, and I think I have one."

The group of four moved quickly to an area of the forest that provided cover, the monster squirrel distracted by the pain of getting shot. George got down on one knee and looked back the way they'd come, Margaret next to him. He kept one eye on the squirrel.

Margaret looked at her husband with new eyes. Holding that shotgun, looking all butch, she wanted him right there and then. She moved closer to him and began to rub her shoulder against his. When he looked over at her, she smiled seductively.

"Okay, when I came back here I noticed where that thing came from. I went to check it out and found a quarry. It's full of some kind of goo. The way it was glowing I bet it was radioactive, too. Someone must be dumping there illegally. It's just a matter of time before we're fighting off fifty foot humming birds and bees as well," George said.

"Then we just need to get out of here and let someone else deal with it." The deputy seemed happy with his idea.

"I have to go back for Loki. My dog needs me," Jennifer said.

"Loki will be fine, dear. What we have to do is get rid of that giant squirrel. That goo might be flammable. If we can get the creature to go back to its cave, we can light it on fire and blow it to hell, trapping it in the cave for good."

"But what if it's not flammable?" Jennifer asked.

"Then we're going to need another plan," Margaret added. Of course her daughter would be negative. "But let's assume it will burn, all right?"

The group watched the giant squirrel as it examined its damaged claw. It looked unhappy, and after a few moments, it turned around and left. The group followed at a distance. The squirrel went back to the quarry and entered a cave, going far enough back to be hidden. The green glow was everywhere.

George felt invigorated. Margaret wanted to jump his bones right now, Jennifer was worried about Loki, and the deputy trailed behind the crazy people wondering if he should run for it.

"I don't think we should touch the barrels," Jennifer exclaimed.

"No kidding," George added and gave his daughter a look, wondering if he was her biological father. "Don't step in any of it, either."

"What are those two red spots?" Margaret asked as she examined the area.

"My guess is, two people who weren't smart enough not to stay clear of that stuff," George mused.

"So, how do we blow up the cave and have it bury the squirrel, and not blow ourselves up at the same time?" Jennifer asked, skeptical.

George had to think hard about that one. The creature had gone into a cave and they had goo that may or may not burn, and may or may not be explosive. With nothing else to try, he decided to plan on the goo being as lethal as dynamite. Now all they needed was a way to execute the plan.

He could try shooting it from a distance, but he didn't know how big the explosion would be, and if it didn't work, he ran the risk of waking the giant squirrel. Then he spotted something that might work.

"Hey, look over there by the mouth of the cave. There's a green goo trail there. I say we light it like it's a fuse and run like hell."

"But it doesn't reach all the way inside and what if it doesn't light?" Jennifer asked again, the skeptic in the group.

George wanted to tell his daughter to be quiet but instead gave her a look that had her quieting down. "It'll work, it has to," he said simply.

Margaret looked at George, admiring the way he was taking charge.

That's my brave husband! she thought proudly.

"And what do you intend to use for a fuse to make the goo trail reach all the way inside?" Jennifer asked, still not willing to let it go. George remained silent this time, having no idea.

Jennifer looked around for something, when she remembered the rope in her backpack. She opened it and took out a nylon rope; only it would be hard to burn.

Maybe, she thought, *if the rope is soaked in that toxic goo, it'll burn...*

"Dad, I think I have an idea. We use this rope, soak it in the gunk, and then light it; the rope can reach the rest of the way inside. If that stuff burns that is."

George got a thoughtful look on his face. "It could work. Okay, you all go and find a good place to seek cover. The last thing we want is this crap raining down on us when it blows. I'll soak the rope and use the shotgun to ignite it from a distance."

The deputy and Jennifer began looking for a place to hide. Margaret stood frozen in place with pure lust. Her husband was finally being the man she'd always wanted him to be. Why it had to be when they were fighting a giant squirrel was something she wanted an answer for. Though she still wanted to take him right there, she followed him to the mouth of the cave where he was using his foot to roll the rope around in the goo.

She leaned in close to him and whispered, "Tonight, after all of this is over, I'm going to rock your world." As she walked away, George realized something had drastically changed with his wife...and he liked it.

At the far end of the quarry, Jennifer found an area with an overhang of rock that would protect them from any falling debris. The rope was soaked in the green goo and all were gathered for the moment of truth.

George hoped to God it worked.

Taking aim, George fired the shotgun, while behind him, Margaret shuddered. The rope caught fire and began to burn, the flame consuming the goo like it was gasoline.

The rope led right to a trail of goo that then led to the barrels of toxic waste. When the flame found the wide pool of goo surrounding the barrels, the explosion was huge.

The ground shook as if an earthquake was beneath the quarry, and the four huddling people could hear the different caverns crumbling as thousands upon thousands of tons of dirt and rock came down.

It seemed much longer, but only a full minute later, the noise stopped.

Dust was everywhere, causing everyone to choke and cover their mouths and noses with arms and shirts so they could breathe. When the dust began to settle, they noticed the opening where the giant squirrel had gone in wasn't fully blocked. Then they saw a huge claw trying to make its way out of the cave, digging at the rocks and dirt.

"It didn't work!" George yelled.

"I'm outta here, you people are crazy." The deputy took off running.

"Wait!" Jennifer reached out to the deputy, but the man was already halfway down the road.

Margaret patted her daughter on the shoulder. "You can do better, dear."

Jennifer almost fell over at the fact that her mother was attempting to reassure her, to actually support her. About to hug her mom, she stopped when the visible claw became a paw.

George took one look at the paw digging its way free and yelled, *"Run!"*

The two women didn't need to be told twice, and scrambled out of the way. George fired a shot at the outcropping over the cave, desperate to do anything to stop the giant squirrel from getting free. His shot caused a landslide, the rock already fractured and cracked from the explosion. The entryway to where the creature hid was finally blocked. With a sigh of relief, the three of them walked into the forest to head home.

"My house is closer, and I think yours might have been destroyed by the creature earlier," Jennifer said.

"Whatever, dear." Margaret said, just glad she and her family were still alive.

Holding onto her husband's arm, Margaret was very happy. She'd married a real man after all. She thought of all the things they could do together now: defensive driving classes, karate, firearms training, police ride-alongs, the list went on and on.

George hoped he could stay awake for what the night had in store for him, but somehow he didn't think he would have a problem. He admitted to being oddly invigorated; perhaps it was the bag of trail mix he'd found in Jennifer's bag.

The giant squirrel gave up trying to get out of the cavern after it collapsed. Turning around, it walked until it reached the back entrance. No sign of the humans were detected here; perhaps it would be better off leaving them alone for now. Plus, it wanted to get that little dog that had tormented it for so long. Crawling back into the center of the cave, it went to sleep.

Jennifer ran into her house while yelling Loki's name. The dog came running up to her, then ran away, but returned a moment later with a tennis ball in her mouth.

George went to the refrigerator to grab something to eat and was shocked by what he found in the fridge.

"Jennifer, what have you been eating? Everything looks like it's gone bad in here."

"Dad, it's just organic. Not that you would know what something looks like naturally grown."

"Honey, potatoes aren't orange naturally—*ever*. You know, all those local farmers you buy from use a water supply that the quarry must have been leaking into for years."

"You don't think the farmers are in danger, do you?"

George looked at his daughter, wondering again if she was really his.

"I think the farmers are fine, honey, but we're moving away from here immediately, somewhere safe, like the inner city."

"Jennifer, go play with your dog for a while, I need some time alone with your father."

Margaret grabbed George by the hand and led him down the hall to the guest room. Jennifer looked at Loki, and the two sat on the couch.

She cradled the dog protectively, and Loki cradled her tennis ball.

"At least we're safe now, Loki. That squirrel is trapped for good."

Loki let out a doggie sigh. Why were humans so naïve? Didn't they know that the giant creature never died the first time it was killed? Didn't they know this was just the beginning?

Jennifer turned on the television to cover the sounds her parents were making, but she fell asleep seconds later, the activities of the past day finally catching up to her.

If she'd watched for longer than a few minutes, she would have seen the coverage of thousands of giant animals of all kinds destroying cities around the world.

BENJAMIN'S VENGEANCE

KRZYSZTOF T. DABROWSKI

He was slowly getting used to it. He had to. He had no other choice. The old woman put the collar on him and attached the lead to it. It was so humiliating—he felt like a slave. The woman was well in her seventies and was twenty kilos overweighed. In her trembling, spotted hand she held a muzzle.

Why was she doing this? Had she ever wondered how unpleasant it was? And what if someone muzzled her—how would she feel then? He turned around. What is this game all about? Why all this dressing up?

Unfortunately, a dog has got to do what a dog has got to do, especially when he is dependant on someone. Sometimes it was to give in to the whims of the old lady. After all, if it wasn't for her, he would be just as skinny as those who were left behind.

Instead of being nice and fat, he would have a keyboard of ribs under his skin. He felt the old woman was getting irritated, but had to show that he didn't like it at all, just for the sake of his pure, congenial perversity.

"Benjamin! Benjamin, turn back at once!" She wanted her trembling, squeaky voice to sound masterful, but it was side-splitting instead. "Benjamin, do you hear me? You nasty, you!"

You're lucky that you give me such good food, he thought. *In any other case I wouldn't stand that chattering.*

He turned back to avoid a beating with the lead. A few times, when he went too far, he got a good thrashing. It hurt. It was an unpleasant variety of everyday routine. She bent to attach the torture tool. Her face, red from anger, was covered with a network of small wrinkles and beads of sweat.

She started to breathe heavily. Was she really enjoying this? He felt an unpleasant odor—some garlic, a bit of onion and the worst one: smell of indigestion coming straight from her intestines.

The smell was horrifying but he couldn't turn away; he would certainly get a beating if he did. That he was absolutely sure of.

He could only take a deep breath and try to survive. It wouldn't be so bad if it wasn't for those trembling, clumsy hands. Unfortunately, snapping always lasted too long.

He felt that he would soon become the world champion in a new discipline: breath holding. The worst thing was that even a champion had to give up sometimes. He felt dizzy. He heard his heartbeat. And the old woman was flabbily fighting with the snap, and the end of this fight wasn't near.

Spring was in full blossom. The sun was shining. The birds were singing joyfully, flirting with one another. There was a scent of freshly mowed grass in the air. Benjamin felt that now was the time to do this. He had been waiting for this moment for far too long.

He squatted down.

"Benjamin! Not on the sidewalk!" his oppressor yelled. "Go on the lawn!"

Oh God, I can't even poop in peace, the annoyed dog thought and went to look for a better—according to her criteria—place. He had suffered so much. Since six in the morning, for three and a half hours, he'd been scratching the door, trying to signal that it was time. That he had to go.

Every day the same thing. Humiliatingly whimpering at the door. He didn't have the courage to demonstratively poop on the carpet, although he often felt like it. He knew far too well what would happen to him. Lead! Pain! Sometimes he thought he was going insane.

Not only the terrifying name, but also leads, collars, muzzles! Additionally, whenever he was getting ready to flirt with and was about to catch some cute female, the old woman was always yelling, "Here!" Then she took him home. He couldn't even relieve himself in peace, because she was beginning to scold. Because something was not the way she wanted! Ugh, what a life...

If it wasn't for the delicious food, he wouldn't stand up to that treadmill. The price was high, however the delicacies he was getting were first class. Everyday some fresh meat. Delicious, delicate dog snacks. Mmmm, yum—yum!

When he was a puppy and lived in a shelter, he was often hungry. He got only scraps, once in two or three days. He had to fight for better bites.

There were plenty of mouths eager to eat. In the winter, he spent days curled up, without ever moving. Every move was a nightmare to his chilled body—it made him feel the cold even more.

Autumn wasn't much better; storms and rain. Wet fur, brrr!

Yes, he had to be honest—it wasn't so bad with the old woman.

Every month the memories became weaker and weaker. Every day he felt more of the poverty and humiliations she was giving him.

"A bad time has come upon us, Benjamin," she sighed with resignation. "We have a problem. No money left. You understand, don't you? My pension is too small for me to buy you the kind of food you're used to. I cannot afford it any more."

More or less, he understood what was going on. The tone in her voice, the troubled look on her face, and the usual time of feeding him with fresh, bloody meat having passed, made him guess what the bad news was about.

It was about his delicacies. He looked at her, asking with his eyes. The old lady reached into the fridge and something rattled in Benjamin's bowl a moment later. It wasn't the sound of meat. The smell was also weird. She put the bowl on the floor. He took a glimpse. No way! Was she joking?

Had she really put a handful of picked chicken bones into his bowl! Was this supposed to be his dinner? Well, she'd decided to tighten his belt. She probably wants to check how much further she can go in the art of humiliating him. The damned sadist!

She knew she was disappointing him, but she couldn't do anything else. Up till then she had often denied herself many things just so her four legged darling could have the best. She was really trying.

She often visited a couple of different food shops and compared prices, to save as much as she could; for Benjamin. Unfortunately, the latest increase in prices destroyed all her efforts. Now, to live through the month they had to live sparingly.

She was looking at her darling doggie. The 'doggie,' a full-grown rottweiler, was looking back at her.

He made a dash. He knocked the old woman down and with one snap of his jaws mutilated her throat. As blood spurted from her arteries, Benjamin reveled in joy.

Ah, fresh, hot meat...

THEIR FAMILIAR

JOHN GROVER

"Foolish girls!" Isabelle pushed the three girls into the house ahead of her and slammed the door behind them. "Damn foolish!" She drew a thick board across the door with trembling hands as the ground shook and the house thundered.

Isabelle's face drained of all color and her eyes widened. She turned to the three cowering adolescents. "What have you done? Playing with the Devil's fire will destroy us all. Who taught you this witchery?"

"We're sorry, Momma," Abigail cried as tears filled her eyes. "We're sorry. We didn't mean to. It wasn't supposed to…"

Her words became a scream as the entire house rocked on its foundation. The dinner table leapt into the air and tumbled over, spilling baskets of harvest fruit and vegetables everywhere. Buckets of well water unleashed rivers as broomsticks flew into the air like they had the day the girls discovered that witchcraft truly did exist. They were shown the trick by the mysterious slave-woman of Salem Village.

"Oh my Lord," Isabelle squealed as she looked out the window. "It comes now…to our house!"

Abigail, her cousin Sarah, and friend Prudence, wailed and dropped to their knees, praying to the heavens for salvation as Abigail's mother pushed herself away from the window…and just in time.

A giant paw crashed through the window and actually tore it and the entire wall apart. The deafening screech of a cat filled the house as the front door crumbled off its hinges. Massive green eyes glared at the shivering girls and the awe-struck mother.

The monstrous cat hissed and reached for the nearest girl and snagged Sarah with its claws, hooking her dress and dragging her through the debris. Her screams were unrelenting as her face burned against the wooden floors and her hands caught splinters, leaving a trail of crimson.

The cat scooped up the flailing Sarah as if she were a mouse and bit into her, tearing clothing and flesh alike. In the distraction, Isabelle and the other two girls fled the house through the obliterated walls and scattered rubble.

The entire village was a frenzy of hysterical people running in every direction. Screams of terror and prayers to God mingled among the din in the girls' ears. Smoke billowed in the air and demolished houses littered the roads in the distance.

Isabelle turned back to see the giant cat still feasting; it was as tall as the trees. Sarah's blood streaked its midnight-black fur, the claws as deadly as swords. It stopped momentarily and eyed the girls. Isabelle's heart sank as she realized it had spotted them.

"To the slave woman!" Isabelle screamed. "She'll know what to do. She'll know how to send it away."

They cut a path away from the panicked crowds as the cat stumbled over their neighbor's house, thrashing it to and fro, wood and bricks raining down from the sky.

A chimney crashed down in front of their paths and the girls fell to the ground.

"My leg, I've hurt it," Prudence called and rubbed her knee.

The cat's roar startled them, the ground shaking again.

"Come, Abigail, help me," Isabelle said and she and her daughter each took one of Prudence's arms and carried the girl to a cluster of trees off the dirt-covered path. They hid among the brush and listened to the terrible cracking and pounding ruckus as the cat trampled its way past them.

A shingled roof sailed across the air and smashed into the trees around them; pieces of it sprinkled onto the ground around them. Isabelle positioned herself over the two girls and shielded them from the assault. Her back took a few poundings but she stayed firm.

A wail pierced Isabelle's ears and she lifted her head to see the giant cat dragging Reverend Parris over the road with its teeth. It played with him as if he was a toy, shaking him from side to side and throwing him back to the ground. It batted him around with its paws again before picking him up and carrying him off.

The cat continued its rampage into the heart of Salem Village as Isabelle looked around for a clear path. "Come." She roused Abigail and Prudence and led them through the trees and down the side of a hill. "Where is she? Where's Tituba?"

"She spoke of retreating to the cave," Abigail replied.

"The cave? Why would she go there? It's forbidden."

"That's where she does her...witchcraft," Prudence called. "Where she showed us."

Isabelle's eyes widened with surprise and fear. "We must find her."

The three continued walking while avoiding the village at all cost. They watched for signs of the gargantuan feline, listening to the sound of its paws battering the countryside, its hisses and screeches pealing through the air. Dusk was settling on the land and soon darkness would be upon them. Then they would have no defense but their sense of hearing and the ability to hide. The cat would smell them. It would pick up their scent and hunt them, using its superior eyesight in the gloom of the darkness and track them down like mice.

The thought of it twisted through Isabelle. She could see the jaws of teeth pooling with puddles of saliva; a pink tongue as big as the roads were wide thirsting for their blood.

Finally, they saw the cave nestled in the woods, hiding among the crowds of thorn bushes and poisonous yew trees. Firelight glowed in the entrance and a shadow danced within. Isabelle knew she was there. Tituba was their only hope now.

A low rumble echoed in the distance and instantly the girls launched into a full-blown run and barreled into the cave, much to the surprise of the slave woman.

She dropped her bowl of stew and stood up. They stared each other down, trading different expressions until Tituba backed herself away from the fire.

"Children? Why have you come back here?" Tituba asked. "This is not the place for you. I forbid you from playing here."

"You must help us," Abigail cried. "Something terrible has happened."

"What has happened my child?"

"Pyewacket is destroying the village!"

"My cat? How is my beloved Pyewacket destroying the village?"

"As if you don't know," Isabelle said and stepped in front of the girls, a twinge of fear holding her back. "You taught the girls your heathen witchcraft, the Devil's power. Now they've brought evil down upon us. The cat is now a monster devouring the good people of Salem! Can't you hear the thunder of its steps and the screams?"

Tituba's mouth was agape, her eyes wide with shock. "I came here to be with my people's Gods and to seek protection from the storm."

"It's no storm," Isabelle said. "It is the Devil's work. Your work."

"No." Tituba shook her head vigorously. "No, it was not I. I told the girls stories of my people, stories of animal spirits and our ways; then I catch them reading my books, playing with my people's sacred items."

"Abigail?" Isabelle turned to her daughter, who cried uncontrollably.

"We didn't mean to, Momma. We only wanted to see the spirit inside Pyewacket. We took Tituba's books and asked the cat's spirit to be revealed. We conjured it with our blood, some nightshade and belladonna from the woods. We didn't know what it would do."

"Oh girls…the Devil tempted you. He waits for us to be weak and foolish. What if the reverend found out about this? You must tell no one else. Not ever."

"What have you children done to my Pyewacket? He has no spirit in him," Tituba announced. "He is just a cat."

"No longer," Isabelle corrected. "He's a monster now. We need your help, Tituba. Make it go away. Stop this evil."

"They are only stories of my people. There may be no remedy for this."

"We must do something."

"Rest here with me," Tituba said. "I will think of something. I will read my books. Hide here, it's safe. Eat…I have enough stew for all."

Isabelle reluctantly accepted the graciousness of the slave woman and the girls hid in the cave. Bowls of stew were passed around as they ate with voracious appetites. Isabelle could see the red around their eyes, how sore they were from weeping.

Prudence continued to favor her knee after eating. Isabelle checked it and cleaned it for her, wiping away the dirt and blood with water Tituba kept in the cave.

"It's just some scratches," Isabelle told her. "Keep it covered and clean. You'll mend."

Isabelle looked around the cave and stared at the animal skins and bones decorating it; she was a bit unsettled by them. She didn't understand her surroundings or the woman giving her sanctuary. There were cut herbs in piles, wooden bowls filled with berries and powders, and shells and beads strung into necklaces.

Throughout the night, the calls of terrorized villagers would echo randomly. The thrashing of tall trees occasionally wafted in the distance, followed by a low rumble. None of them slept.

Tituba read her books by firelight and mumbled to herself. She gathered herbs and salt into a stone bowl and ground it with a round rock the size of her fist.

Isabelle lay across the ground beside her daughter with one eye open, watching Tituba work. She listened to the fire crackle and felt the cool air moving through her hair. Glancing down at her bonnet sitting on the ground, she saw it was dusted with dirt, splinters of wood, and what she thought might be blood, which appeared black in the weak firelight.

Her gaze met the slave woman's eyes briefly. "Thank you," she whispered.

"It is not over yet," Tituba answered. "We are not yet safe. The beast will smell the girl's wound. There is nothing that can be done. It will come for us and we will face it."

Panic swept into Isabelle's heart and soul but she remained calm. "What are we going to do?" Her lips trembled. "I'll pray to the Lord." Isabelle murmured to herself, her lips moving swiftly.

Tituba sighed and realized how terrified this woman was for herself and the children. "If it worked once it can work again," she told Isabelle. "The children worked real magic. What they have done can be undone."

"It's the Devil's witchcraft," Isabelle said. "It'll destroy us all."

"No, not the Devil. It is of nature. This power is all around us if we just look."

Silence passed between them as Tituba continued to work. Eventually the night took its toll and Isabelle fell asleep, cradling Abigail in her arms.

Prudence slept on her other side, snoring softly, a sound not unlike a purr.

Sunlight streamed into the cave and struck Isabelle directly in the face. For the first time in hours, a smile crossed her lips. She thought it had all been a dream. Nothing but a dream, a fanciful figment of her imagination, of fantasies born of boredom and superstitions.

Her theories were instantly shattered as the cave rumbled. A loud screech filled the cave as Isabelle and the girls screamed. Dirt and rocks fell all around them and they jumped to their feet and clung to each other.

Huge rubble crashed to the cave floor. Some shattered the cooking pot above the dying fire, sending embers showering through the air.

They looked up and saw fierce green eyes glaring at them from outside the cave entrance. More screams erupted as Tituba fought her way to the front of the women; she held a pouch in her hands.

"Pyewacket!" she cried. "Stop this terrible killing!"

The cat paused momentarily and then hissed with spite. An enormous paw thrust into the cave and swatted the slave woman.

Tituba rolled across the cave and hit a wall. A dazed look washed over her face and the pouch fell from her hands.

"Behind me!" Isabelle called to the girls. They maneuvered around her, nearly paralyzed with fear, rivers of tears flowing down their faces.

The group backed away from the cat paw searching for them. They headed for the rear to hide when Prudence suddenly winced and grabbed hold of her knee. Blood seeped from the bandage and she struggled to walk.

"Prudence, walk with us!" Isabelle yelled, almost angered now. "Keep walking."

"My knee...my knee!"

The paw swung hard and caught Prudence on the shoulder, a razor-sharp claw impaling the girl and nearly severing the arm from the socket.

Prudence went down hard and smashed her face on the cave floor. Her horrible screams were muffled by the blood in her mouth. She squirmed on the ground and attempted to crawl towards the dumbstruck Isabelle, until Pyewacket clamped its paw across the girl's waist and dragged her towards it awaiting mouth.

"Prudence no!" Abigail screamed. "Prudie...oh dear Lord, Prudie..."

"Don't look, Abigail." Isabelle grabbed her daughter's face and buried it against her chest. Chomping sounds echoed throughout the cave, cracking bones, tearing flesh, a hellish symphony that threatened the sanity of everyone.

When the awful sounds stopped, Isabelle looked back and saw the cat's paw stretching in again, reaching and clawing to get hold of another morsel.

A claw hovered above and Isabelle stood up to it defiantly. She shoved Abigail against the back wall and stood in front of her, blocking Pyewacket's reach.

"You won't take my daughter!" Isabelle yelled. "You hear me, foul beast?

You won't take her!"

The paw loomed above her, ready to strike. The claw dripped scarlet as it lifted high.

Tituba sprang into action and emptied the contents of her pouch onto Pyewacket's leg. She gestured with both hands and recited the words from her books that were committed to memory. Hours of studying overnight allowed her to unleash her final defense against the giant cat and its rampage of death.

Strange powder burned the cat's fur and it began to smolder and then, in a blinding flash of light, the cat roared one last time and transformed.

Moments later, Pyewacket the cat strolled into the cave, back to its normal size and purring. The cat ran instantly to its master and curled around Tituba's leg as if nothing had happened.

Isabelle's face relaxed and she hugged Abigail as tightly as she could. She turned and looked at Tituba and the two exchanged half-smiles.

A giggle of relief escaped Abigail as she wiped her plump, tear-soaked cheeks.

"Praise the Lord," Isabelle said.

In the days that followed, Salem Village began to repair itself by rebuilding homes and replanting crops and enlisting the help of nearby towns. However, an air of paranoia and fear had swept the village. Would this happen again? It was clear now that some in the village consorted with the Devil and practiced witchcraft. Salem Village was indeed plagued by witches.

The giant cat was only the beginning, and soon, other horrors were unleashed on the village…giant toads, giant crows…all manner of abominations.

The villagers knew all too well that midnight Sabbaths under pale moonlight occurred; the rubbing of oils on naked bodies to achieve flight with broomsticks. It was rumored that three girls had charmed broomsticks into the air and were seen reading black books and playing with black cats.

The cat that attacked the village had been black.

Some in the village whispered of seeing Abigail involved, seeing her remove her bonnet and let her hair down, perhaps even dancing in the woods by the cave.

Isabelle heard the stories. She watched the people grow mad with their hysteria. They wanted to blame someone for the tragedies that never seemed to end; the blighting of crops, the death of children, disease and sickness, the cat. She knew it wouldn't be long before they came for Abigail, came for her only daughter. She couldn't let them. She wouldn't let them.

She had an idea to save her daughter.

"You will say this, Abigail," Isabelle said and took hold of the girl's wrists and looked her right in the eyes. "You must to save yourself."

"But it's a lie, Momma," Abigail protested.

"Do you want them to take you away? Do you know what they'll do to you if you're proven to be a witch? You'll be executed. It's not your fault. You didn't know what you were doing or what the book was for."

"But Momma."

"Silence daughter. You were bewitched. Bewitched by Tituba."

"Tituba only told us stories…we stole the book. Momma, please…"

"No, she bewitched you with her witch powers. I saw her spirit at the window at night. She came to you in your bedroom and made you take the book so you could be like her. I see it all now."

"Momma…"

"Hush child, I can hear them." Isabelle ran to the window and saw the group of men walking down the path to her home. Her husband was in the fields and it was too late to get him. She was alone. "The new preacher, Reverend Lawson and Constable Mathers are coming now. They've come for you!"

"No!" Abigail screamed. "Momma, don't let them take me…don't!" She ran to her mother and hugged her.

"It'll be all right," Isabelle said. "Now do as I say," Isabelle whispered into Abigail's ear as a hard knock came to the door.

With hesitation, Isabelle approached the door and opened it slowly, her hands trembling. Grim faces leered at her and the men asked her to let them enter.

"We have come to ask your daughter Abigail about the affliction of the cat and other acts of witchcraft," Reverend Lawson said in a stern manner.

At the word 'witchcraft,' Abigail screamed and threw herself to the floor. She writhed violently and rolled under the dinner table. She got on her hands and knees and screeched as the cat had then spouted all manner of strange words and animal sounds. With another scream, she threw herself from under the table and over to the back wall.

"My dear Lord!" Isabelle called. "She's been be-witched…afflicted!"

"Who has done this to your girl?" the constable asked.

"Tituba," Abigail said between groans and moans. "The slave woman Tituba."

"I've seen Tituba's spirit at my daughter's window," Isabelle offered. "She afflicted her and the other girls; tricked them into reading the Devil's books. That's how the cat became a monster. It was Tituba's cat Pyewacket."

Stunned looks came over the men. They looked at each other and then at the thrashing Abigail. "I knew it," Reverend Lawson said. "We have allowed that witch to remain in our midst for too long. We must find her and rid Salem Village of this devil. Where can she be found?"

"She's in the cave outside of the village," Isabelle said.

"Come," Constable Mathers called. "The woman is to be arrested and tried for witchcraft. Thou shalt not suffer a witch to live."

The men turned and headed back down the path in a rage, their calls and grunts following them all the way.

Abigail went silent and stood up. She walked into her mother's waiting arms. Isabelle could see the tears in her daughter's eyes. She wiped them dry with her fingers. "No tears, my sweet Abigail." She kissed the top of Abigail's head and cradled her tightly. "It will all be forgotten soon."

So began the nightmare that would seize Salem for years to come.

GRASSMAN

PD PUFFINBURGER

Almost all Americans know of the Lewis and Clark expedition but very few people know about the failed expedition that was sent out before that. When President Jefferson hadn't heard from Wilson George, the leader of the first expedition, he sent scouts out to find the lost party.

They followed the same trail George's expedition had taken, and in the northern-west part of what is now Ohio, they found their last camp. They found that something had attacked the party and looked to have killed them all. In a nearby cave, the search party found torn-up, bloody clothes, and the journal of Paul Orndorf, the second-in-command of the expedition.

Only a few people read the journal and they were sworn to secrecy, but over time, they told their families and the story was passed down from father to son, mother to daughter.

The journal was given to the President, and after he read it, he threw it in the fireplace to destroy it forever. But a few charred pages were saved from the flames by a chambermaid after the President left the room.

What follows are those pages.

July 13th 1803

I am very excited to get under way, my good friend Wilson George chose me to accompany him and several other men to head an expedition into the land known as the Louisiana Purchase that President Jefferson is about to procure. He wanted to learn more about the land and decided to send George to scout it out. We know that there are hostile Indians to the west but we have hired an Indian tracker to lead the way and the man claims he can speak the language of the savages. I hope Umpopa, as we call him, knows what he's doing. I definitely do not want to go out into the wild with someone that does not know what they are doing.

We have hired several other men, toughs and thugs mostly, but they are strong brutes, and that is what we need to carry our supplies and equipment. Wilson has bought their loyalty with wealth and the promise of more wealth when we return. I suspect these men have been pirates or raiders at one time or another, but the promise of money should be enough to keep them in line.

With everything packed and ready to go, we will set out in the morning. We are to sail up river, as that will lead us into the wild. The excitement of it is overwhelming to me. I shall miss my wife but this will make my career and fortune; then I will never have to leave her again.

July 14th

After saying our goodbyes, we left. The burly men are paddling up-river as I write this and my excitement is un-bounding. Their muscles bulge as they paddle the canoes and I can only imagine how hard it is for them to keep going. They have been paddling for hours. I don't know how they can do it. So far, none of them has complained about the task as of yet.

July 15th to July 29th

There was nothing of significance, only the day to day aches and pains Orndorf suffered. These pages have been discarded due to nature of the passages.

July 30th

The men are restless and they have been fighting among themselves. They say that something is following us. Every time we stop, they go out to hunt for it, but whatever it is stays out of the sights of their guns. One man, his name was William Tanner, went out and never returned. We heard screaming, horrible screaming in the woods; it lasted for several minutes and then stopped.

The men ran towards the screaming but all they found was blood and torn clothes, the signs of a struggle apparent. They brought everything back to have Wilson examine it.

All that was left were bloody clothes that had been ripped to shreds, the blood dripping off them. I have never seen so much blood. In addition to the clothes, the men found intestines; something had torn the man's guts out and then carried off his body. I asked Umpopa what would do such a thing, and he couldn't answer the question. Umpopa says we should leave this place and seek a different route. He is terrified about something. He told me we had traveled far and there are no Indian tribes this far north. I begged Wilson to let us go back but he would hear nothing of it. He was going to do what Jefferson told him to do even if it meant all of us losing our lives.

July 30th

At eleven p.m. we all heard strange howling in the woods all around us. I have to admit I was terrified. Wilson wouldn't let the men build a fire so we are in total darkness. While I sat there and trembled in fear, I saw a spark, then a small flame of a match as a candle was lit. I was thrilled at seeing the darkness leave even just a little. The flame went out as soon as the candle was lit, and then a scream filled the darkness. The man who had lit the candle was screaming, and I had to put my hands over my ears so I wouldn't have to hear him. Then gunfire filled the night and a few more men screamed. Then everything was quiet. The quiet was worse than the screaming. I sat there on the ground, listening, but could hear nothing. I remained there for what felt like an eternity.

Then a torch lit and I could see it was Wilson. He started giving orders to build fires, a lot of fires and the men quickly went to work. I stood up and went to him and together we walked around the camp, looking for anything out of the ordinary. When we found the man that had lit the candle, he was sitting in his own urine and feces, rocking back and forth. He kept saying, "that face, that face" over and over. The man had clearly lost his mind.

Then he told us:

"I lit a candle to see what was attacking us and then I saw its face, it was covered in red hair. The face was black as tar, its eyes were dead looking, like a dead person's eyes. They had no feelings or kindness in them, just death. It wanted to kill me. As it grabbed me and pulled me close, I saw that its nose was large and flat. When it breathed, it blew snot on me, then opened its mouth and there was nothing but huge, sharp, pointed teeth. Its breath smelled of dead rotten meat. The candle burned its lips that were stuck far out and it grunted in pain, then threw me to the ground. That's where I stayed till now when you found me."

After he finished telling the story, he went back to rocking back and forth. The man hasn't spoke since and is now led around by his friend tied to a rope. The rest of the night the men stayed awake, gathering wood to burn to keep the fires high to scare off whatever attacked us. Later we heard howls far off; they lasted for hours. They wouldn't stop and I thought I was going to lose my mind. They sounded like the howls of victory and then changed to howls of blood lust and wants of death.

I trembled in fear.

August 1st
The men still feel that something is following us. I hope it's not what attacked us last night.

August 1st

At mid-afternoon, a man that was scouting ahead came running back to the main party with tales of large red furry men that tried to attack him at a river crossing. I think the heat has cooked the man's brain, but he is certain of what he saw, the poor fool. After he told Wilson the entire story, he pulled his pistol out and shot himself in the head. The musket ball entered his head at the temple and exited out his ear. The entire thing happened in a moment that felt slow to me. A large chunk of skull flew out in front of the ball, then pink, soupy-looking brain matter flew out a second later, to be followed by slime and blood. The poor bastard fell to the ground, dead. It's the second dead man I have seen, and I couldn't look at the red and pink fluids seeping out and pooling up on the ground without getting sick. I don't think I could ever get used to seeing a dead man.

Wilson pulled me aside to record the story the man had told him:

"The man said he was looking for a way to cross the river when he came upon a group of large red hairy ape man things that appeared to be catching fish. They seemed to be fighting amongst themselves over something. A big one over seven feet tall picked up one that was about six feet tall and threw it in the river out of rage. When the six foot tall one came out of the water, it saw the man hiding in the bushes and it pointed at him and grunted. The rest of them saw him and they started throwing rocks at him. He was so scared he just stood there, not knowing what to do until finally a rock whizzed by his head and he thought to run. The things charged across the river like it was a shallow stream, and chased him. Every time he looked back they were closer and closer. When he was a few hundred yards from the camp, he could feel hot sour breath on his neck, so he ran harder but couldn't get far enough ahead. A large hairy hand grabbed his shoulder and lifted him off the ground, and he felt his feet running in the air, then the thing slipped and they both went down. He rolled and then the thing rolled on top of him. He could smell the thing and the stench of it was horrendous and instantly made him throw up. It smelled like shit and sour sweat mixed with body odor and rotten meat. After he threw up, he turned and ran again. He looked back once to see the thing eating his vomit, and in a few seconds he was in the camp. He looked back one more time to see the creature was gone; the thing had disappeared. That was when he found us."

The story would have been hard to believe if the past thirty-six hours hadn't happened.

August 1st

A few hours after dark, we made camp with large fires. The moon is full, so seeing our surroundings is not that difficult. Grunting noises are coming from the woods and I have moved closer to Wilson. I'm starting to think the men with the tales of the furry men might be right. Wilson thinks me a coward and laughed at me. He hired me to record the journey, and he knows I am not a fighting man, but the noises are chilling me down to the bone and I don't think I will sleep tonight.

The grunts sound like one of them is giving commands to the others. Later, around midnight, stones flew into the camp. We had to keep moving so they wouldn't hit us. One man was hit in the head; the stone was as big as a watermelon and it crushed his skull. I didn't go look at him because I can't take looking at any more dead men. Finally, the stones stopped flying and the howling began. I sat down next to a fire and held my ears; the howling is so maddening it pierces the ear and shoots through the brain. I would go insane if I listened to it for very long. The men began shooting into the woods towards the howls. I hope they kill what-ever those things are. I want to go home.

August 2nd

This morning I woke un-rested, as the noise and fear kept me awake most of the night. I thought I dreamed of a man screaming for hours, but Wilson told me it was no dream. He found a man's arm, a few pieces of clothing and lots of blood. Something stole him out of the camp, dragged him into the woods, and slaugh-tered him. I want to go home, but Wilson won't even listen to such a suggestion. For some reason we have lost a keg of gun powder, it has simply disappeared. The creatures seem to know that it is the power of our firearms.

Umpopa begged Wilson to leave this place and told us of things he heard as a child. He was told of men that live in the woods that are covered in hair and stand twice as tall as a man, and have the strength to tear small trees out by the roots. His grandfather ran into one of them once and it threw a boulder at him that was as big as a bear. The Indians had a name for them that I don't understand but Umpopa says in English it means grassman, because they tear up grass and carry it away. He's terrified as am I.

August 3rd

We have been walking for so long my feet are covered in blis-ters. Wilson says we will stop for a few days to rest when we are away from the monsters that plague us. He wants to find a good campsite near a river away from them. I can't wait since my legs, ass, back, and arms hurt so badly that if I was not around a gang of toughs I believe I would cry. The men already hate me. They think I am too weak and small and a coward because I don't use firearms, plus that I write. I tried to tell them that it is my job to write but they just laugh. The only man that talks to me beside Wilson is a small stocky man that is forever kissing my ass. He thinks that when we get back to civilization I will help him secure a job; he is a fool. When we are done here, I will never speak to him again, if we even make it back to civilization.

There was no contact with whatever the things are that attacked us as of yet, and hopefully there won't be. We are far from where we were attacked by the hairy beasts. I really hope they didn't follow us.

August 3rd

Late afternoon, we stopped. Wilson found a lightly wooded area close by to a slow-moving river. We will rest here for a few days to hunt, fish, and relax. The men are building the camp now, then they will unpack everything and I will finally be able to sleep in a real bed instead of on the ground.

August 3rd

Late tonight there was a loud howling that woke everyone up. Umpopa screamed that it was them; they had followed us and they were going to kill us for being in their woods. Whatever it was howled for hours; the men set out to find whatever it was but it was too dark to see anything so they returned after a few minutes.

Whatever it was finally stopped howling only after the men started shooting into the woods with their muskets. I have to admit I was terrified, but joining in and shooting with the men did make me feel better.

The howling had moved back a half mile but I have no doubt will return shortly. They will not let us sleep and we are all so very tired.

August 4th

The howling went on all night. Sometimes it was close and other times it was far away. Wilson said they were getting into position to attack, but the attack never came. Something has stolen all our food. We didn't have much and what was left of our meat and fish was gone when we woke this morning. Umpopa said it was them and the howling was a distraction so one of them could come into the camp and steal our food. Wilson is angry at the men who were on watch. We have been setting a watch at night, but the men fell asleep after the howling stopped. Now we are tired, starving, and too afraid to leave the camp. I fear they have us right where they want us, for these things are intelligent; maybe more than us.

August 4th

In the afternoon, Wilson and I were out exploring and hunting for game. He thought he would set an example for the men to follow, showing them that we were not afraid, nor should they be. I am very afraid. After walking an hour, we heard a crying noise that sounded half human and half animal. We searched for the sound and came across a strange-looking mound.

On closer inspection, we could see that it was hundreds and hundreds of saplings woven together. The structure was amazingly strong as we were both able to climb on top if it without it sagging or falling down. We thought the Indians must have built it, but Umpopa said there were no Indians that built homes like it

So we tried to make one of our own, and after a few hours, had accomplished nothing but making our hands sore and bloody. Whatever had built it definitely knew what it was doing. We hadn't even noticed that it had a doorway until we searched around the entire thing. It was thirty feet long, almost twelve feet wide and six feet high. The door was small compared to the rest of the structure. We had to crawl inside and saw several holes that had been scooped out of the dirt and looked like beds of some type. Leaves and large amounts of grass were lying in the holes to pad it. Inside the third hole was a small ape-looking thing. Umpopa demanded we leave it and should flee from the structure, and that whatever it was scared him badly. He then turned and ran out of the structure and we haven't seen him since. Wilson was thrilled about the creature and picked it up as it hissed and smacked at him, but the thing tired quickly and it seemed weak and frail. The ugly little thing's legs looked like they didn't work right, as they were smaller and twisted than the rest of it, nor did they move. We could tell that it was a boy because we could see it's penis through the reddish brown hair covering its body. The smell of the thing was the worst smell I have ever smelled.

I thought Umpopa was right, that we should leave the thing alone and leave, but Wilson wouldn't have it. He wanted it and was planning on taking it back to Washington to show it to Jefferson. I pleaded with him to leave it alone, that the thing probably had family and they wouldn't leave it for long. The thing appeared to be a baby. I knew what its parents looked like, and I didn't want be there when they returned. Wilson finally left the structure, but he refused to leave the little ape-thing behind, so we took it with us. I knew it was a bad idea, but time will tell.

Back at the camp, the men demanded Wilson take it back to the mound and they started to pack up their things to leave. They were leaving and I was going with them. To hell with this trip! I have had enough. Wilson told them they weren't going anywhere and to prove his point he shot one of the men in the chest. I thought he had gone mad, but he explained that if we had the child, the others would leave us alone. Later he told me he had to shoot one of the men to get the others back in line. He knows a lot more about these types of men than I do so I didn't question him further.

August 4th

Early in the evening we heard screaming howls that came from the direction of the mound. It was the most unnerving sound I have ever heard. The men were in a panic and the firearms were passed out. The little ape started screaming back to whatever it was that was screaming in the woods. A laborer, Pete Spooner, ran over to it and smashed it in the head to shut it up. Wilson was furious at him for killing his pet. I thought he was going to shoot the man, but I think he realized we were about to need every man we had. The screaming howls stopped after a few minutes, but soon after they were replaced by the screams of a man. I thought it had to be Umpopa. The little ape's parents had found him and probably had torn him to pieces. I fear that when the sun goes all the way down we will suffer the same fate.

Wilson seemed to know that we were about to have a battle with the creatures so he had one of the men build large fires all around the camp, and kept them stocked with dry wood. He hoped that whatever they were out there, that they were afraid of fire. He was wrong.

Around ten at night the howling began again. They seemed to be trying to call out to something. I think it's probably the dead baby. They came closer and closer until the howls sounded like they were right beside of us. My skin was chilled and I couldn't stop shaking, even though it was summer and over ninety degrees. I felt like I was frozen.

While the howls continued in all directions, a large ape man jumped over the flames, grabbed Philip Jones, then jumped back over the fire. They were howling to distract us; these things were definitely a lot smarter than we had thought. The one that grabbed

Jones looked like the baby one but a lot bigger; it had the same color fur and the same god-awful face, but it was over seven feet tall and was covered in muscle.

That night, the air was filled with Jones' screams; he sounded like he was in agony. Then it stopped and it was eerily still. Then a round object came flying into the camp and struck Wilson in the chest and knocked him down.

The brute Pete picked it up and looked at it, it was Jones' head. It had been torn off his body. The amount of strength it must have taken to do that was incredible. That was all I could think about, not that he was dead or anything so mundane, but the thought of the strength of those things and how they were circling around our camp. Wilson slapped me across the face to get my attention.

"We're surrounded by those things, you have to stop your writing and take up a rifle!" he screamed at me.

I don't know what good that would do since he knows I am a terrible shot. So after he walked away from me I just dropped the rifle onto the ground.

I feel someone should be recording these events seeing as how we are all about to die. The thought didn't scare me for some reason. I think these creatures have no problem with me, as I have not wronged them in any way—somehow I know this to be true.

After Wilson got the men to calm down and focus on the task at hand, they patrolled around in a circle, waiting for the creatures to attack again. The howling began again and we were all on alert. If they were true to form, they would grab one of us again during the howling.

A minute into the horrific bellowing, stones began to fly into the camp; most of them were the size of pumpkins. They came from all directions and some were avoidable, but some slammed into the tents and fires.

One of the laborers, I don't know his name, was hit in the face with one that was bigger than his head. It smacked into him and his skull shattered like a hardboiled egg. It cracked and his brains began to seep out of the cracks.

I never knew that the human head had so much blood in it, or that our brains were so big. I watched the cracked pieces fall apart, then his brain fell out, all before his body dropped to the ground.

In the middle of the attack, another ape man jumped down from a tree. It grabbed a laborer and bit into his neck. It spat the chunk of meat out on the ground as the laborer's body flopped over, then the creature ran to another man named Phil Pearce. It grabbed the man's head and ripped his face clean off. I didn't think it was possible but the thing did this easily and made the task look easy.

Wilson and the other men shot at it. A few bullets found their way into its chest, but it didn't seem to notice, and it was still able to jump over the fires that were burning out of control.

Wilson and the men grouped together and stood side by side to protect each other. I felt it was futile to fight these monsters since they didn't seem to die when shot, and they could kill us whenever it pleased them.

The men cursed me for being a coward, but I know I am not. I just think it is pointless to fight these things. We have seen what they can do, and that our firearms won't stop them. If we had any sense, we would have left this place as soon as we found the little ape baby.

The men are complaining about not having gunpowder left to fight them off. The fools didn't realize that their bullets did nothing to the creatures that I now believe are demons that have been cast out of Hell.

Hours passed by slowly and it is now well after midnight. The men and I are getting tired but the apes continue to howl and throw stones at us.

A man named Howard Lease left the group to make a run for it, but he did not get far. He screamed for hours and has just now stopped. I guess they kept him alive to torture him. There are only four of us remaining. Myself, Wilson, Pete, and a man named Michael. I fear we don't have long. I am sure they will kill us before the sun rises.

An hour ago they charged into the camp and we scattered in different directions. I ran to the river, waded across it, and the darkness of the woods is overwhelming. I stumbled around in the woods for a while and I could see a few of them behind me, chasing me.

They are getting closer and closer. I found a cave to hide in and luckily I was smart enough to grab one of the small lanterns when I ran, so now I can see my way around the cave. The lantern has been burning all night and I don't think there is much oil left. The thought of sitting in the dark is as horrifying as is the feeling that I was wrong about them not wanting to kill me. I guess they see me as a threat like the other men. I have crawled as far into the cave as possible.

The lantern is going out, it is barely putting out any light at all, and I can hear the creatures searching the cave for me. They came in here a few minutes ago, sniffing the air through their huge nostrils and I think they can smell me. This cave has many chambers and the one I have chosen I hope they can't fit down.

They are at the opening of the chamber now, they have found me, but they can't fit down the opening to get to me. One is standing guard and the other one has left. I assume I am to be waited out and starved.

I was wrong again. The one that left came back with a small one compared to the others, but he is still bigger than me and he is crawling to me right now.

My death is certain. I can see him better now. He is the most god-awful thing I have ever seen; they are demons from Hell.

His face is black as night, the eyes are filled with death, the teeth long and sharp, and I can already feel them tearing into my flesh when he is close enough. He is inching his way closer and closer to me and I have no place to go. I am at the back of the chamber.

His claws are long and sharp and he keeps slashing at me as I pull myself tighter into the chamber. He has ripped into my leg several times, and the pain is horrible.

He will be on me in seconds. I wish I could hold my wife one last time...

IT CAME FROM BLACK SWAMP

DANE T. HATCHELL

Terrence Hastings closed one eye while pulling at the barbed hook stuck in the lower lip of the catfish. The fish refused to make the task any easier, struggling to flip out of his firm grip. The layer of slime coating its skin made him afraid it would squirt out of his hand and get away.

The catfish stared back at him with bulging eyes, begging with a sad face for a return to its nurturing water home. The *whiskers* above its lip and under its chin gave it the appearance of a wise Chinese man. Terrence could have sworn he heard the fish curse when the hook popped free.

Careful to avoid the pectoral fins tipped with irritating toxin, he let it drop into the ice chest with the rest of his catch. Not a bad haul so far, having almost enough for the night's meal. This would make the third time this week having fish for dinner. He didn't mind, and he knew his wife wouldn't either.

He pulled out a fat red worm from the bait box, threading it carefully on the hook, then returned his expanding buttocks to his lounge chair at the end of the pier. He dropped the hook into the water. The plastic bobber floated on the surface, looking like a big red eyeball staring at the sky.

"Hi, honey, how's the fishing today?" Patricia asked.

He barely glanced at his wife. "Can't complain. I did hook a couple of bullheads, but tossed them back in the bayou. Funny, when we lived in Minnesota, we'd eat those things, but there's so many channel catfish here in Louisiana, we can be choosy. Channel cats taste so much better."

"They sure do," Patricia agreed.

"I guess it all has to do with the diet. Bullheads will eat just about anything, including dead fish. Channel cats only eat live bait."

"We've been here for two months now. You're not getting tired of the same routine, are you?"

"Hell, no. I lived the first sixty-two years of my life in the frozen north. I'm enjoying my retirement, feeling warm and toasty in this subtropical weather. Living by the water is a lifelong dream, and I'm gonna live this dream till the day I die." Terrence lifted his line to check the bait.

"It certainly is 'warm and toasty' out here. A little bit too much for me. I just wanted to come and see about you. Don't let time get away."

"Baby, I got all the time in the world," he said, looking up at the blue sky and basking in his new, stress-free lifestyle.

Patricia walked down the pier towards the house, careful to avoid remnants of discarded fish guts and bird poop.

"Hey, I got a big one!" Terrence shouted.

Patricia turned to see her husband lift a large channel cat from the water, the pole bending from the weight to the point that she thought it might break.

"Look at the size of it! I bet it weighs ten pounds!" He stood at the end of the pier, holding his prize before him for his wife to admire.

Before Patricia could utter a word, a huge white gator leaped out of the water behind Terrence. A long massive mouth spread wide, showing rows of pointed teeth, and they clamped down across Terrence's chest, pulling him into the water.

It was so sudden that Patricia didn't believe her eyes. Her husband was there one second, and gone the next.

"Terrence…" she said softly in disbelief. "Terrence!" Panic was setting in. She ran to the end of the pier, calling his name.

Terrence plunged into a netherworld of cool wet darkness. The air bubbled out of his lungs as two inch teeth sank through his soft skin, finding bone. It had happened so fast, hitting him like a powerful locomotive from behind.

The water by the pier boiled as the enormous, white alligator spun over and over, subduing its prey until the struggle ended.

As Terrence's consciousness faded, he watched his last few bubbles of air float to the surface.

His living dream was over.

Clovis Gilchrist sat on his porch, cutting trash fish harvested from his traps into strips for bait. Blue crab season was at its peak. His morning haul netted over twelve dozen of the biggest and fattest crabs he'd seen in the last twenty of his fifty years of life.

Lake Maurepas connected Lake Pontchartrain through Pass Manchac; otherwise known as 'Black Swamp' by the locals, as the infamous Black Swamp was located on the northern section of the pass. Gunther Gilchrist, Clovis's father, built the cypress wood, three-room house on Black Swamp in the early '50s. He ignored the folklore of the swamp witch Addie, and of the tortured souls haunting the crystal waters, a result from an unnamed hurricane killing all but twenty residents of the near town of Frenier in 1915. Gunther purchased the ten acres of land his house now sat on for only a hundred dollars.

A studious man of German descent, Gunther married a young Cajun woman named Bertile. The swamp and the two lakes it connected harbored a bounty of fish and crustaceans, providing an endless supply of food; the excess sold for cold hard cash at the local fish market. By fate and heritage, the rugged but simple lifestyle was passed on to Clovis, their only child.

Clovis' parents died within six months of each other, before he reached the age of fifteen, taken by the Grim Reaper in the form of lung cancer, though neither smoked. There were those who blamed the swamp witch and her evil spells. Others blamed the ghosts that drifted along Black Swamp, jealous of those who walked among the living.

Spying a large black cockroach following the trail of fresh fish drippings on the porch boards, Clovis took careful aim and spat a wad of warm, tobacco-enriched spittle on the roach's head.

"Take dat, you disgusting bastard. Get yourself on outta here."

Though only a lowly insect, its species had survived a hundred million years of evolution by sensing when to flee and live another day. It turned, heading back to the pile of rotting firewood near the side of the house.

The distinct cadence of an Evinrude 250 hummed down the pass. Clovis could identify any boat motor by its sound alone. Engine noises were similar to the tones of people's voices. He knew this particular engine belonged to the sheriff of St. John the Baptist Parish.

His heart skipped a beat at the thought of the sheriff snooping around. Self-preservation took control, directing his attention toward the sixty-quart ice chest near his front door. He sprang to his feet, letting the fish and knife fall to the porch as he rushed over and grabbed the handle of the cooler, intending to hide it inside the house. It was full of twice the legal limit of speckled trout from his fishing trip the day before.

Giving it a mighty tug, anticipating over fifty pounds of fish and ice, Clovis jerked it off the porch and crashed off balance against the front door, bruising his shoulder.

The ice chest was empty!

His son, who he affectionately nicknamed 'Rooter,' had apparently had taken him up on his invitation for cooler full of fresh fish. *If you want 'em come get 'em. You clean 'em and they're yours,* Clovis remembered saying.

The sheriff was halfway down the pier, his arms swinging gorilla-like by his side. Sheriff Michael Browning filled his forty-four inch waist pants with that 'no ass at all' look in the rear, the back end practically caved in. His bottom lip bulged from a quarter can of Skoal, but his lip was in more proportion with his face than the beer keg gut he sported with the rest of his body.

Clovis remembered the sheriff from his younger days, how fit and trim he was from a stint in the U.S. Marines. Sitting at a desk job had its way of adding on a few pounds each year. Sheriff Browning now found himself tipping the scale near three hundred.

"Clovis Gilchrist, now just what in heaven's name are you doing standing there with that shit-eating grin smeared across your face?" Browning asked.

"I don't know what you're talkin' 'bout, Sheriff. I was just thinkin' bout how my ice chest is empty and I got no fish to eat."

"You can save your sad stories for someone else. I've heard them all before. I'm only here to talk to you about gator hunting."

"Whoa, Sheriff. Hold it right now. I got tags for every gator I fish outta the swamp."

Browning lifted his hands and shook his head. "I'm not here to start any shit, Clovis. But I ain't gonna take no shit either." Browning stopped, the words he was about to say tasted like cod liver oil. "I need your help."

Genuinely stunned, Clovis stuck his right pinky in his ear and jostled it about. "You said you need my help?"

"Don't make this harder on me than it is. You can think of it as helping the community," the sheriff said. "You've been keeping up with the news, the missing people on Pass Manchac?"

Clovis closed one eye. "I hear things. I travel Black Swamp every day of my life."

"The fourth person to come up missing in the last six months happened three days ago. We suspected gators all along, but we got an eyewitness on this one. The victim's wife reported that the gator grabbed her husband as he stood on the edge of the pier in front of their house. The man killer should be easy enough for you to identify. It's an albino, and it has to be pretty big for it to get that high out of the water to grab him."

As if believing the stories over the last several months for the first time, Clovis's eyes turned as big as saucers. He uttered two words, "Ol' Lu."

"Huh? Oh, you mean that old wives tale of the swamp witch's pet gator."

"Dat ain't no wives tale," Clovis retorted. "The swamp witch is angry. She warned the town dat if that con-du-minium was built, she'd curse the waters."

"That senile old woman Addie Landry? She can't even gum the kernels off an ear of corn. The only curse that woman ever knew of is when she was young enough to still have her period."

"She may be old, she may be weak, but her magic is strong. I can't help you, Sheriff, you on you're on. The best thing for you to do is pull the permit for construction right now. They's just clearin' the land, there's still time."

Browning lowered his head. He knew the power local legends had over the people. This one though, he hoped Clovis had grown out of; age having a way of shattering both the wonders and fears in life.

"Well, Clovis, I do appreciate your time. You let me know if you change your mind."

"I ain't changin' it, Sheriff."

"Okay. How about your son, Albert? You taught him everything you know. I'm glad he decided to make more of his life and got an education. But there ain't nothin' you can do that he can't match."

Clovis sighed. "Maybe, maybe not. I learned the boy real good. He's his own man now. Gator season is short; he helps me make my limit at season's end. You have to ask him yourself, Sheriff. If he's smart, he'll say no."

Browning sensed the fear harboring inside of Clovis. It was so powerful it brought a slight chill up his spine.

Rooter Gilchrist huddled inside his Ford King Ranch 250 for the fifth night in a row, mindlessly rubbed the St. Christopher medal hanging from his neck for luck. The medal was one of the few possessions that linked him with his mother; she'd died before he reached the age of five.

Rooter earned his nickname from his insatiable curiosity as an infant. A pile of clean clothes waiting for someone to fold was a mountain to explore. What mystery hid between the sheets of a bed? Rooter always took the challenge. Even couch cushions proved to be doors leading to hidden treasure. He delved right in with no fear of the unknown.

This is one hell of a way to spend my vacation, he thought. A sentiment his wife, Claire, and his seven-year-old son, Gaston, shared. He'd put the annual beach trip to Florida on hold. One of the motives for sacrificing his family fun was the ten thousand dollar reward for the capturing or killing of the alligator. The other, and more important, was to protect his financial investment.

Two of Cyprus Point Condominium's primary goals were to free the wealthy residents of New Orleans, and the greater area, from the concrete and steel of urban life—and their money—by offering the latest in luxury living, with the access to Black Swamp and the adjoining lakes just a step outside their door.

The recent ups and downs of the stock market motivated Rooter to invest his savings in a local business that 'guarantied' to triple his investment within six months of completion. The only way he knew to put any controversy out of the minds of potential buyers was to eliminate the menace of a killer alligator.

His hope of killing the beast quickly and salvaging a few days on white sands and turquoise water had ended the night before. Though a total of ten alligators took the bait thus far, Old Lu remained free to haunt the waters.

Rooter's GPS tracker beeped three times, pulling him from his thoughts and back to the dark waters of the Black Swamp.

Exiting the truck and giving his body a quick dousing of mosquito repellent, he waited for his target to travel fifty yards before trailing him in his twenty foot bass boat.

Hunting alligators normally involved a baited hook hanging a foot or so above the water. Rooter used a whole fresh chicken from the supermarket, hanging only from a string, with no hook, as he didn't believe even the strongest of hooks could hold Old Lu. The idea was for the alligator to take the bait and go sleep off the meal. The GPS transmitter hidden in the cavity of the chicken would end up in the gator's belly, and lead Rooter directly to it.

But this gator was different from the others, traveling almost twice as fast, and not stopping to rest within the hour of swallowing the bait. Rooter had a good feeling that he'd found Old Lu, especially when it turned up a narrow tributary flowing into Pass Manchac alongside the actual Black Swamp area.

That good feeling gave way to foreboding fear as every story his father had ever told him about Black Swamp and the witch rolled through his mind.

You stay away from there, son, if it's the last thing you do. Give swamp witch Addie her peace, and she'll give you yours, he remembered his father saying on more than one occasion. A lesson Rooter always adhered to—till now.

He'd invested too much time in this endeavor already. He shook the fear off as ignorant superstition, and sped toward his target.

On the horizon, the swamp witch's shack loomed against the orange light of a full moon. Its outline reminded Rooter of a haunted house in a picture book his son Gaston loved. The front of the house was so dark that if it had any windows, it was impossible to tell. There was no way of knowing if Addie was on her porch waiting, and watching.

The blip on the GPS locator had him twenty feet from the gator. Careful not to shine his flashlight in the direction of the house, he scanned the waters, looking for the telltale signs of the resting gator.

In less than a minute, he found it. The beam of his light bounced off what first appeared to be an empty red Coca Cola can. He knew different. It was the eye of an alligator, and from the size of it, a huge one.

It was difficult to tell if it was Old Lu at first; the gator's body hid under a patch of lily pads. But as it snaked its way parallel to his boat through the lilies, there was no doubt it was Old Lu, which was short for Lucifer.

The reptile clearly exceeded twenty feet in length. Rooter estimated it weighed over fifteen hundred pounds. The only albino alligators he'd seen were at the Audubon Zoo in New Orleans. This one would be the largest ever on record, looking like the creature that time forgot.

Rooter picked up his Rock River Arms AR15, complete with night-vision laser scope. A descendent of the Late Cretaceous period, Lucifer turned towards him with that alligator smile that made the back of Rooter's neck tingle. That wicked smile was one of knowing. *The joke was on you*, or more specifically, *the joke was you; just a soft morsel about to fill the belly of the beast.*

The red dot of the laser danced between the eyes of the alligator, and a single shot cracked through the songs of insects, bringing a creepy silence over the swamp; it was then followed by the unnerving scream of a woman.

Lucifer lay still in the water. His legs rose from underneath and floated on the surface.

Rooter searched the bank, using the night-vision in hopes of finding the source of the scream. He questioned if it was a really a woman's scream he'd heard.

Maybe it was just a startled heron and was only my imagination, he wondered.

A shadowy figure appeared at the end of the pier in a long black robe. The moon lifted above her shack as if on her command, bathing her in its dim light. The witch lifted her gnarled cane made from corkscrew willow. "You have committed the greatest desecration to the lost souls of the waters since the storm banished them to wander the face of the Earth."

Rooter froze; her words seemed like long needles penetrating his spine.

Ethereal fireflies formed a mist, and swirled above the dead body of Lucifer. The wind blew Rooter's hair across his face as faint voices suffering from toil and abuse whispered around him.

Rooter relived the sorrows of a hundred departed souls. They drowned him in a sea of despair, and filled the emptiness he felt with a sinister conscience and mindset intent on revenge.

The swamp witch lowered her cane. "It is said, 'an eye for an eye and a tooth for a tooth.' The evil that you have caused the innocent will take you a hundred lifetimes to repay. You do not have a hundred life times to give. You are cursed, you and your family. Until the old man of Black Swamp is replaced, and the lost souls can once again find a safe harbor to dwell, until the sky opens and all the souls of humanity are called home to heaven."

Rooter collapsed, falling out of the boat, the waters of the Black Swamp swallowing him whole.

"Good evening, ladies and gentlemen. We begin the six o' clock edition of Channel 4 News with two tragic events that have authorities and locals scratching their heads. One of Lake Manchac's own, Albert Gilchrist, age thirty, was reported missing by his wife, Claire, this morning when he failed to return from an alligator hunt, sanctioned by the local sheriff.

"Gilchrist was on a mission to capture or kill a reported twenty foot long albino alligator. Legends of the giant albino alligator have circled these parts for the past eighty years. His boat was found empty around noon today, floating down Pass Manchac near Black Swamp. Authorities sought local resident Addie Landry for questioning on Gilchrist's possible whereabouts. No one was home at her residence. And now the news gets even stranger. Shortly after seven this morning, at the Cyprus Point development located on Pass Manchac, a creature described by one man as 'part alligator and part man,' attacked a crew of five heavy equipment operators.

"Robert Sanchez said that the creature attacked with uncanny speed, mauling his four companions to death. Sanchez narrowly escaped by running to Highway 44 and hitching a ride on an eighteen-wheeler. Blood, but no bodies were found at the scene.

Someone had driven four pieces of earth-moving equipment at the site directly into the waters of Pass Manchac. The owner says that the two bulldozers, excavator, and dump truck are total losses. Authorities are questioning the authenticity of Sanchez's story. The FBI has been contacted to see if the events are retaliation from a Mexican drug lord, whose drug ring was recently broken up in St. John the Baptist Parish. Now, here's Donna, with the brighter side of the news."

"You want me to move the umbrella? You're in the sun," Clovis said.

"No, that last frozen daiquiri made me cold. I'd like to catch some rays right now," Claire said, repositioning her swim top.

Clovis took another beer from the cooler and brushed the chips of ice off the top before popping it open.

Claire let out a huge sigh. "None of this seems real. It's been a month since Rooter disappeared and I've been in a haze ever since. I don't even know what I'm doing on Pontchartrain Beach, like nothing happened at all."

"It's July 4th, little one. The world, she still turns. Not just your world, but Gaston's, too. I know he misses his daddy, but look at him out there, playing in the sand with his friends. He needs to be around other people. So do you. You're still a young woman. I'll be here for you and Gaston, but you need a man in your life, and Gaston, he needs a daddy."

"Stop it! My mind isn't thinking like that right now. I don't even know if it's even possible, ever. There's such a hole in my heart…" Claire stopped as the tears came.

"The swamp, she's a dangerous place. It's always been dat way. People watch too much TV, think dat modern convenience can change the wild of the land. Mankind, he can only push so hard against nature. Nature forgive to a point, but once that threshold is reached, Nature, she get her revenge," he said.

The shrill alert from a lifeguard's whistle cut through the air. Claire stood up from her chair before Clovis had pulled his mouth away from a gulp of beer. Gaston and the boys building the sandcastle were no longer there.

A distorted voice over a megaphone blasted, "Everyone get out of the water, now! Make your way to the beach area. Get out of the water now!"

Claire ran with sand flying, towards the crowd gathered by the water. Clovis winced in pain from arthritic knees while chasing after her. From the lifeguard's perspective, sitting twelve feet above the sand, all he could see was something in the water overtake the swimmers the farthest from the beach. A momentary thrashing left each swimmer floating lifeless. No one cried for help, there wasn't time.

The lifeguard pushed through the crowd of gawkers, commanding everyone to leave, and to get out of the water. Most preceded to the shore, but some intentionally lagged behind, wanting to be the last one out.

"Say, dude, why'd you make us get out?" a teenage boy asked, pulling the back of the lifeguard's shirt.

The lifeguard turned. "Hands off! We've got a situation. Off the beach, now!"

A ten-year-old girl was the first to scream. She did so when a wave deposited a severed head at her feet.

"Oh my God! Someone's head!" a fat old woman in a black bikini yelled, before fainting and falling face first near the surf.

A severed arm arrived next, and then another head, a young girl's this time. Waves pushed the torsos of four other bodies into view seconds later. Claire saw Gaston standing in the back of the crowd, peering around a tall man's hairy leg. She breathed out a sigh of relief and slowed to a fast walk.

Without warning, the throng of people turned and ran straight for her, screaming in terror, and knocked Gaston over and trampled him into the sand.

Claire yelled his name just as Clovis ran in front of her, wrapping his arms around her chest. The mass of people ran past, only one bumping into Clovis. Claire tore herself from his embrace and ran to the side of her son, lying still in the sand.

Standing in the water not twenty feet away from the two, Clovis saw why the people had fled in panic, and his mouth fell open in amazement.

The monstrosity stood on two legs, holding the lifeguard by the throat with its alligator teeth. It had the head and neck of an alligator, the rest more like a man. Its arms and legs were uncannily human, except for the rough alligator-like skin. The claws from its four-fingered hand ripped the lifeguard's lower abdomen, spilling his intestines into the foamy, brackish waters of Lake Pontchartrain.

Gaston woke while Claire sat gently beside him, patting his cheek. A large *goose-egg* of a bump was above his left eye, where someone's knee had caught him in the stampede. Her attention was only on her son, and she almost jumped out of her skin when Clovis yelled for her to run. The Man-Gator slung its head to the side, releasing the dead lifeguard, hissing like an angry dragon.

Every hair on Claire's body stood on end as she turned to see the Man-Gator drop to all fours and charge toward her.

Clovis raced past her, coming between his loved ones and the creature. The Man-Gator stopped and turned, its tail arching through the air and smashing Clovis on the right side of his chest.

Clovis tumbled into the sand, his mind spinning towards oblivion, and crying out in agony from his broken ribs.

Once again, the Man-Gator hissed, angry at the world. Clovis laid in the shadow of the magnificent creature, mesmerized by a certain beauty found in its uniqueness, a perfect killing machine.

Then, Clovis understood.

The Man-Gator bent over him, its mouth agape with rows of blood-stained teeth, the gore from its victims still clearly wedged between them.

While Clovis waited to die, the sun reflected off a gold St. Christopher medal that hung from a chain around the Man-Gator's neck. It once belonged to Clovis' wife, the one his son had worn in her memory.

Clovis closed his eyes and repeated his departed wife's favorite prayer, waiting for the deadly jaws to snatch his life away. Each second passing felt like a minute while he lay frozen in fear.

When death didn't immediately overtake him, he looked up to see the creature no longer standing over him.

Claire screamed from behind. Rolling to his stomach, Clovis turned and watched the Man-Gator snatch Claire in his arms, running on two legs back to the Lake.

Gaston yelled out for his mommy, his voice hoarse from strain.

As Clovis struggled through the pain to stand, the Man-Gator and his prey disappeared into the water. Each step Clovis managed to take sent a wave of sharp knives through his body. It hurt even to breathe. By the time he reached the shore, the Man-Gator and Claire were so far away he could barely see them bobbing between the waves.

Gaston ran up to him. Clovis dropped to his knees and hugged his only grandchild.

Clovis severed the heartstrings pulling at him to stay with Gaston. If he had any chance of finding Claire alive, he had to act now. If there was any chance that Rooter could be returned to normal, he had to act now, and he had to act alone. No one believed in the swamp witch's magic. The sheriff and his deputies would shoot first and ask questions later.

The first ambulance arrived minutes later. Clovis handed Gaston to the EMT as the woman exited the driver's side door. He told her that the boy had a head injury, and then quickly hurried away. Running to his truck on aching legs, he hopped in, started the engine, and burned rubber as he headed for Saint Gabriel Catholic Church.

Once inside the church, Clovis met with Father Presley, and told him to have someone go and stay with Gaston at the hospital, while he went to look for Claire. He gave the father the briefest of details on the kidnapping, and didn't included anything about the Man-Gator. Instead, he changed the story to some crazed man at the beach taking her by gunpoint and fleeing in a boat.

Clovis demanded that Father Presley perform Last Rites on him, in case he lost his life in the attempt to rescue her. Fearing Clovis' sanity and his personal safety, Father Presley complied after hearing his confessional. The father performed the ancient ritual, ensuring Clovis' entrance into heaven.

After thanking him, Clovis drove home and gathered weapons for what might be his final conflict.

By the time Clovis pulled up to the end of Addie's pier, the sun had gone below the treeline, casting eerie shadows that were silhouetted in the orange fire of moss-filtered light.

He was certain the swamp witch knew of his arrival, as he raced up the tributary at full speed. When he turned off his outboard motor, the roar of the engine gave way to a woman's cry from within the witch's shack. It was unmistakably Claire's voice.

As Clovis stepped out of the boat and onto the pier, a fresh wave of pain from broken ribs nearly dropped him to his knees. Fighting nausea, the cries from Claire helped him push past his physical chains, and he staggered to the door.

With his double barrel shotgun before him, he kicked open the door and yelled, "Don't move or I'll shoot!"

Claire lay spread-eagle, naked on the rough wooden floor in the one room shack. Her hands were tied above her head to a bedpost, and ropes were tied to each ankle and nailed into the floor.

The Man-Gator hissed as it rested on all fours between Clovis and Claire. The old witch stood next to a small metal bucket of smoldering roots, which filled the air with an acrid odor that reminded Clovis of mothballs and ammonia.

"Your devil sacrifice stops now! Let my Claire go!" Clovis demanded.

The Man-Gator crouched lower, as if ready to make a leap on command. Clovis cocked back one hammer on the shotgun. His wife's rosary dangled from the barrel like a strand of tensile on a Christmas tree branch.

"That gun is useless here," the witch said.

The shotgun in Clovis' hands turned as cold as liquid nitrogen, completely numbing his palms and fingers. The gun fell to the floor with a thud.

"If you do not leave now, you will die," the witch hissed.

"I'll leave when you give me Claire, and when you return my son to me," Clovis said, feeling some sensation returning to his fingers.

"Your son must pay for his sins. His debt is great. His family must pay, too," the witch said.

Clovis lifted his shirt, revealing six sticks of dynamite wrapped in gray duct tape around his waist. The dynamite was left over from simpler times when 'fishing' with explosives was a sure way to earn fast cash.

"D'is will end in one of two ways. Either I get what I want, or we all die." He popped the safety guard off the trigger switch, his finger in position on the button.

"Stop!" The witch yelled; the Man-Gator stood on his legs and hissed again.

Clovis' fingers jerked nervously, almost triggering the explosives.

"You will do nothing but bring harm to everyone in Black Swamp if you do that," the witch said.

"Then the smart thing to do is to give me what I want," Clovis said.

The witch mumbled something in a tongue that had died centuries before. Then said, "Very well."

The Man-Gator fell to the floor and cut the ropes holding Claire's feet with one slash of its sharp nails, then did the same to free her arms. Claire hadn't uttered a word from the time Clovis had broken into the shack, seemingly disoriented from the torture.

"Claire, come to me," Clovis called.

She steadied herself and stood up, as if she were on a boat casting about on troubled waters, then managed to shuffle to Clovis' side.

"My boat is at the end of the pier," he whispered. "Get in and get as far away from here. As long as you can still see the shack, you're too close. If I return to the pier, come back and get me. You'll know if I'm not comin' back." He pointed to the dynamite around his waist. Claire saw it as if it were for the first time.

"You two, leave now," the witch commanded.

Clovis pushed Claire out of the front door. "Go now, hurry," then returned inside.

"I want the other half of the bargain now. I want my son put back to normal," Clovis demanded.

"You have the woman and your life. Leave now, while you still can," the witch hissed.

"I keep my word, old crone. I leave with my son normal, or we all die here."

"Your son brought the curse on himself. He still has to pay!"

Clovis stood rock solid, his finger set to push the detonator. "I count to three, then I push the button. One…two…three!"

Grinding his teeth and closing his eyes, he went to push the button, but his finger didn't respond. The witch spoke in a low voice, calling enforcement from the netherworld to do her bidding.

Clovis opened his eyes to see the room swirl with ethereal plasma, mystical blue and green flashes appearing. He pushed against the invasion of darkness assaulting his mind, determined to regain control. He would not be denied!

The witch felt the power of his resistance, and it knocked her backward as if something invisible had slammed into her.

His body shaking, Clovis felt the force that held his finger still start to give. He was winning, and he prayed the witch would beg him to stop and reverse her spell on Rooter.

The Man-Gator stood still as a statue, its soul adrift between the two worlds that clashed.

Knowing the outcome, the witch slipped out of the shack through a side door, casting a final incantation spell to protect herself. Clovis snapped free of the spell and his finger moved to the button. The dynamite exploded before he realized his victory was bitter sweet.

Sitting naked and shaking from her ordeal, Clair felt the shockwave seconds after the house splintered into a million pieces and a huge ball of fire turned to black smoke, rising to the heavens. Almost numb from shock, and knowing that Gaston would never see his grandfather again, she started the motor and headed for safety. The sheriff and two other boats of armed State Troopers met her not long after she reached the main waterway of Pass Manchac.

Dahlia, Claire's younger sister, waited for two pieces of bread to pop up from the toaster. She'd come to live with Claire and Gaston two days after Sheriff Browning found Claire at Black Swamp. Staying with Claire meant that she wouldn't be able to graduate from SLU next year as she'd hoped. But it was more important to skip the fall semester, and help Claire and Gaston adjust to life without Rooter and Clovis.

Claire was about two months into her pregnancy. It was one of those untimely acts of fate when the woman discovers she's with child after the father unexpectedly passes away.

Claire's house was located directly on Lake Maurepas, with a full view of the lake from the glass walls all along the rear of the house. Dahlia loved to spend her quiet time sipping on wine and watching the sailboats and fishing boats pass by.

The toaster jumped, and two dark brown crowns of toast appeared, bringing Dahlia's mind back to the present.

Claire sat at the table, staring blankly into her cup of steaming coffee.

"You want me to scramble you some eggs?" Dahlia asked, putting the toast on Claire's plate.

"No, toast is fine. Gaston may want some eggs though," Claire said.

"Gaston's eaten already. It's eleven o' clock."

"Oh, sorry. I forgot I overslept. I'm feeling very strange today," Claire said.

"Strange? Do you think there's something wrong with the baby? Do you want me to call the doctor and see if he can work you in?"

Claire nibbled on a piece of toast. "No, don't do that. My stomach feels kind of weird but it's probably just gas," Claire said.

"Just gas? Well, if you start feeling any worse, tell me and I'll call the doctor. You don't need to be taking any chances."

"I know. I know," Clare agreed.

They finished breakfast, discussing what to have for dinner that night. Claire helped Dahlia clean the dishes, and excused herself, going for the bathroom

While washing her hands, sharp pains jabbed at her stomach. She hurried and sat on the toilet. Gas rumbled out of her, echoing off the sides of the porcelain bowl. Feeling immediate relief, she leaned back and relaxed.

Suddenly, a stabbing pain filled her abdomen, causing her to buckle forward. She immediately knew this was more than a simple gas pain, fearing for the welfare of her unborn child.

Before Claire could call for Dahlia, it happened again. Her insides felt as if they were about to explode from between her legs. Digging her fingers underneath the toilet seat, she watched between her spread thighs as something inside her started to move.

A head began to crown out of her vaginal opening. No, it wasn't a head. At only two months, the fetus would be surrounded by its embryonic sack. This was…something else.

It pushed out, splashing toilet water on her thighs. It was a medium sized egg.

With the foreign object out of her, she felt well enough to lift herself off the toilet, and sat on the floor.

She had no idea what was going on, and didn't begin to know how to explain it to Dahlia, much less a doctor in an emergency room. They would think her insane.

In the toilet, pecking noises came from inside the egg, and as it began to crack, the small face of a tiny albino alligator broke through the shell. Claire watched amazed, and questioned her sanity.

The reptile breached itself from the shell, and floated in the toilet water, looking up at her like a grinning log with nothing but evil and malevolence on its mind.

Claire reached up and pulled down on the toilet handle, evacuating the tank and flooding the bowl with fresh water. The tiny creature tumbled around as the whirling pool of water sent it down into the plumbing, and directly into Lake Maurepas. The house was old, the plumbing had never been connected to a modern sewer system.

Pushing itself along the waters with its tail, Lucifer returned reborn into the world. He fed upon small frogs and insects as he lazily made his way towards Black Swamp.

He felt the swamp witch and the host of wandering souls eagerly awaiting his arrival.

THREE IN A GRAVE

TERRY ALEXANDER

Martha's Story

Martha Dickerson ran through the thick forest, her heart beating madly in her chest. She held her aching side, her lungs burning like fire. Leaning against an oak tree, Martha gulped air like she was drowning.

A bullet kicked up dirt near her feet.

"You're running the wrong way, bitch! Go straight north, stay on the path."

"What's wrong with you?" she panted, tears streaming down her cheeks. "Why are you doing this, Russell?"

"Because I can," he chuckled. "Because I can."

Martha ran her fingers through her dull red hair and wiped the sweat from her forehead. She pushed away from the tree into a stumbling, lopsided gait. The strap on her flip-flop snapped after a dozen steps and flew off to land on the ground five feet away. She kept running, desperate to escape the madman behind her.

He'd looked like a nice guy when he stopped to pick her up on highway 69. Russell O'Shea had a good looking face and the cutest smile of any man she'd seen in a long time. That and the promise of a ride to the Texas state line convinced her to hop in his pickup truck. It was the biggest mistake of her life.

Earlier.

Russell shook two cigarettes from his pack and returned it to his shirt pocket. "Care for one?" he offered.

"You bet." She accepted eagerly. "I haven't had a smoke in a week."

"I've got some cold beer in the ice chest, if you're interested." He thumbed the lighter wheel and puffed the cigarette to life and passed it to his passenger.

"Damn straight I'm interested." She rummaged through the Styrofoam box and lifted two chilled cans into the air. "I'm dry. I'd drink warm rabbit piss if you had any." She popped the top and drained half the can in a single gulp. "Man, that's good stuff." She smacked her lips.

"Well then, just sit back and enjoy yourself for a couple of hours. As long as we've got cigs and brews we're good." He smiled broadly, showing even, pearly white teeth.

Martha felt her heart melt inside.

"I've got a delivery to make in Durant. You're welcome to go along for the ride or I'll drop you off on the highway." He tilted the can to his lips.

"What're you delivering?" She smiled crookedly, trying to hide the bad spot on one of her front teeth. She should have seen a dentist months ago, but lacked the funds. "Something green and leafy, I'll bet."

"Are you a cop? You don't look like a cop." His eyes fastened on her body, tracing the leafy vine tattoo that circled her leg from her ankle and disappeared under her high cut-off jean shorts.

"I'm not a fucking cop." She drained the beer can and dropped the empty in the chest and fished another from the ice. "Just drive. I'll holler when I want out."

"All right then." The smile returned to his face. "We'll have a party later on if you're game."

"I'm a born partier." She opened her second beer, sipping at the chilled brew.

He stared at the tattoo. "Where does the vine go?"

"It weaves around my leg and ends in a big red rose; the bloom circles my pussy," she said.

"I'd like to see that." Russell inhaled deeply on the cigarette.

"You may get the chance if you're lucky," she winked.

He turned off the highway onto a secondary road. After two miles, he abandoned the narrow asphalt ribbon, taking a sharp right onto a dirt road.

"Damn, this friend of yours really lives in the sticks." Martha glanced through the windows at the dust-covered weeds and scrub growth choking the drainage ditch.

"In our business, you can't live on the main street in town." He patted his shirt pocket for the cigarettes. "Care for another?" he shook two free.

"Sure why not." She plucked it from his fingers.

"It's only a couple miles to my buddy's house. Don't worry, it'll be worth the time." He passed her the lighter.

"This had better be a kick ass party." She puffed the cigarette to life.

"It will be." He reached over and patted her hand. "It will be."

Martha snatched her hand back quickly, feeling a pin prick behind her knuckles. A single blood drop welled from a small puncture wound. "What the fuck did you do?" she shouted. Her vision blurred, swimming in and out of focus. "What the hell did you do to m…" She slumped to the side, her glassy eyes staring out the window.

"This is a dress rehearsal, baby, and you're the guest of honor."

Martha opened her eyes slowly. She blinked several times against the sun's afternoon glare.

"It's about time you woke up." Russell kicked the bottom of her left flip-flop.

Martha's gaze settled on her captor's smiling face. He sat on a dead fall, a cigarette dangling from his lips. She moved her hands and feet, surprised to find she wasn't tied up. When she looked at her clothes, she saw that the shirt and cutoff's appeared undisturbed.

"I didn't get any while you were out, if that's what you're thinkin'." Russell dropped the cigarette to the ground and smashed it out under his boot sole. "You really don't appeal to me."

Her mouth felt dry as cotton. "What the fuck is going on?" she croaked.

"We're gonna play a game." He lifted a .22 magnum from the ground and laid the weapon across his knee. "The pickup is half a mile north of here." He let the key ring dangle from his fingers, and tossed it in the dirt at her feet. "You've got a thirty second head start. If you can make it to the pickup before I kill you, I'll let you drive back to town and get the police."

"You crazy bastard." She snatched the keys from the ground and jumped to her feet. "What the hell is wrong with you? Were you abused as a child?"

"Your time is running." Russell glanced at his watch. "You've got twenty-five seconds."

Martha slipped the keys in the front pocket of her cutoffs and darted up the trail. Within fifty feet, she stumbled into a briar patch. The thorns tore at her unprotected legs and arms. Blood beaded from numerous scratches and mixed with the sweat coating her body. Crimson streaks ran down her limbs and dripped to the ground.

Prickly grass and rocks tortured her unprotected flesh. Each step sent shards of agony shooting up her legs. She gritted her teeth and kept moving, placing one foot in front of the other. She stumbled and fell to her knees, peeling the skin away from her shins.

"Get up," Russell's rough voice sounded behind her. "Get your ass up and run." He fired a round near her leg. Hot dirt peppered her skin.

Martha rose slowly. "Please. Please let me go. I won't tell anyone, I swear. You can fuck me. I'll suck your dick, anything you want. Just let me live."

"Run, bitch," Russell snarled. A look of pure evil marred the face that Martha had considered handsome only hours before.

She broke into a half-hearted trot, dragging her right leg behind her. Where's the truck? She stared through the trees, hoping to spot the dark green pickup. *It's got to be close. Where did he leave it?* she thought. The muscles in her legs quivered uncontrollably. Her feet became numb. *I can't go much farther. Where is the damn truck?*

She tripped and fell and knew it was over. Russell caught up to her a few seconds later.

"You can stop now." He laid the barrel of the rifle on her shoulder. "I want to show you something."

"No," she whined. "Please don't kill me." Tears filled her eyes. "I tried. I really tried to find the pickup."

"Quit bawling and get up." The barrel moved to the center of her back and shoved her forward. "Before I kill you, you have one last job to do."

She stumbled into a large clearing. A small creek flowed on the north side. The water looked clear, so inviting. She rushed to the edge, collapsing on all fours and burying her face in the cool refreshing goodness.

A hand fisted in her hair and yanked her back. "Nothing for you." Powerful arms threw her into the middle of several small, grass-covered mounds. She lay on the ground sobbing, trying to fill her empty lungs.

"Why are you doing this to me? Why?"

"You'll find a shovel behind that tree." He moved to a tree stump near the creek and sat down. "That's a good spot to dig." He pointed the rifle to a small section near the center of the clearing. "The grounds nice and soft there."

"Please don't do this. Please let me live," she blubbered.

"You can die now, or you can live a little longer while I tell you a story." He calmly pulled a cigarette from his pack and lit up. "This place is special to me. Some of my best memories are buried here."

Martha stared at the dried blood on her feet as she crossed to the tree, the shovel propped against the far side, the blade driven into the dirt. She returned to the assigned spot and placed the tip on the ground. She cringed in pain as her aching foot tried to drive the blade into the earth. Instead, she stabbed downward using her arms and shoulders to drive the edge into the soil.

"That's Mrs. Ryan's cat over there," he said. The tip of the cigarette glowed cherry red as he inhaled. "That's the first thing I ever killed." He pointed to a small mound by a wild rose bush. "I crushed its skull with a hammer." He grinned broadly showing his perfect teeth. "It was a hell of a rush, greatest feeling I ever had. Gave me a big time boner. It was all I could do to keep from cumming in my jeans."

"Is that when you became a sick fuck?" she panted.

"Watch your mouth. It'd be easy to finish that grave." The rifle centered on her chest. "My second trophy was Leslie Varner's dog. Damn mutt bit me on the ankle once. Fucker's teeth caught in the seam and ripped my pants up past my knee. I remember Leslie laughing at me. I never forgave her for that. My mom really tanned my hide when I got home from school. Let me tell you, she wore my butt out. Then one day, I saw that dog wiggle through the yard fence, and I got it to follow me to the railroad bridge." A look of absolute bliss crossed his face.

Martha paused. She leaned on the shovel handle, breathing heavily. "You think that makes you special? Everyone's had it rough at one time or another in life."

"I'm special because I change things and I've got the gun." He grinned. "I hung that mutt from the railroad bridge. Damn thing kicked its life away in a couple of minutes. That's the grave over there." He nodded to a patch of dirt on the far side of the clearing.

Russell craned his neck, looking at the depth of the hole she was digging. "You should go a little deeper. I don't want a varmint to dig you up and scatter your bones everywhere."

She threw the shovel to the ground. "Fuck you, I'm not digging anymore." Her bloody hands fisted on her hips. "Kill me if you want to, but I'm through digging."

Russell rose to his feet, leaving the rifle leaning against the stump. He walked toward her slowly, his thumbs hooked in his belt loops. "Whatever you say, baby." His right hand disappeared behind his back, and a second later, the bore of a small pistol was pressed against Martha's forehead. "Whatever you say."

A hot explosion of pain centered in Martha's forehead. She fell to the ground, pawing at the pile of loose earth. A line of blood ran from the small hole. It pooled in the corners of her eyes and curled around her nose. A hard soled boot rolled her into the grave. She stared at Russell through a red mist, as the first shovelful of dirt hit her face.

The worms feasted on Martha's flesh. The seasons changed. The summer's heat gave way to the crispness of fall and the bone chilling cold of winter. Martha lay covered in her blanket of dirt with a thick topping of snow, sleeping the sleep of the dead.

Far above the Earth, a large meteorite broke apart in the far regions of space. Its glow lit up the early morning sky with an assortment of colors. Bright reds and orange tinted the sky. Brilliant blues glowed, as they burned up in the atmosphere. The dull green rocks survived, making the journey to Earth mostly intact. A small piece no larger than a baseball crashed into the ground in the small clearing. The rock glowed with a vibrant emerald fire. The energy leeched into the forgotten bodies underground.

Russell's Story

A light rain fell on the saturated ground. Water stood in the tire ruts of the pickup. Russell left the rifle in the rack behind the seat, opting instead to only carry the pistol. He donned a thick cap as protection against the rain and exited the vehicle. Water sluiced around his foot and he sank three inches into the mud. The suction threatened to pull the rubber boots from his feet.

He rubbed the scratch marks along his cheek. "You really got me good, you fucking bitch; put up a good fight." He dumped the corpse on the rain-soaked ground. The falling rain popped against the plastic sheet. He sat on the same stump he'd used over a year ago and replayed his latest adventure in his mind.

Things hadn't gone as planned. The constant rain had ruined his carefully constructed scheme. Leslie Varner's body, wrapped in thick plastic, lay crumpled on the floorboard. Her head was covered in garbage bags to keep the blood from reaching the carpet. Russell planned on killing her at his special place, but she'd fought back furiously and in a fit of anger, he'd pulled his pistol and shot her in the forehead.

The drive to his private cemetery proved to be nerve wracking. He constantly checked his mirrors, expecting to see the flashing lights of a police cruiser closing behind him. Russell chain-smoked a pack of cigarettes to keep his nerves under some semblance of control. At last, he finally arrived at the access road; a pig trail in the middle of nowhere.

Shouldering the corpse, he walked through the rain, his feet slipping in the slick gunk of rotting leaves. He waded through mud and water a foot deep. The thick mud stuck to his boots, adding to the weight. He fell several times during his trek, but through sheer perseverance arrived at the clearing.

He filled his tired lungs with air. Patting his shirt pocket for his cigarettes, he found that the rain had soaked the tobacco and paper. He threw them to the ground in disgust. "You put me through a lot of hell today, Leslie. I wanted to watch you dig your own grave like that other bitch. I've got to give you credit though, you showed a lot of moxie."

He rose from his perch to fetch the shovel from its hiding place, then stopped suddenly to stare at the open mounds. Each appeared to have burst open from the inside. The short hair at the back of his neck tingled. "What the hell is going on here?"

He first thought the police had stumbled onto the small graveyard and removed all the bodies, but the notion quickly vanished from his mind.

The sound of a cracking twig caused him to turned around, and as he did, his eyes went wide in amazement to see Martha step out from behind a massive oak, the shovel gripped tightly in her rotting fist.

"Were you looking for this?" A dull green luminance colored her empty eye sockets. Dried flesh clung to her bones. A few tuffs of hair remained on her glistening skull and green mucus dripped from her chin, dotting her exposed ribs. "We've been waiting for you to return."

"What the fuck?" Russell stepped back. He felt small sharp teeth nipping at his heel, and he looked down to see a decomposed human skeleton worrying his pant leg. The teeth were unable to penetrate the thick rubber boots. He kicked at the animated bones.

Licking his lips nervously, he stared in horror as all the animals he'd killed through the years formed a circle around him. Half rotten corpses of raccoons and squirrels, along with several cats and dogs, glared at him with glowing green eyes. Mrs. Ryan's cat, its crushed skull held together by moss and bits of yellow fur, swatted at him.

"We've been very patient, Russell." Martha said in a thick, screechy voice. Russell strained to understand her words. "We knew you'd be back." She glanced at the plastic-covered lump of flesh. "Is she the one? Is she the one that broke your heart? Is she the one that made you a killer?"

Russell snatched the .22 from his rear pocket, his earlier fear forgotten for the moment. "Stand the fuck back."

A guttural laugh burst from Martha's rotten throat. "I'm not afraid of death any more. You can't kill me twice."

Russell pulled the trigger and the gun popped in his hand. Shards of bone filled the air and a small hole appeared in Martha's face. Her dried flesh pulled back along her cheeks in a grotesque semblance of a smile.

"Remember what you told me a year ago?" She moved toward him on wobbly legs. "You have the keys in your pocket. The pickup's a half mile away. You have a thirty second head start."

"You stupid, bitch. You can't catch me, hell, you can't run. You couldn't run when you were alive," he sneered.

"Yes, but I've learned a few tricks in the last year." Her eye sockets glowed brighter. She lifted a small green rock the size of a baseball, holding it up for him to see.

The plastic behind Russell began to pop and rustle. Leslie Varner rolled from her plastic coffin. Her stiff hands reached up and tore the trash bag from her head, leaving a torn, ruffled, duct-taped necklace around her throat. Her dead eyes stared at the trees and circled around the clearing, settling on the man who'd ended her life.

Her fingers explored the small hole in her forehead, coming away with a smear of thick congealed blood. "You shot me. You asshole, you fucking shot me." Leslie clambered awkwardly to her feet, standing on shaky legs.

"I've got more surprises for you, Russell," Martha said and gestured at a wild rose vine growing a few feet away from him. Immediately, a thorny limb wrapped around his wrist. The sharp points cut a deep line into his flesh.

Russell jerked away from the painful embrace. He fired the pistol at Leslie, the bullet hitting her chest. The woman smiled as she advanced.

A bony hand caught Russell at the elbow and spun him around. "Get moving." Martha's rotten face was mere inches from his nose. Her thick, putrid stench nearly gagged him. "Your time is running out. You've got ten seconds left." Russell turned and sprinted to his pickup, his boots sliding over the slick ground.

"Ten, nine, eight..." Leslie counted.

Russell splashed to the ground when his boots got stuck in the mud. He yanked his feet of them, running in his socks for greater speed. In his haste to get away, he'd left the pistol lying in the mud. He remembered Leslie from their high school days. The girl was going to be a track star in her younger days, excelling in long distance races.

"Seven, six, five."

He risked a glance over his shoulder. Leslie dropped into a runner's stance and the ember of fear smoldering in his gut became a small flame.

"Four, three, two, one, go!" Leslie screamed, her feet splashing in the water as she began to run.

Russell darted into the woods, abandoning the path. He knew the forest well, and believed he could keep ahead of the dead woman long enough to reach the pickup truck and escape.

"Catch him and bring him back to me!" Martha shouted. "Bring him back!" Russell's soaked shirt stuck to him like a second skin. His breath came in ragged gasps. He ran out of wind quickly and slowed his pace.

I've got to use my head, he thought. *I know these woods.* He moved slowly through the thick foliage using all his woodland skills.

"You ain't gonna catch me. This is my backyard," he mumbled. "No one can find me in here."

He walked on the wet leaves to eliminate his tracks on the muddy ground, jumping from rock to rock when they were handy. Unknown to Russell, tiny skeletal figures moved above him through the trees and followed his scent trail. One of the partially-decayed squirrels scampered down the tree until it was eye level with a panting Russell.

He glanced to his side as the dead animal leaped at his face. Chisel-like teeth caught the fleshy portion of his nose, biting through the soft tissue.

"Damn it!" he screamed. His hands closed around the small bones and pulled. The skeleton broke to pieces and only the skull remained. The teeth were still buried in his flesh. Russell pried the jaws from his nose and threw it against a large stone. The shiny skull shattered into a thousand pieces.

"So that's your game!" he shouted. "Well, it ain't gonna work! Do you hear me, bitches? It ain't gonna work!"

"You shouldn't shout like that." Leslie appeared behind him. "It gives your position away."

Russell ran, weaving his way through the trees. He expected to hear the splashing of Leslie's running feet behind him but didn't so he risked a glimpse over his shoulder. The walking corpse was still in the same spot. A smile split her pasty-white face.

She's enjoying this, he thought. *She's actually hunting me!*

The parallel struck him instantly and the flame of fear rolling in his guts burned brighter. *They're not going to get me!*

Russell dashed through the thick leafy cover, his woodsman skills forgotten. He ran across the grass and mud, leaving large deep impressions in the wet dirt.

A skeleton dropped from the trees. Small pieces of desiccated gray fur clung to the dead raccoon. The jaws opened wide, and sharp teeth closed on his ear lobe, biting through the flesh.

Russell slapped the dead animal from his shoulder, losing part of his ear in the process. Blood flowed onto his rain-soaked shoulder. Another one darted from ground cover and sharp claws locked onto his sock-covered foot. Dagger like teeth sank into his ankle. Russell hopped on one foot, yelping in pain. His fists pounded the cat's crushed skull to wet powder. Poison Ivy vines pulled away from the trees, wrapping around his arms and legs. Russell gasped through his open mouth as he tried to fight his way to freedom. He glanced through the trees. Leslie slowly walked toward him. Over her shoulder, he saw his green pickup not fifty yards away.

"You lose," she smiled. The vines tightened around Russell's body. Leslie bent and lifted the free end of the vine from the ground, using it as a leash. "Come on, Martha wants to see you."

"You can't do this to me! Damn it, you can't do me this way!" Russell twisted and turned, trying to free himself. The vines resisted his efforts and squeezed tighter.

"You did it to us." Leslie yanked the vine, pulling him to her side. "It's only fair for you to meet the same end."

"No!" he pulled away, digging his feet in the ground. His feet slid out from under him. He floundered in the mud, as Leslie dragged him back to the tiny cemetery.

"Here he is," Leslie said when they'd arrived. She tossed the vine at Martha's feet.

Martha drove the shovel point into the dirt. "You know the routine."

"No! No, I'm not going to do it! I'm not." He slowly stood up. The vine fell away, lying in a coil around his ankles. He stood proud and defiant, staring at his two victims.

Martha aimed the pistol at Russell's head. "You dropped this when you left. So, do you want to die now or do you want a few more minutes of life?" She fired a round into the ground at his feet.

"Stop, I'll dig, I'll dig." He swallowed the knot in his throat. "I'll dig." His tender feet couldn't push the shovel into the rain-soaked soil, so he used his hands to shape the grave.

"Make it deep. We don't want the varmints to dig us up." Leslie sat on the stump at the far side of the graveyard.

"Us?" Russell repeated. "What do you mean 'us'?"

"All of us. We'll be together for eternity." Martha waved the pistol at Russell. "Now dig."

After an hour, a panting, exhausted Russell produced a six foot hole approximately four feet deep. He paused to rest.

"That's deep enough." Martha crossed the clearing, and pressed the muzzle of the .22 against Russell's forehead. "Time to say goodbye."

"Wait! Hang on a minute. It's not enough." Leslie jumped to her feet. "I want more. He needs to suffer."

"What do you have in mind?" Martha's inhuman stare fastened on the newly dead woman.

The corners of Leslie's mouth twisted into a smile. "If he moves, shoot him." She met Russell's panic-stricken eyes. "You've dreamed of me doing this to you since junior high school. I hope it was worth the wait." She went to him and loosened his belt and pants, letting them bunch around his ankles, then yanked his boxers down to his knees. Her cold hands wrapped around his penis; the member shriveled against her touch. "It's not very impressive, is it?" Leslie glanced at Martha.

Martha shrugged. A chunk of dead flesh fell from her shoulder. "I've seen bigger."

Leslie's mouth enveloped his manhood. Russell closed his eyes as the dead lips manipulated him, enjoying the sensation. Though cold, it was still wet. But then his eyes suddenly popped open, and his face stretched in a look of sheer terror and anguish. "No! No, not that!" he screamed as agony filled him to his very core.

Warm blood filled Leslie's mouth and flowed around her lips. Russell pulled away from the cold slimy embrace, screaming. Looking down, his groin was spurting blood in thick spurts, in rhythm to his beating heart. Martha fired then, and a small hole appeared in Russell's forehead. He crumpled to his knees and fell into the water pooling in the bottom of the grave.

Martha lifted the green stone from the muddy soil, its glow fading. "The energy is nearly gone, our time is over," she mumbled.

Her decayed, bony arm reached back and tossed the stone as far as she could. It landed in the creek thirty feet away. The two women crawled into the fresh grave. The rain fell harder, washing the pile of soil into the hole, and covering the bodies.

CHAMBER OF THE CRYSTAL SKULLS

KELLY M. HUDSON

I

Revelations

"What the hell?" were the last intelligible words to drip off the lips of Rodrigo Vasquez, as the head of Dr. Thomas Morrow grew tiny blue legs and feet from its severed neck, and then proceeded to dash across the floor of the cave, run up Rodrigo's right leg, and chomp on his testicles.

Amidst the screams and the cries for help, Dr. Morrow's head worked hard, the teeth gnashing and chewing, the barbed tongue tearing through the thin fabric of Rodrigo's khaki pants, the teeth finally finding the testes. The head crunched down with an almost delightful glee as a tickled laugh tittered from Morrow's mouth, mixing with the screeching of the Mexican to form a strange tapestry of sound that echoed off the walls of the small chamber, where the five crystal skulls had sat, undisturbed, for centuries.

Greg Summers stepped back, part of him shocked and the other part full of wonder, the metal plate in his forehead buzzing and popping. All around him, his colleagues were falling to their knees, holding the sides of their skulls and screeching in agony. Greg was the only one, besides Rodrigo their guide and Sandra, the graduate assistant, who weren't affected by what was going on in the room, that dreadful cavity, deep in Mt. Taholiche.

What had happened? What was happening? It was hard to say. When they broke the seal on the room, the vault where the long-sought after crystal skulls supposedly resided, a deep thrumming began. Greg recalled how his bowels had loosened at the sound and he feared he was going to defecate in his pants. They all stood and stared at the dais the crystal skulls sat on, each one the size of a cantaloupe, unvarnished and appearing as if they hadn't been touched in centuries. They all also experienced the same sense of dread and terror as the thrumming grew louder and the skulls gave off an eerie blue glow.

They were all men of science, undaunted by superstitions and folk tales, but were now confronted with something they instinctively knew wasn't of the natural world.

Rodrigo, who had lingered behind the others as they stepped into the room, pushed the door the rest of the way open and joined them inside. The sweet, gentle smile on his sunburned face froze as he realized something wasn't right.

He'd been thrilled and chipper the entire trip, the promises of rich rewards dancing like dreams in his mind. He'd found an immeasurable treasure and was delighted to bring it to the rest of the world.

He didn't look happy now, on the floor, Dr. Morrow's head buried between his legs, slurping and eating its way up into Rodrigo's crotch, past the penis, into the lower abdominal cavity. Rodrigo's body spasmed, he shit himself, and died, his brown eyes locking on Greg's and holding them until they could see no more.

A hand touched Greg's arm and he screamed until he realized it was Sandra, just as stunned and afraid as he was, reaching out on some primal impulse to feel connected to someone, anyone, and in that connection, take some comfort.

She was gorgeous, the stereotypical blonde beauty old scientists took under their wing for their good looks rather than their brains, but Sandra was much more than her blue eyes and fair skin; she was smart. Far more intelligent than anyone Greg had ever met, in fact—smarter than he was. During the trip, including the meetings they'd held prior to their departure, he'd tried to hit on her but was met with a cold wall of ice. It didn't bother him much, though, because he had always been a spectacular disaster with women. Why should this time be any different?

She warmed up to him when they'd reached the jungle. All the other scientists were older, in their fifties and early sixties, where Greg had just turned forty. Eventually, because he was closest to her age, they got to talking and he found her not only charming, but engaging.

She knew more than he'd forgotten and it intimidated him a little, if he was to be honest, but he also found it intriguing.

All of that had flown out the window now. The other scientists were on the floor, still screaming and crying and beating their fists furiously against the rocky ground beneath them.

The thrumming had grown louder and more insistent and Greg could feel the steel plate in his head—earned on a different jungle expedition in South America five years ago—vibrate so hard he thought his brains would explode.

There were eight of them on this trip, six scientists, Sandra, and Rodrigo, plus the four guides they'd left behind in another chamber. Dr. Morrow was the head of the expedition and the first to fall.

He'd collapsed and everyone had watched in horror as his head popped off his shoulders like a zit on a teenager's face. It exploded in a pool of blood and blue bile, rolling on the floor until it hit the dais upon which the five crystal skulls were displayed.

When it made contact, the head spun in a counter-clockwise direction, and as it did, the other men all fell—except for Rodrigo, Greg, and Sandra—and began screaming. That's when Dr. Morrow's head sprouted two long and sinewy blue legs from the stump in its neck.

They scrabbled on the ground until they found purchase and the head propped up, rocking back and forth, wobbling, and then found its balance. Dr. Morrow's eyes searched those still standing, those unaffected, and as they did, they glossed over, a thick coat of greenish pus bubbling from under the eyelids and dribbling down his cheeks, mixing with the pouring snot and blood flowing from his nose and dripping onto the floor.

His lips opened and he screeched a tittering laugh that sounded like a hyena on speed, and then the head ran for Rodrigo and…

There was Dr. Michael Stand, PHD from Harvard, head of their cultural studies division. He was sixty and chubby, with a gray goatee that matched his eyes. Also down there was Dr. Merle Lynn, fifty-five and author of a revered treatise on South American indigenous peoples. He was bald and skinny, rather like an umbrella without its material—all skeletal and frail. Next to him was Dr. Dan Gere, the youngest besides Greg at fifty-years-old and perhaps the strongest.

He was in fine shape, with bristling muscles and stamina to match a work horse. And last was Dr. Lee Ho Fook, sixty-five, a leading geneticist with a taste for ancient South American folklore. He was the oldest and the smartest, tall and thin, with thick jowls like a bulldog and a high-pitched voice that made him sound like a woman. He was Sandra's mentor.

Dr. Stand was the next to go, his head pulling free of its body even as his hand held on for dear life, trying to keep his head attached. Greg watched as the muscles strained and then burst, tendons stretching and snapping, until all that held the neck to the shoulders were a few strands of thick, fatty skin. These, too, popped and his head rolled just as Dr. Morrow's had, rolling until it butted against the dais and spun.

As it did, tentacles sprouted from his ears and nose, long and blue, pointed at the ends with hard, sharp claws and covered in a viscous, greenish fluid. The tentacles knotted up at three points on each one, becoming knuckles, as Dr. Stand's head sat up like a crab. His eyes were glazed just like Dr. Morrow's, and when he opened his mouth, a deep, sonorous sound blew out, lilting and disturbing all at once. His tongue flickered from between his teeth. It was long and skinny and barbed on each side. It licked the excess fluid that had run from his eyes and matted in his goatee. Between slurps, he sang in that deep voice, the words an ancient and forgotten language, rhythmic and lulling.

Dr. Lynn's head came off, like the others, but different. It creaked and crackled, turning right and then left, swiveling farther each time, the bones snapping, until it turned completely around, then around again.

It spun, the flesh wrinkling along the neck and then it shot off, rocketing across the floor, skipping and skidding, stopping when it slammed against the dais. Long arms, like those of an octopus, sprouted from the stump of its neck, slithering out and wiggling in the air. His eyes opened as greenish fluid poured from them down his nose and dripped into his mouth.

His lips pursed together and tiny bubbles foamed from the corners. He glided next to Dr. Stand and took his place there, no sounds coming from his mouth but the constant bubbling.

Sandra and Greg shrank back against the wall, too frightened and fascinated to move. They hugged each other and watched, unable to take their eyes from the spectacle unfolding in front of them.

Dr. Gere's head was perhaps the most gruesome to watch as it separated from its neck. It was a slow process because his muscles were so thick and toned. So when his head bent backwards and touched between his shoulder blades, even though his Adam's apple ripped through the flesh, the head wouldn't come off.

His head twisted right then left, violently wrenching back and forth, the skin in front where his neck had torn open glistening with blood and greenish fluid, slowly splitting. But it wasn't enough; the muscles held firm.

A great howl peeled from his mouth, echoing off the walls, the sound of fingernails raking across a chalkboard, a screeching pitch that caused Sandra's left eardrum to burst. She collapsed to her knees, holding the side of her head, as blood pulsed between her fingers.

At last, Dr. Gere's head came free. It popped like a cork from a champagne bottle and bounced over by the dais. His eyes blinked clear the greenish fluid they were emitting and turned a deep blue, his iris' clouding over and staining the whites of his eyes until they resembled a cobalt crayon. Long fins, like those of a shark, sliced out of his head from the stump of his neck, just above both ears, and at the top of his skull. They were short and thick, resembling runners on a sled.

His head lolled to one side as the fins grew until he rested between two of them, his face tilted to his right. He moaned and spat out a wad of green phlegm and rocked in place for a moment. The head rolled over next to Dr. Lynn's head.

Greg could see tiny feelers, about a centimeter thick and black in color, grow from each of the fins. They helped Dr. Gere's head, guiding it as it rolled and then stopped.

The final head was Dr. Fook's, and his was the worst of them all. It ripped free from his body with hardly any trouble because he was so old and frail, the bones snapping like dry sticks, the skin folding and almost melting away. His head rolled and touched the dais, just like the others, and began to vibrate.

Greenish fluid sprayed from his tear ducts, coating the floor around him, mixing with the blood that was still frothing from his stump. His nostrils flared and kept spreading until they tore open and peeled back and up his face, exposing the jutting bone underneath.

The skin from his nose oozed and melted down his cheeks, freezing there in a hiss of steam, and then contracted, pulling his fleshy jowls up like they were on marionette strings.

His large cheeks ripped free from his jaw line and spread out, the nostril flesh hardened now and acting like attached muscles, revealing the inside of Dr. Fook's mouth, his tobacco-stained teeth crooked and small. The jowls lifted higher and higher, the skin spreading out, thinner and thinner, until they fanned, six inches each in length. The muscular nostril skin pulled them and let them go, over and over again, faster and faster, until the cheeks flapped and buzzed. Once the rapidity of the fluttering grew so fast that the jowls were nothing but a pink and red blur, the head took flight, lifting off the stone floor and hovering three feet off the ground.

"You've got to be kidding me," Greg said, his face long and white.

The crystal skulls, sitting on the dais, glowed bright blue. They were nearly transparent, with just a slight fog where the brains would be if they were actual heads for actual bodies. Their glow was hypnotizing and they were the first thing that the group saw when they stumbled into the chamber. Greg remembered laughing when Dr. Gere turned to Dr. Stand and said, "Nothing like that awful movie, are they?" Dr. Stand had flushed red with rage. He'd been a consultant on said film and had been deeply embarrassed when it turned out as rotten as it had. He didn't have any trouble, though, bragging about all the money he'd made.

Now the skulls were brighter, so intense Greg and Sandra had to shield their eyes.

"Humans," a voice said, coming from out of the thrum. It was deep and hollow, ancient and heavy.

"We have returned, humans!" the voice said. It actually wasn't one single voice, but five, blended in such unison that it sounded like one. "Bow before your masters!"

Greg, in a moment of sheer insanity or maybe just good old fashioned courage, spat on the floor between him and the five heads. "Go to hell," he said. His voice quivered and his knees shook, but somehow the words flew from his lips and filled the room with his defiance.

"You would mock us?" the voice asked. "We, your masters? We, your gods? We, the most powerful beings in the universe?"

"Is this really happening?" Sandra turned to Greg, her eyes wide, a mixture of fear and wonder. "Is this a dream?"

Greg shook his head. "No. This is all bat shit is what it is."

"Silence!" the voice said. "You will speak only when spoken to."

"Okay," Greg said. "Who are you? Why did you do that to our friends?"

"We are the Skonari. We are the gods who built this land. We are the ones you worshipped so long ago. We are the ones who guided human hands to paint pictures in the fields for our Father in the Sky to see, the ones you sacrificed your young and virtuous to. We controlled the weather and the seasons and your very fortunes. We are the Skonari."

"Never heard of you," Greg said.

"If you're so powerful, then how did you end up here?" Sandra asked.

It was a good question, one Greg should have asked if he wasn't so damned angry. And where did this rage come from?

Was it a coping mechanism, some way to keep his mind from snapping? He reached up and massaged his temples.

The plate in his head was really hurting, each word the voice said making it shake and buzz so that it felt like it was about to burst from his forehead.

"A shaman, a magic man, tricked us, sealing us in these skulls and then trapping us in this room," the voice said. "Here we have stayed for hundreds of years."

"Boo, hoo," Greg said. Sandra punched his arm and gave him a fierce look. But his blood had been roused now, his head hurt, and his temper—which had always been bad—was raised. There was no turning back. "You must not be so powerful if a stupid, barbaric human tricked you."

The doctors' heads shook, their mouths opening and emitting various high-pitched squeals.

"We would have taken you," the voice said to Greg. "But something blocked us."

The plate, Greg figured. And for the first time in over a year, he was glad he had it.

"And you are female, and weak, therefore not worthy of becoming a vessel for us," the voice said to Sandra.

She folded her arms across her ample chest and flipped them the finger. "Go fuck yourselves," she said, hissing between her teeth.

"Enough!" the voice screamed. Greg fell to his knees, the pain in his head so intense that he was blinded for a moment. His vision was bright white and then dull again as his sight flared out and came back.

"Now you die!" the voice thundered.

Dr. Morrow's head shrieked and charged Greg and Sandra, screeching, "Yi, Yi, Yi!" over and over again. His small blue feet slapped on the stone floor as he scampered forward, teeth gnashing the air, eager for their flesh.

Greg cowered back against the wall, the pain in his head too much to overcome. Sandra snarled, reared back and kicked Dr. Morrow's head, the toe of her boot catching him between the eyes, punting the head back across the room.

The head spun and flew and crashed into the others, scattering them like bowling pins. Sandra reached out and grabbed Greg's arm, hauling him to his feet.

"Run!" she shouted and then she was gone, out the entrance of the chamber and down the tunnel. Greg was right behind her, never bothering to look back.

The five heads righted themselves and took off in pursuit.

II
Chase

The tunnels deep inside Mt. Taholiche were long and twisting, the roof of the caves sometimes no more than four feet tall. Rodrigo had brought a group of fellow helpers in when he first discovered the cave that led to the Chamber, and they had posted torches at regular intervals through the twisting, dark passageways.

Those same men, four in all, were just down at the end of the tunnel that led to the Chamber, forbidden by Rodrigo to come any further for fear they would scare the whites who'd come to pick the mountain clean of its treasure.

They'd heard the screaming and the thrumming and although they were frightened, they didn't move, because through Rodrigo, they had earned more money in the last few months than they'd received over a lifetime. To say they were poor would be an understatement; to say they were cowards would be a lie.

But when Sandra and Greg emerged from the cacophony of madness and burst into the small tunnel, their faces white and their bodies shaking with fear, the guides had their doubts.

"Run!" Sandra yelled as she trundled past them, Greg hot on her heels. The men fell to one side, confused and unsure what to do. What had happened to Rodrigo? If he was hurt or dead, would they still get paid? One of them, Miguel, a small, wiry fellow with sunburned skin and dark, hard eyes, said that they should go search for Rodrigo. The others called him a fool. He spat at their feet and was just about to tell them where they could go when Dr. Fook's head flew into the tunnel, his cheeks flapping and buzzing the air, his eyes red with fire, freezing the men in their places.

Dr. Fook laughed, his voice echoing in the chamber, as his eyes grew brighter and redder by the second. The men all watched, too terrified to move, as twin beams shot from Dr. Fook's eyes and sliced Miguel's legs in two at the knees. Miguel fell into a heap of screaming, scorched flesh, holding his stumps where his calves had been, his expression pleading for help.

None was coming. The other heads appeared, Dr. Morrow's running rapidly across the ground and up the leg of one of the guides, a stoop-shouldered man named Doug. The blue toes dug into Doug's flesh, until through sheer momentum and strength, Dr. Morrow was eye-level with the poor man's throat. He opened his mouth and his barbed tongue shot out, drilling a hole in the larynx of the man, blood gushing out on all sides. Once he was anchored, Dr. Morrow thrashed his mouth to and fro, tearing large chunks from the man's neck, eating his way through until he struck the backbone. All of this happened so fast that the man didn't even have time to collapse, his body finally spasming into a heap of urine, blood, and shit.

Dr. Gere's head rolled in next, careening like an out-of-control boulder. The fins kept the head moving and the feelers directed its course as his eyes rolled inside and out, always keeping focus on what lay ahead. The head smashed into one of the guides, a tall man named Antonio, and shattered both of the man's legs. Antonio screamed and tried to crawl away as Dr. Gere rolled up on top of him, and stopping at the middle point of the man's back, suddenly spun in place, like a basketball on a fingertip, the fins spreading and the feelers pointing out sharp and deadly.

Blood sprayed from Antonio's back as the feelers and fins cut through his thin clothes and then his flesh, the head burrowing down into Antonio until it had sliced through his spine to touch the cold stone floor through the man's torn stomach.

Dr. Gere's head paused for a moment, spun a bit, adjusted, and closed his eyes, the greenish fluid dribbling down his cheeks and mixing with Antonio's blood. The head sat there for a few seconds, not moving, simply floating in the pulsing blood and innards of Antonio, before the feelers grew out and wiggled like worms, reaching into the closest arteries, attaching, and then slurping up the blood. Dr. Gere's head swelled like a fat leech as his lips parted into a deep and pleasant smile.

Dr. Lynn's head slithered along the side of the cave, slipping and sliding across the dark rocks, leaving a slimy trail of green ooze, heading straight for the final guide, a young man named Pierre. He was the poorest of the group and a second cousin to Rodrigo, brought along only because Rodrigo's wife had insisted.

Now, Pierre was running for his life from a head with octopus arms and legs, slinking over cold walls, its mouth frothing with tiny blue bubbles, boiling and popping in loud bursts. Pierre stumbled and fell, catching his hands on a pair of jagged, broken rocks in front of him.

They sliced his palms open and blood dribbled down his arms as he righted himself just in time for Dr. Lynn to leap from the wall and land on his legs. The octopus arms tangled in Pierre's ankles and tripped him up. He fell to the ground again, this time on his back, and held his bloody hands up to beg for mercy as Dr. Lynn squiggled over his legs and up his body, coming to a stop on his stomach. Dr. Lynn's mouth fizzed and he spat twice, two long, arcing gobs of blue phlegm, both landing directly into Pierre's open cuts as if guided there by an unseen force.

Dr. Lynn hopped off the boy's stomach and watched as Pierre squirmed, the poison from the spit working its way through his system. In a matter of moments, Pierre went docile and then stood, zombie-like, teetering back and forth on the balls of his feet, slack-jawed and staring at nothing.

Dr. Fook's head went over and studied Pierre for a moment. "Excellent," he said, his voice choked and high-pitched. "Put him to work. You know what to do. The rest of you, get the girl and kill the other human."

Dr. Stand, Dr. Morrow, and Dr. Gere's heads all sped from the small room in hot pursuit of Sandra and Greg.

Meanwhile, Sandra and Greg were very lost in their attempt to escape. Neither had paid much attention on their journey inside the mountain, a combination of pure anticipation of a major discovery and their reliance on Rodrigo. Now, however, they weren't sure which way was which, and every turn they took left them with at least two more options on where to go. Finally, after a fruitless five minutes of going in circles, Sandra held up her hand.

They both bent over, gasping for air. Greg was worn out, his legs weak and his lungs burning. Still, his eyes and mind were very much on alert, so when Sandra bent over and the top of her shirt fell open, revealing the top swell of her magnificent breasts, he couldn't help but look, a wry smile on his face. It was funny, he thought. Here he was, running for his life, and he still had the time to look at a pair of breasts out of the corner of his eyes.

"We need to get it together," Sandra said. She righted herself and looked around. "We need to go that way." She pointed behind her.

"We already went that way and it led us here," he said.

"Yes, but there was an offshoot to the right, remember?"

"We took that one and it led back to the same spot which led us here," he said.

"No. That was in the tunnel before this one," she said. "That's the way out, I'm sure of it."

Greg wasn't so sure. But she was smarter than him, and pretty, so he shrugged his shoulders and went with it. "Let's go, then."

Sandra took point and led them out the small room into another twisting, tight corridor. Most of the tunnels were cramped, wet, dark, with low-hanging ceilings. It was hot, too, which was unlike most caves Greg had ever been in. Sweat dripped into his eyes and stained his shirt, his back aching, as he had to spend half the time crouched over like a hunchback. The sight of Sandra's ass, bobbing ahead of him in the light of his flashlight kept him motivated, and the monstrous heads that were probably in pursuit. They'd heard the screams of Rodrigo's men as they ran for their lives, but those had died down a little while ago. The silence that followed was almost worse than the cries of terror.

"Up here," Sandra said. There was a small passage to their right and she slipped through it, Greg close behind.

He ran face-first into her bent behind and bounced back. It was like getting hit with two pillows.

"What are you doing?" she said, annoyed.

"You stopped." He was grinning.

"Come on."

He followed, keeping his ears open for any sounds, but couldn't hear anything over the scraping of their boots on the stone ground and the panting of their breaths, hot, heavy and desperate.

Sandra suddenly stood up, and when he came out behind her, he saw why.

They'd entered another cavern, this one with a forty foot tall ceiling and a big, open space. Earlier, when traveling to the chamber with the crystal skulls, they had passed through this room. It was about fifty yards wide and long and had several offshoot corridors on each side. There was an altar at one end, four feet off the ground, covered in moss and small tufts of grass that stuck up between cracks in the rocks.

"We were here before," she stated.

"Yeah, but which entrance did we use?" Greg asked.

They stood for a moment, evaluating their situation. Finally, Sandra said, "We can eliminate the ones behind us."

Greg grunted and counted the open passages across the hall from them. There were five.

From somewhere at the back of them, something screamed. It was loud and long and full of anger. Greg's heart froze in his chest and he stumbled over next to Sandra and put his arms around her. He hugged her tight, frightened, his legs quivering. She squirmed from his grip and shot him a disgusted look.

"Don't lose your head," she said. She pointed at the middle passage. "Let's try that one. It's as good as any."

Dr. Morrow's head scuttled into the room, howling mad. "Yi! Yi! Yi!" it screeched.

Greg screamed and shoved Sandra out of the way as he ran towards the middle passage. She tripped and fell as Dr. Morrow's head was followed in quick succession by Dr. Stand—who scuttled in like a giant spider with a human head—and Dr. Gere, rolling in like an out of control bowling ball. Dr. Stand joined Dr. Morrow as they closed in on Sandra, and Dr. Gere tumbled quickly after Greg, who was already in the corridor and on his way.

Sandra swung her foot and kicked Dr. Stand, but it only knocked him off-course for a moment. His crab legs pierced her thighs and calves as it scampered up her body and came to rest on her torso, just below her breasts. She threw a jab at the head that bounced off, ineffective. Dr. Morrow ran around her and stopped right next to her head.

"Yi! Yi! Yi!" it bellowed and kicked her in the temple.

Her head recoiled from the impact and her eyes fluttered closed as she passed out.

Dr. Gere was closing in on Greg, who had to slow down and duck as the passage before him became smaller, tighter, and lower to the ground. Soon, he was on his hands and knees, crawling as fast as he could. He could hear Dr. Gere behind him, gaining ground, rolling with little impediment.

Greg whimpered and kept his head low. He didn't remember having to crawl like this at all during their initial entrance into the mountain and he knew, deep down, that this wasn't the way he'd come in. He just hoped the corridor didn't dead-end.

A sizzling pain lanced his right butt cheek and he screamed as Dr. Gere caught up to him at last and bit his ass. He kicked his legs furiously behind him, hitting the disembodied head with an infuriated series of blows to keep it off him. It was futile. For every kick he landed, Dr. Gere bit a chunk out from his legs. By the time Greg was crawling on his stomach, the ceiling was so low he could barely wiggle through, he was bleeding in dozens of places; Dr. Gere's attack never stopped.

His fingers clawed the dirt and ground in front of him. He couldn't see anything, having dropped the flashlight back when he'd first been bitten. It was dark and damp and his only recourse was to feel his way along. Tiny, slimy things crawled over his arms and face, sending surges of panic stabbing through his chest. But he kept going. He had no choice; that thing was at his feet and even though it was slowed by the narrowing and collapsing passage, it was still getting a good bite in every now and then.

His hands hit solid rock in front of him and he knew this was it, his run for freedom was over. He'd come to the end of the passageway and now he'd be eaten alive by the rolling head of his former friend and colleague. With a desperate barrage of punches, Greg pummeled the rock in front of him, hoping against hope for a miracle.

The rocks broke and sunlight blinded him. Hot, humid air licked his face like the Devil's tongue and he tumbled from the passage and fell into the jungle surrounding the mountain.

He was on a small rise. He lost his grip and skidded down a hill, scraping up his elbows and shins until he landed against something hard and metal that knocked the breath from his lungs. He looked up.

The jeep. Their jeep. The other vehicles were there, in a semi-circle. He'd escaped the mountain and was free! He quickly checked over his shoulder to see if Dr. Gere's head was near but he heard nothing other than the normal sounds of the jungle.

A bird squawked to his left, some other small animal sneezed on his right. The trees rustled in a slight breeze. Another bird chirped somewhere.

It was hot out, the air thick as a wad of wet toilet paper, and it clung to him like a leech, drawing out whatever strength he had left. He opened the door of the jeep and grabbed a bottle of water from the cooler, taking a long, deep drink. His head ached and his legs throbbed where he'd been bitten. He would have to dress those, but first he had to decide what to do next.

Sandra was in there, alone, captured by those fiends. Rational thought dictated he run, as fast as he could; take the jeep and get some local help. But his heart spoke other words, more seductive whispers. It told him about how grateful she'd be if he charged in, the big hero, and saved her life. His chest swelled with pride. He'd always wanted to be a hero. But how? How could he fight demonically possessed, disembodied heads with supernatural powers?

His eyes flickered to the back of the jeep, where the weapons were kept, a just-in-case measure if things went badly on the trip. There was a shotgun, pump action, and it was loaded. He'd fired a rifle once, at a target range during a science conference in Vegas, and he was a pretty fair shot. With a shotgun, he didn't have to be perfectly accurate. With a shotgun, he could blast those evil heads back to the hell they came from. He could save the day.

Greg grabbed the shotgun and a pocket full of shells. After drinking the rest of his water, he urinated, and marched back to the cave entrance, a determined smile on his face.

III

Conflagration

Greg crept down the tunnel. It was big, open and wide, the way he and the others had originally entered the mountain, and soon, he was deep inside the caverns, the natural light from outside gone, replaced by the dim glow of the nearly, burnt-out torches the guides had placed upon their initial entrance.

Greg followed those torches, their embers leading him to where he wanted to go.

Deep in the caves came the echoing sounds of laughter and the chittering of what sounded like a hyena. Then there were screams, human screams, and these were followed by unearthly howls, cries from the darkest depths of the human soul. They echoed off the walls, pressing in on him, threatening to suffocate his ears and his senses with their unnatural noise. Parts of his brain told him it wasn't too late. He could turn around and leave! Flee for his life and count himself lucky.

Sandra's screams drove those inner voices away.

He could tell it was her because the wails were different than the others. These came most certainly from a human, not from some beast or foul creature. Despite his very legitimate fears, he knew he had to keep going.

Surprisingly, he met no resistance. He traveled further and further into the mountain, until at last he came upon the opening to the large chamber with the altar. The closer he was, the louder the noises became; more furious now that he was there. In this cavern, he realized, the final battle for his life and Sandra's was about to take place.

He skulked over behind a boulder and crouched down. From his vantage point, he could see the entire cavern. And what he saw made his blood boil and freeze, all at once.

Sandra was splayed out at the foot of the altar, completely naked, her arms and legs staked into the stone floor, and bound by ropes tied to some sort of spikes. She was magnificent, in a damsel-in-distress kind of way. Pangs of guilt stabbed Greg's heart but he couldn't help how he felt. He stared at her breasts, large and beautiful, jiggling with each cry, and at her rosy pink nipples, stiff with fear and slick with sweat. She had a perfect body, the shape of the proverbial hourglass, with strong, tanned arms, legs and gorgeous bikini lines around all the right places. There was a tuft of blonde hair between her legs, proving she was a true blonde, and for a moment he watched, captivated, as her pubic hairs stirred in the breeze blowing through the cavern.

All around her, the doctors' heads were gathered, humming and communicating with each other in strange tongues. Every now and then one of them would emit a strange noise, one that corresponded with the ruckus he'd heard on his way to them. Sometimes one of them would become animated and talk excitedly, but most of the time they hardly moved, sitting still, as if waiting for something.

Pierre entered and left the room, each trip bringing in one of the crystal skulls, where he placed it on the altar, facing out into the chamber. There were three there now and Pierre was just coming in with another. What the skulls were doing on the altar and what these horrible creatures were up to was not readily apparent.

Greg bided his time.

At last, Pierre left and returned with the final skull, and once it was in place, all five glowed bright blue and thrummed as they had before, earlier in the day. Pierre, his duty done, fell to his knees, his face melting into a taffy-mix of flesh and green fluids, blood and bone. Within seconds his head collapsed inward and his body slumped, quivering, to the floor. Two more seconds and he stopped moving.

"Let us commence," boomed the ethereal voice. The droning in the room pulsed against the steel plate in Greg's head, sending waves of nausea through his body. He bit his bottom lip and fought through them, straining to pay attention to what was happening before him.

"What are you going to do to me?" Sandra asked, her voice a mixture of defiance and fear.

"We are going to impregnate you," the voice said. "You will carry our offspring, born into this world to enslave and destroy mankind."

Dr. Stand's head crawled over between her legs, its appendages clacking on the stone floor. It crept up and settled directly in front of her pubic mound, its eyes glistening with the greenish ooze as its tongue rapidly licked its lips.

"Please, no," Sandra whimpered.

"Commence!" the voice thundered.

Dr. Stand's mouth opened and the lips stretched and split, green and red pus blubbering from the wounds. A large phallus slid from the round opening. It glistened with a brackish-green fluid that coated its girth, which was as thick as a body-builder's forearm. Heat vapors fumed in the air around it as the member pulsed with excitement. From the tip, a drop of blue liquid dripped and splattered on Sandra's pubic hair, matting it into a thick, tangled wad. The head moved back and positioned the throbbing penis, which looked human but was engorged so thick and tight it was monstrous to behold, at the entrance to her vagina.

Greg figured this was his moment to step in, to save the day. He was just about to stand when, suddenly, Dr. Fook cried out.

"Halt!" Dr. Fook fluttered over from where he'd been hovering by the crystal skulls and landed on Sandra's stomach. "Something is not right!"

He laid his ear against her pelvis and listened intently. When he raised his head, disappointment and confusion filled his eyes.

"She cannot have children," he declared.

Sandra cried out in triumph. "That's because I'm on the pill, you morons!" She laughed like a maniac. "You idiots missed women's lib, didn't you?"

Dr. Fook flew back to the skulls on the altar, angry and inflamed. He squinted and barked a command at Dr. Lynn, whose head wiggled over the floor and stopped inches from Sandra's chest.

"Rape her," the voice boomed.

It was now or never. If Greg was going to be a hero, this was the moment. He steeled his courage, took a deep swallow, and strode into the cavern.

As he did, Dr. Lynn spat two bubbling and sizzling green wads onto each of Sandra's breasts. The liquid fizzled and burned her nipples as she screamed in agony. Between her legs, Dr. Stand dipped his head and prepared to thrust the penis forward.

Greg yelled and pumped a round into the chamber of the shotgun, then fired. The pellets peppered the ground inches from Sandra's head, almost hitting her. Dr. Stand withdrew, having never entered her, and scrambled back, the penis tip spurting globs of blue fluid. Dr. Lynn followed, joining his brethren by the altar, their heads clicking together like some kind of Three Stooges skit.

On the ground, the most awful things were happening to Sandra. Greg halted his advance and looked at her, appalled and shocked at what he saw.

Where the green spit had hit her breasts and foamed, it dribbled off to the side as her nipples blew up to three times their natural size, the hard flesh trembling and shivering. The tips split in two vertically, and a tiny insect head pushed its way out, one from each breast. The creatures being birthed resembled a common fly, with a similar head but colored blue instead of red, and they were much bigger, about the size of Greg's thumbnail. Each fly tore free, wet with a greenish fluid, and buzzed up into the air, taking flight. Sandra's nipples peeled open as the first flies were followed by another and another. Soon, a dozen came from each breast; the small monsters filled the air above her, hovering like a swarm of mosquitoes. The unearthly voice barked commands in a strange tongue and the flies turned as one and flew straight at Greg.

The flies swarmed his face, swooping in and taking tiny bites of his flesh. Within seconds his left cheek was nearly devoured, just a series of bleeding strips, jagged pieces of beef jerky.

He screamed and fanned his head but it did no good; each time he raised his hand the flies would gnaw on them, tearing chunks out and spitting them to the side. They were like flying piranha, only smaller and much quicker. As Greg stumbled back in an attempt to get away from them, he knew if he didn't do something drastic he would be dead in a matter of moments.

He dropped to his knees, the flies falling with him, buzzing about his head, swooping and diving and chewing. He raised the shotgun, placed it in front of his face and pointed upward, then he turned his face, ducked quickly, and pulled the trigger.

The force of the blast, a combination of the gunpowder and pellets, shredded most of the cloud of flies. They sizzled from the heat and screamed, hundreds of tiny, shrill, dying voices.

The right side of Greg's face was scorched from the shotgun, his eardrum ruptured and trickling blood, and his hair was smoldering, but he was alive, at least, and most of the flies were dead.

The surviving flies, stunned from the concussion of the discharge, fluttered in the air and fell to the cold stone floor. Greg, shuffling on his knees, disoriented, saw them and immediately went to work, smashing them with his fists, grinding them into the ground until only a few were left.

When he finished, he fell onto his back, gasping for air, wishing to God that he'd taken a jeep and fled instead of coming back, trying to be a hero.

Sandra's screams roused him from his fugue. He lifted what was left of his ruined head, the right side seared and smoking, the left tatters of raw flesh, and stared at her. She was sitting up, her breasts melted down over her stomach like candle wax.

She pointed at the heads of the doctors, at the horror that was being unleashed right in front of them.

The heads had rolled next to each other and were vibrating, humming along with the thrum of the crystal skulls on the altar. Dr. Morrow's head sat up and squatted down as Dr. Gere's head rolled over and bounced on top of it, resting there.

Dr. Lynn was next, squirming and wiggling his way up over his colleague's heads and sitting down. Dr. Stand's head followed, its crab legs skittering and digging into the flesh of its comrades until it sat on Dr. Lynn. The final piece was Dr. Fook, who flapped over and came to a gentle rest at the apex of the stacked heads.

Greg's hand searched for the shotgun he'd dropped, his instincts screaming for him to run.

A giant pop echoed around the chamber, followed by a cracking and groaning. The heads hummed as one, the sound growing louder by the second.

The metal plate in Greg's head rang out and he fell back to his knees, screaming in agony. Even if he wanted to flee, there was no way for him to now.

Long, thick limbs grew from the sides of all the heads, starting with Dr. Fook. They twisted and turned, digging into the heads below like long vines of ivy.

The creepers pulsed, glowing blue as greenish bile secreted from small holes, coating the heads in a thick, viscous fluid. The heads fused, the limbs tying them to each other as the bile glued them together.

Dr. Fook's cheeks flapped furiously, and the heads, now one long mass with their individual, distinct faces staring forward, tottered and rose. At the bottom, Dr. Morrow's legs grew fatter and stronger. They strained at the bulk but lifted, and the heads, now one obscene totem pole, screamed and charged forward.

Sandra tried to roll out of the way but was caught under the feet of Dr. Morrow. Her legs were crushed, the bones pounded into bloody powder. Laser beams arced from Dr. Fook's eyes, slicing Sandra in half at the waist. She screamed and tried to crawl away but the totem pole jumped up into the air, landing on her back, the blue feet stomping her into the ground.

Two silicon pouches exploded from her breasts, shooting in opposite directions across the chamber and ricocheting off the walls as the totem pole crunched the rest of her under foot, until there was nothing left but a bloody smear and a mop of blonde hair.

Greg had regained his feet and staggered forward, all his plans forever destroyed. He didn't save Sandra, and instead had ended up watching her die as a new monstrosity rose up to murder him, too. He was no longer a warrior, no longer a man hoping for redemption or glory.

He was now a man with nothing left to lose. He was a very, very dangerous man.

He sprinted towards the totem pole even as it ran towards him, his shotgun raised. He pulled the trigger, sending a spray of buckshot into the middle of the totem pole.

The tiny pellets sheared Dr. Stand's face off, shredding the throbbing and dripping penis into thousands of glittering shards. Dr. Stand screamed and a green gas farted from his face as his head suddenly collapsed, empty and dead. The other heads crunched down as they trundled forward, undaunted.

Greg fired again. This time it was Dr. Lynn's head that exploded in a green mist of charred bones and brains. The totem pole contracted again, growing smaller.

Another blast and there went Dr. Gere's head, bursting into a fog of green blood and flesh.

Just two heads remained now, the top and the bottom, Dr. Morrow and Dr. Fook, and they were only five yards away and closing fast.

Greg pumped the shotgun as Dr. Fook's eyes shot out twin laser beams. They caught Greg's left side, burning a clean hole through him just above his hip. He screamed and fired the shotgun, aiming for Dr. Fook. The pellets found their mark and left behind only a steaming green pile of flapping cheeks and the back of Dr. Fook's head. The rest of the buckshot dissipated into the air.

Dr. Morrow, the last of the living heads, barreled forward, shrieking, "Yi! Yi! Yi!" Greg stopped, pumped the shotgun, aimed, and fired. The chamber clicked empty. He was out of shells.

Instead of giving up, and digging through his pockets in a useless panic, searching for extra shells, he simply flipped the weapon, catching it by the barrel, and he leaned back and waited for Dr. Morrow to close the short distance between them.

That's when Greg, an average golfer at best, swung through the greatest drive of his life.

Dr. Morrow's head shot through the air, screeching, "Yi! Yi! Yi!" as it spun, plummeted, and shattered on a jagged rock, splitting in two like a rotten pumpkin. His brains spilled out in a pile of green and blue gunk, plopping onto the ground with a wet smack.

Greg wobbled, digging the shotgun into the stone floor to keep from falling. He was tired, beyond exhausted, and his mind was ready to shut down and fall into a deep sleep.

"Foolish human," the voice said. It was coming from the crystal skulls. They pulsed blue with every word spoken. "You may have destroyed our vessels, but you cannot destroy us."

"Oh, yeah?" Greg said. He smiled, angry and weary, lifting the shotgun and stumbling towards the altar.

"No! Stop! What are you doing?" the voice demanded, panicked.

"Oh, yeah?" Greg lifted the shotgun like a club.

"Do not do this! We command you! Do not do this!" the voice shrieked.

"Suck it," Greg said. He swung the shotgun down, butt-first, and shattered the skull closest to him. It fell into hundreds of pieces, littering the altar.

The voice squealed in anguish and begged Greg to stop as he raised the shotgun again and destroyed the next skull, then the next. There were only two left as he staggered in place, out of his mind, giggling like a maniac.

"Suck it," Greg said again. With one swipe, he smashed the final two, stepping back and watching with special pleasure as they crumbled and crashed to the ground.

The entire area was bathed in a hush, like a breath about to be taken in but not quite yet. It was eerie but pleasing, given the earlier chaos. Greg laughed, his mirth echoing off the walls and filling the emptiness.

He didn't know what he was going to do next, or how he was going to explain what had happened to his team, but at the moment, he didn't care. He was alive. He had survived. And although he hadn't saved anyone else, at least he'd destroyed the evil.

"Foolish human!" the voice boomed.

Greg looked up. Five blue vapors, each the shape of a skull and the size of a large boulder, shimmered over the shards of the smashed crystal skulls. Their faces leered as they hovered, emanating a fog of pure, undiluted malevolence.

"You have done what we could not do! You have freed us! Only by the action of free will, by the choice of a human to crush the skulls, could we be freed! And you, foolish mortal, have done so!" the voice thundered and laughed.

"No," Greg said. He fell to his knees and dropped the shotgun.

"Yes!" the voice shouted. The floating blue skull vapors swirled in the air, forming a mini-cyclone. They blew over to Greg and surrounded him. "Now, accept your reward!"

"Well, shit," he said. They would be his last words.

The vapors eddied and churned, spinning around Greg until they lifted him up and twirled him in mid-air. He screamed as his body twisted up into a long funnel, his bones cracking, breaking and smashing flat, blood squirting from every open orifice, gushing from his eyes, nose, mouth, penis and anus, until he was squeezed flat and long like a piece of bread dough.

The vapors flung what was left of him against the wall and flew down the tunnel leading to the outside as his body shattered like the skulls had, raining pieces of flesh onto the ground.

When the vapors reached the exit and were outside, they separated and hovered in the air, five blue skulls once more, and measured the land in each direction as far as they could see.

They had once ruled this part of the world, and now that they were free once more, they would rule it again.

With a cackle, the skulls flew off to reshape the world in their dreaded image.

ABOUT THE WRITERS

Terry Alexander lives on a small farm near Porum, Oklahoma with his wife Phyllis. They have three children and nine grandchildren. His work has been published by Living Dead Press, Static Movement, Moonstone Books and at frontiertales.com. He is a member of the Oklahoma Writers Federation, Ozark Writers League, The Arkansas ridge Writers and The Fictioneers

Krzysztof T. Dąbrowski is a polish writer. In Oct. 2008 he was awarded in a "In the circle of sensation" literary contest organized by Portalkryminalny.pl. In Oct. 2008 a story collection titled "Deathbirth" was published by Armoryka publishing house. In Nov. 2008, the story "Deathbirth" won the "Story of the Month" competition of American Literary Magazine Bartleby Snopes. In 2009 - publication in slovak PLAYBOY. V.2010 - Second book: "Anima vilis" (Initium publishing house). He stories have been in many countries: USA, UK, Germany, Slovak, Czech Republic, Spain, Russia, Brazil, Argentina, Hungary and Mexico.

P. A. Douglas is a full time nationally touring singer-songwriter living in South East Texas. His debut novel "The End: A Zombie Novel" was released in July 2011 by Living Dead Press. To hear music, watch video blogs and more from his touring antics, visit his website. www.indie-inside.com

Anthony Giangregorio is the author of 37 novels, almost all of them about zombies, and has edited over 30 anthologies.

His work has appeared in Dead Science by Coscomentertainment, Dead Worlds: Undead Stories Volumes 1-7, and Wolves of War by Library of the Living Dead Press. He also has stories in End of Days: An Apocalyptic Anthology Vol. 1-5, the Book of the Dead series Vol. 1-6 by LDP, Zombie Zoology by Severed Press, and two anthologies with Pill Hill Press.

He's also the creator of the popular action/zombie series titled Deadwater and his action/ horror novel Dead Rage is being optioned for a movie. Check out his website at www.undeadpress.com.

Scott T. Goudsward lives and writes in New England. Writing seriously since 1992, he is a founding member of the Essex Writer's and Artists Guild and is also in NEHW (New England Horror Writers.) His published works include Shadows Over New England and Shadows Over Florida. Both books have made the HWA Stoker preilm ballot and been nominated for The Rondo Award. His first novel "Trailer Trash" was published in 2007 and he has edited the anthology "Traps."

John Grover is a dark fiction author residing in Massachusetts. Some of his more recent credits include: Best New Zombie Tales Vol 1 by Books of the Dead Press, The Book of Cannibals by Living Dead Press, The Vermin Anthology, The Northern Haunts Anthology by Shroud Publishing, The Zombology Series by Library of the Living Dead Press, Morpheus Tales, Wrong World, The Willows, Alien Skin Magazine, Aurora Wolf and more.

He's the author of several collections, including the recently released Feminine Wiles, sixteen tales of wicked women as well as various chapbooks, anthologies, and more. Please visit his website www.shadowtales.com http://www.shadowtales.com for more information.

Dane T. Hatchell lives in Baton Rouge, LA. He has stories appearing in over fifteen different anthologies from Living Dead Press. You can contact Dane at Enadious@gmail.com.

Kelly M. Hudson was born in Kentucky and currently resides in California. He loves horror and has over a dozen stories published in various anthologies, as well as a novel called The Turning published by Living Dead Press and available on Amazon.com and other places. If you wish to know more about Kelly, please visit his website www.kellymhudson.com for links to other stories and news.

Kelly M. Hudson grew up in Kentucky watching cowboy movies and loving rock and roll. He currently lives in California and is the author of two novels, The Turning, and Men of Perdition, both published by Living Dead Press and available at Amazon.com. You can find out more about Kelly and his work by visiting www.kellymhudson.com where you'll find links to stories he's had published and how to find him on Facebook and Twitter.

Matt Kurtz writes twisted tales for fun in his spare time. His fiction can be found in anthologies from Pill Hill Press, Living Dead Press, Blood Bound Books, Comet Press and "Necrotic Tissue" Magazine.

Adam P. Lewis is an author within the horror genre. He has written numerous short stories, essays, and reviews published by Wicked East Press, Pill Hill Press, Living Dead Press, Static Movement, Dark Quest Books, Open Casket Press and Ambrotos Press. For more information follow Adam P. Lewis at http://www.facebook.com/adamlewis518.

Kevin Lewis is a graduate of Emerson College. His horror fiction has appeared in online horror publications such as Blood Moon Rising Magazine, MicroHorror, and Sonar4 Science Fiction and Horror Ezine. His short story, "Get Me Out Of Here!" will be published in the upcoming anthology, Groanology 2: Monsters, Madness, and Mayhem. He's a member of New England Horror Writers (NEHW) and resides in Massachusetts.

Suzanne Robb's debut novel Z-Boat will be released soon. Her stories are in current and upcoming anthologies with Coscom Entertainment, Pill Hill Press, Wicked East Press, Rymfire eBooks, Library of the Living Dead, Post Mortem Press, Norgus Press, May December Publications, Living Dead Press, and Hidden Thoughts Press. In her free time she reads, watches movies, plays with her dog, and enjoys chocolate and Legos.

For more check out Ramblings of an Anxiety Ridden Mind at http://suzannerobb.blogspot.com

Brennon Thompson lives in the Midwest, with his wife and cat. His latest tale "InBox" appears in "The Big Book of Bizarro" anthology from Burning Bulb Publishing. He's also currently working on two novels: titled: BRAIN GOO and TOUCHED.